BATTLETECH:
VISIONS OF REBIRTH
FOUNDING OF THE CLANS, BOOK TWO

BY RANDALL N. BILLS

BATTLETECH: VISIONS OF REBIRTH
By Randall N. Bills
Cover art by Ken Coleman
Interior art by Alan Blackwell, Doug Chaffee, Brent Evans, Harri Kallio, David Kerber,
    Chris Lewis, Duane Loose
Cover design by David Kerber

©2021 The Topps Company, Inc. All Rights Reserved. *BattleTech & MechWarrior* are registered trademarks and/or trademarks of The Topps Company, Inc., in the United States and/or other countries. Catalyst Game Labs and the Catalyst Game Labs logo are trademarks of InMediaRes Productions LLC. No part of this work may be reproduced, stored in a retrieval system, or transmitted in any form or by any means, without the prior permission in writing of the Copyright Owner, nor be otherwise circulated in any form other than that in which it is published.

Printed in USA.

Published by Catalyst Game Labs,
an imprint of InMediaRes Productions, LLC
7108 S. Pheasant Ridge Drive • Spokane, WA 99224

To my magnificent children: Bryn Kevin, Ryana Nikol, and Kenyon Aleksandr, along with my new daughter-in-law, Emilee Kirkman. Every single day I thank my Heavenly Parents for the gift of you in my life.

ACKNOWLEDGMENTS

I've known many authors who cannot understand working in a shared universe, preferring their own creations. And I can respect that. But for me, the shared universe is as exciting and challenging as it is rewarding. Working collectively with a group of talented, passionate individuals is one of the great joys in my creative life. Finding a way to tell new, epic stories with a skein of preexisting continuity is just...fabulous.

And when writing a *BattleTech* novel, there's always a huge pile of books on the table. (As I write this, there are eighteen sourcebooks I've referenced, not to mention several novels and the corroborating details of Sarna.net.) A huge thank you to all the authors who have contributed to a thirty-five-year-old universe that's still dynamic and growing.

But for these specific novels, I would like to thank two in particular—friends, colleagues, and more: Chris Hartford and Christoffer "Bones" Trossen. Their magnum opus work *Reunification War*, the twin *Liberation of Terra* volumes, and *Operation Klondike* (along with Chris's *The Clans: Warriors of Kerensky*) were invaluable resources.

FOREWORD

In 2004, I was at the Essen Game Fair, working with the great Fantasy Productions crew. (After the close of FASA Corporation in early 2001, Fantasy Productions formed FanPro US and acquired the license from WizKids to continue tabletop game and fiction publication; I was employed as the FanPro US *BattleTech* Line Developer from 2001 through 2007, while working many of those years also full-time for WizKids.)

I was feeling pretty good. We'd published numerous *BattleTech* sourcebooks by this point, including a new *Technical Readout*, keeping the line alive and starting to grow it again. And we were starting to work on the material that eventually would see publication in the *Dawn of the Jihad* sourcebook, which would launch the line into a whole new era.

During a long, relaxing evening there, we began talking more and more about fiction and the stories we might tell. And the idea coalesced that despite everything written about the Clans at that point, there was no fiction that delved into that history and fully explored those origins.

A trilogy was formed in that evening. A series of novels that would open on 5 November 2784, as the SLDF prepared to jump away from New Samarkand into the unknown, and would end decades later after Operation Klondike. It was a crazy, ambitious project, but one we all felt would finally cover this chapter of lore as it deserved. What's more, it would be a wonderful homage, in my own way, to what is still my favorite *BattleTech* novel, *Heir to the Dragon*.

The first novel, *Fall from Glory*, was published in German in 2006, followed a few years later by the second, *Visions of Rebirth*. The details—and the secrets—from those books were folded appropriately into a variety of sourcebooks that would see publication after the fact, including one of my all-time favorite sourcebooks, *Operation Klondike*. Unfortunately—and much to my chagrin—the third book was never written, and the years slipped by as I kept exceptionally busy in a variety of ways.

I'm just as busy now, of course, if not even more so. However, Loren Coleman used the Kickstarter as a way to challenge me to finally finish off this grand, epic tale. A challenge I accepted. But as I delved into these stories once more, and came face-to-face with the characters I'd embraced all those years ago, I realized there was a little more I wanted to explore. A little more I wanted to tell. So while I worked with the wonderful Sharon Turner Mulvihill to re-edit the entire series (she was the primary editor at both FASA and WizKids), we also worked to nip and tuck and even expand as necessary, creating what we hope is the definitive edition of these books. Being able to draw a few of the new elements crafted in those previous sourcebooks back into these expansions was particularly satisfying. As with the first novel, I took the opportunity to fold in some interludes that I hope will bring the story of these wounded characters to life with greater passion and understanding.

It's been far, far longer than I ever imagined. But as we begin the journey to finish this long-awaited chapter of *BattleTech*, I am reminded of how much joy I find in this work. I am always so humble and grateful to be a part of this fantastic community and work alongside such creative people. To share a love of this universe, and to have had a hand in expanding it in such great, wonderful ways.

I hope you enjoy the reading as much as I did the creation!

—Randall N. Bills
January 2021

PROLOGUE

MCKENNA-CLASS WARSHIP *MCKENNA'S PRIDE*
NEAR ORBIT, STRANA MECHTY
KERENSKY CLUSTER
8 JUNE 2802

Déjà vu eddied through Raymond Sainze until he struggled to breathe.

"Now that's an impressive sight," said Windham Khatib, at his side.

Nostrils flaring—dragging in air to calm his ragged heartbeat—Raymond turned away from the view of a metallic constellation of shuttles, fighters, and DropShips searing bloody furrows across a thousand-kilometer-wide swath of Strana Mechty's upper atmosphere.

Shifting slightly under the weight of the final braking maneuver, Raymond opened his mouth to speak and paused, stunned to realize the stale air of the WarShip actually made it *more* difficult to breathe. How many long years on New Samarkand's *Shiro's Hope Olympus*-class space station? And now it seemed he couldn't stand breathing recycled air. He shook his head at such a weakness.

How my brothers would laugh at me. He tried to speak again, but found recollections stopping up his tongue and occluding his sight until he stared down a long tunnel of memories.

Dead.

I'm the youngest. And we knew war was coming to the Inner Sphere. Which is why we left. And in my homeland, the Dragon would be the first to declare himself First Lord of the dead Star League and launch a war. And the Sword of Light regiments would be in the vanguard, with my brothers hitting worlds in the first waves of such a conflict. They're likely dead...perhaps along with my parents.

How many years...

Raymond stood transfixed, his thoughts hammering through him, leaving him standing on a precipice of years that separated him from all he knew. As surely as the thousand light years separated him physically from the edge of the Inner Sphere, he knew it likely was changed beyond anything he might recognize. That any of them might recognize.

Such thoughts always held a special place in the back of his mind, carving out their existence like peregrine falcons on a cliff face; tenacious and unwilling to give ground. Yet this déjà vu had them bubbling to the surface like long-undisturbed scum on a pond suddenly churning with swamp gas, dredging up its dark and awful secrets to lay exposed under brilliant, stark sunlight.

"Cat got your tongue?" Windham said, laughing lightly, his merry eyes taking away the sting.

The jesting tone from a longtime friend shattered the grip of his reverie and allowed Raymond to breathe again. Stale air or not, he dragged in a huge lungful, trying to banish his own thoughts as well as the déjà vu that still tried to ensnare him with its wickedly barbed seductions.

"Memories..." he finally got out around a tongue too thick and dry. He ran his teeth across the tip until tears started in his eyes, working moisture back into his mouth.

"Ah. Those. They can get you in trouble, Raymond, if you're not careful. Just look at Andery." His tone dropped at the end.

Despite his usual calm, Raymond glanced over his shoulder before he could stop, taking in the bridge of the *McKenna's Pride*. Dozens of navy personnel occupied the large area, all frantically talking into headsets and reviewing information on three times as many monitors as there were people, trying to coordinate the mammoth drop of the final men and women arriving. He marveled at their ability to continue working despite the obvious excitement of *arrival*, and knew they'd continue working without a hitch as they entered orbit and microgravity returned. In the center, the giant holotank showed the system in detail, with hundreds of icons swirling around the central view of a planet, each icon representing a ship of the incoming fleet.

And after this final grounding of personnel, there would be no others. Even if anyone left on the Pentagon Worlds eventually came—which everyone doubted—they would likely face the *Pride*'s guns before they could answer any questions.

Raymond turned back toward the large ferroglass viewport, disgusted at his lapse. After all, they didn't want to draw the attention of Nicholas again. Anything but that, regardless how Andery championed him.

"I know. I know. Just stunned by how much time has passed since I found myself stuck on this ship, outbound with the General and his Exodus."

He could see Windham take a moment, as though running numbers in his head. "Has it really been eighteen years since New Samarkand?" Windham asked in wonder, scratching his huge, black beard absentmindedly. "Doesn't seem possible."

"Exactly." They fell into silence, watching the magnificent vista below. Raymond knew the planet had been surveyed in 2792—known it *before* the informational datapads began circulating to acquaint everyone with their new home—and hosted a thriving colony. But it was still just a colony. What would they make of the massive influx of personnel bombarding them? What would the world make of it? *Nearly one million people, once more unto the breach...can we survive?*

He slowly stretched out his hand and placed it flat against the ferroglass. Though he knew he couldn't feel the vacuum of space, his mind played tricks for a moment, and it almost seemed as though his hand were going numb, raising goose bumps and eliciting an involuntary shiver.

> *Metal seeds fall unknowing*
> *Nurture in blindness*
> *Sunset old, sunrise new; hope.*

"Such poetry sings to my heart," Windham said softly.

Raymond jerked his hand away from the ferroglass as though burned and turned quickly to Windham. "I didn't mean to speak out loud."

"But you did. And despite years of separation and acceptance, your Combine heritage sings true. A warrior's eye, but the heart of poet. You simply say what everyone else wants to, but can't find the words. Can't find a hundred, much less your haiku that paints our current picture so well. And in so few brushstrokes."

Raymond turned back as a new wave of DropShips and small craft hove into view from around the stern and under the keel of the *Pride*. "How bad do you think it will get?" he asked quietly. He knew such discussions were discouraged, and on the bridge they might be particularly troublesome, but he couldn't stop himself. And aside from Andery, Raymond knew Windham better than anyone. Knew him to be man of God, a man who would not betray a confidence.

The hubbub of activity across the bridge swirled around them as Windham remained silent and Raymond wondered if he'd heard the question. Just as he began to voice it once more, Windham spoke.

"Bad, Raymond. You were there, like the rest of us. You saw it as clearly as I did."

"I know. But how could it get worse?"

"I don't think all of the mothballed equipment has been found yet. There're still piles of small arms to find, not to mention how many BattleMechs and vehicles? And heaven forbid they find the WarShips; at least those'll prove a lot more difficult for them to activate. And in a civil war—and don't you for a second believe it's anything else—it always gets nasty before it can get better. *Very* nasty."

Raymond slowly shook his head, stretching his neck, feeling the pull of his single-suit. "Will they come after us? Will they hunt down our second exodus?"

Windham turned his bearded face to regard Raymond, then responded. "I don't think so. We've escaped for now."

"I hope so."

"So do I," Windham said, the sorrow in his voice enough for both of them. They'd seen enough Star League Defense Force personnel killing one another to last a lifetime; the civilian massacres and death tolls everyone tried to forget.

After a moment, Windham spoke again. "Not to mention, if the various warlords and remaining SLDF combat commands batter each other down as much as I think they will...well, some of the colonies might have a lot more to worry about than killing each other. The Pentagon Worlds are not kind to those who forget how long and hard we fought to tame them. A little slack in the leash and they'll be back to their wild ways quick as you like."

Raymond shifted, his short-cropped black hair waving lazily, glad for the magnetic slips that kept him firmly anchored as microgravity asserted itself with the cessation of thrust. Yet again memories of years spent in zero-g flooded and he couldn't help the sardonic smile that creased his lips.

"Something funny?"

"No, just memories again."

"Like I said, dangerous."

"I know."

"*All personnel logged for the* Heliophus, Targen, *and* Amber Sands *vessels are scheduled for departure in one hour,*" a metallic voice echoed through the depths of the spacecraft. "*Access to assigned ships will be closed twenty minutes before departure.*"

They glanced at one another, knowing it was time to go—neither wanted the tongue-lashing from their superior over missing their billet—yet unable to pull away just yet. Both had expected Andery to arrive some time ago; the delay probably meant some new trouble between him and his brother. They shied away from that problem. Plenty of other issues to overcome in the short term, much less *that* Gordian knot.

"Déjà vu." Windham finally spoke, causing Raymond to start slightly as his friend echoed his own sentiments. Despite the intervening minutes since Raymond had had the same thought, the entire scene still reeked of it, dragging out memories so clear and near they prodded dully, painfully, like scabrous fingers incessantly scraping his skin; no banishment possible.

"*Hai...*" he said slowly, falling back on the long-unused language of his birth. "I feel it, too."

Windham scratched his beard again, pulling at the thick curls, then spoke. "Sixteen years. Just a few days past sixteen years since we stood in almost this exact spot on this bridge and looked down at Eden."

"So many hopes and dreams laid before us," Raymond continued softly. "All to come crashing down, as our old identities and hatreds surfaced. Will we make it work this time?"

"Or will we conquer this world, only to find ourselves falling upon one another again?" Windham continued.

"Will history repeat itself?"

"*Exactly*," they said simultaneously. Despite the gravity of their words, they found a smile for one another; the heartfelt, knowledgeable curve of lips that only comes to those who've experienced great pain and hardship together, yet still find the strength to carry on, chin up and nose to the grindstone.

"We'll just have to make it work this time," Windham finally said.

"*Hai.*" Raymond glanced around one last time as they both felt the pull of the minutes bleeding away until they faced their uncertain future and tried to wrestle it to the ground. Yet they'd done it before. They could only hope they'd do it better this time. "Where's Andery?"

"Not coming, looks like."

Quick eye contact; no words needed.

Nicholas.

"At least we don't need to listen to Nicholas's daily speeches anymore," Raymond said, voice low as he surreptitiously glanced around to make sure no one was too close.

Windham slowly nodded, apparently mulling over similar thoughts. "And yet, I've spoken with others. Carson, who spoke to Truscott, and others who've very discreetly asked around," he continued, lowered voice matching Raymond's. "And while we may feel it's overkill, he's selling his vision. And after months of travel and everyone onboard watching holovids nearly daily, he's made a lasting impression. Whether we agree with it or not, he's made a good start. A very good start. I think Andery's right."

Raymond nodded in agreement. *Andery just might be right.* They still needed Nicholas. And yet. If Aleksandr Kerensky, the Great General himself, the hero of the Star League, who led millions of men, women, and children on their first exodus to build a new Star League from the fallen and war-ravaged past, had failed, leaving the war now exploding in the wake of his death—how could his oldest son succeed?

Glancing back out the viewport, a thought came. As the two men grasped arms in a firm handshake of friendship and longtime camaraderie before turning to begin the trip to their waiting DropShips, a name surfaced. A name that just might make it all work.

After all, Raymond knew full well that little brothers were there to nag their older siblings into line. Despite the wistfulness of such thoughts and the minor ache of sorrow they brought—knowing he'd never see his older brothers again—it seemed to firm his resolve, lifting his maudlin spirit.

Raymond passed from the bridge into the long corridor, with the name on his lips—*Andery.*

BOOK ONE

"Somewhere between obsession and compulsion is impulse."

—Alexander Pushkin

CHAPTER 1

COLOSSUS-CLASS DROPSHIP *JACOB'S LADDER*
DESCENT, STRANA MECHTY
KERENSKY CLUSTER
9 JUNE 2802

Muscles slowly relaxing, Andery fell away into the arms of his beloved.

Head nestled into the curve of her lap, her breast pressed against the top of his head; he could feel the rhythm of her heart. A matching beat to the pounding thrust of the DropShip as it entered the atmosphere and attempted to keep them from spinning out of control to vaporize in a fiery death that would send their ashes sailing across the world's jet streams, forever floating. Forever free.

If only...

A thousand visions unfolded like an orchestrated symphony, blossoming a canopy of possibilities, of probabilities. Of what the manacles of the future held. For him.

Andery snuggled closer, knowing that at times the mere presence of his soul mate seemed the catalyst to such bizarre flights of fantasy. But for once he didn't care; tried burrowing deeper.

"God, I've missed you," he said, the words muffled in her thigh. Sliding his left arm around her waist, he companionably dipped several fingers under her shirt to feel the blessed warmth of her skin; calloused tips finding scars from her terrible childhood. Instead of the sorrow it once evoked, an emotional wave began to rise and crest. Understanding only he knew of such secrets; only he shared the knowledge of not just her flesh, but the luminous being within. He snaked his other arm over her thighs and pulled her to him like a drowning man.

"How many times can you speak such words?" she said, her voice echoing in the small berth.

As with the feel of her body, he drank in the strange delicacy of her accent and ofttimes odd phrasings that brought a smile to his face. Knowing none would hear words coated with such tenderness. Only him.

"A thousand lifetimes are not enough."

She laughed, setting her belly dancing against his face. He twisted as best he could to look up. Found her silhouette falling across him as she leaned in to block the wan light of the single overhead fluorescent in the berth. Twin dark, mysterious eyes found his, despite the shadows swallowing her features. He could trace every contour of her face blindfolded without ever touching it.

"Is not Raymond the poet? Will you now take up that pastime?"

He laughed as well, pulling himself back into a sitting position; contemplated taking off the lap belt, but decided against it as a new wave of vibrations hummed through the twenty-thousand-ton vessel. He swept his arms out and composed his face into a dramatic expression, then declaimed:

> *"Roses bloom florid red lips*
> *Tongue, ear, cheek, neck, more*
> *Lifetimes in moments, ever"*

"Do not leave your job."

They fell into each other's arms, laughing over their own silliness as only two best friends can.

The laughter slowly faded into silence (or as silent as is possible on a DropShip burning through reentry), leaving Andery almost breathless. "How did we go so long without seeing each other? How many years?"

Dana leaned back against the bulkhead, slipped her cool fingers into his and quirked a half-smile as she canted her head in his direction. "Duty."

He tried not to flinch, but couldn't help it; he had expected a reaction from her, but received none. *Of course she would know. Somehow, she always does.*

He took a deep breath, glanced at the ubiquitously Spartan bulkhead and tried to keep the sigh from slipping past his lips. Her squeezing his hand told him he failed. *Does anything get past her?*

He swung his head back in her direction, saw himself reflected in her eyes and smiled tiredly. *No...and that's the beauty of it.*

"Nicholas," she finally said.

"*Aff.*"

She tilted her head, as though searching for something in his face, then responded. "Your '*aff*' only seems to come out when you have something you do not want to face. Do you know that?"

He opened his mouth to deny, then snapped it shut and sheepishly nodded. "How do you know me so well?"

She smiled—that precise curve of lips reserved only for him—and nodded in return. "I know myself."

He shook his head at such an answer. *Should've known.* "Well, if you know me so well, then what happened?"

Her smile bloomed at the challenge. "Nicholas reminded you of your responsibilities."

"And?"

"You cannot turn away from the expectations of the people. They need you."

"But that's just it," he said, losing most of the good mood he'd managed to recapture after the endless hours of talk with Nicholas. "What expectations? Sure, maybe some in the military might care about my opinion—" he still struggled with that concept, regardless of the evidence, "—but what civilian knows my name? What do they care what I think?"

She raised her hand to lay it gently against his cheek, her knowing eyes almost too much for him to bear. "Andery, you are so naïve at times. So caught up in your own life you cannot see what transpires around you. The holovid talk shows. The magazines. The screen thrown up around you."

"What?" he began, trying to forget her soft flesh pressing against his cheek. "What screen?"

"The screen your brother puts up to protect you from prying eyes. You are not your father, or Nicholas. However, you cannot think such adoration would fall upon the Kerensky name and not touch all who bear it. The average citizen may not know much about you, but the above-average citizen knows your name, if not everything about you, but generally respects your obvious desire for privacy. And for those who might not respect it..." she shrugged, as though that explained it all. "Your brother has provided precautions."

He shook his head, pulling away slightly, trying to fumble through what she was saying. *Is it possible? How?* "How is this... why didn't you tell me?"

She shrugged again, and raised her eyebrows, her gaze definitely not asking forgiveness. "I am sorry, Andery, but you never brought it up and I did not think..." She trailed off.

In their years together, he could only think of a handful of times when she had irritated him, and this was one. *You didn't think I could be stupid enough to* not *notice.*

He closed his eyes and once more leaned back against the bulkhead, feeling the cold metal hard against his scalp, prickling his flesh. *But I was stupid enough.* Irritation kindled a degree higher, sputtering and sparking for anger.

As though in answer, the ship hit a particularly turbulent patch of spiraling wind, shuddering the vessel like a toy in the throes of a child's tantrum.

The sudden weight of her against his left side as the ship slewed smothered the flames. *Those flames are for me anyway. Always for me.*

"I am sorry."

"I'm the one who should be sorry. Stupid. How long has this been going on?"

Her shrug shifted his weight, providing an answer he did not need eyes to see. And likely was all the answer he would receive.

"Andery," she said, pulling away from him.

He remained silent, content to wallow in his darkness, until her insistent fingers pulled his chin toward her; like a doll, he couldn't resist opening his eyes in response.

"You are simply too passionate. You immerse yourself so thoroughly in your circumstances and in what is going on around you, you become oblivious to all else."

He chuckled, darkly. "So either I'm selfish or arrogant."

"Neither. Both."

"Huh?" Leave it to his Dana to come up with an answer like that.

"It simply is who you are. All you need to do is learn to lift your eyes to encompass a larger whole. And I know you will pour as much dedication, love, and obsession into that whole as you do everything else about your life."

Andery narrowed his eyes slightly, turning them into sparkling, murky depths, and smiled his half smile. "So you want me to share all of my obsessions?"

"Do not distract me," she purred, then leaned closer, until their lips almost touched. "Not everything, Andery, not everything. But you must learn to share a great part of you. With so few of us choosing this second exodus, we will all need to fulfill greater needs. And yours, I am afraid, will be greater than just about anyone else's."

He closed his eyes against her harsh truth, then leaned into her soft flesh and drank in the strength that would sustain him; unflinching support, regardless of what might come. Though he could not yet begin to think of sacrificing for the greater good (*look what that got my father!*) he knew he could do it for her.

For Dana, he could do anything.

CHAPTER 2

ALPHA BIVOUAC, NEAR STRANA PRIME
NOVY TERRA
STRANA MECHTY
KERENSKY CLUSTER
11 JUNE 2802

The black armband chafed.

Andery chided himself for such an exaggeration. *How can I feel a light silk armband through my sleeve?* Yet as he neared his brother's command tent, it seemed to chafe all the more, transforming into a lead weight through some strange reverse alchemy. A weight threatening to drag him to a stop.

Yet Andery forged on, determined to attend this meeting; determined to not shy away from this day. *Of all days. Regrets will not keep me from what I need to do. For Dana.*

A sudden wash of air and a high-pitched *hum* that tingled his fingernails and drove sharp, quick jolts down his spine announced the arrival of a hovercar. It slewed expertly around the corner of a far Quonset hut as he passed a final tent and headed toward a pair of guards standing sentry like two hulking mastiffs.

The whine crescendoed, and Andery's speed slowed to a crawl as the hovercar's fans whipped up the alien soil and spun it into his face like a cyclone. Clenching his eyes shut, spitting out grit that brought spores of alien tastes and smells to his senses, Andery mentally unclenched nerves and unhitched shoulders suddenly strung tight as myomer bundles.

He laughed inwardly, despite the coming unpleasantness. *How long have you lived on an alien world, and suddenly you're back to your "issues" again?* Andery shook his head, his dirty-blond locks actually tickling his ears. *Need to cut my hair. And need to pave this dirt field we're calling home. Hell. Got plenty of ferrocrete in Strana Prime, just over the blasted hills. Why does Niki feel we need to camp out in the rough?*

The sound scraping along his nerve endings cut off like a turned spigot and the silence oppressed as much as the previous banshee wail. The servo whine of a door opening pulled his eyes, and Andery watched as the gull wing slid up to disgorge a portly fellow in a neo-business suit, looking to be in his mid-seventies, with a balding head, low forehead, and dark, beady eyes. *A predator, that one.*

The man glanced quickly in Andery's direction, then down as if in distaste at the annoyance of placing his well-made shoes on dirt, and swept toward the tent as though accompanied by the fanfare of a thousand trumpets; he moved past the guards as if they were statues. Andery looked back at the hovercar, noticing for the first time the logo writ large on the side paneling, and his stomach fell.

That's *the planetary governor? Good lord. Not a predator. More like a vulture.* Forgetting about the metaphorical weight of his armband, Andery leaped toward the tent opening. *Hope I'm not too late.*

He slid into the tent and stopped dead at the tension seething in the room. *Already?* He slowly shook his head and took in the unfolding scene.

Though a large tent, his brother kept it spartan to the point of austere. A large holotable dominated the center, with a half-dozen folding chairs placed at uneven intervals. A large desk occupied the very back of the tent, and three closed and locked quick-stack shelving units covered one wall. Except for the microfiber poly-myomer weave—charged to rigidity to create an even surface for the floor—nothing else was in the tent except for the planetary governor, Nicholas, and Andery. He glanced around, wondering when the rest of the staff would show, then belatedly realized this meeting would only include the three of them.

Andery looked at his brother, noticing an identical black armband. He shifted his gaze to the governor, taking in an unadorned sleeve. *Uh-oh. This could get nasty.*

He almost sidled back out through the flap opening. Neither man was aware of Andery's presence. *Would be so easy.* He clenched his fists, slowly opened them and raised his right hand to feel the sensual texture of the armband; almost as soft as Dana's skin under moonlight.

No. That was the old me. No longer.

He cleared his throat and stepped boldly into the room.

Nicholas's icy eyes centered on Andery, and for a moment he imagined he saw a slight thaw before they dropped to subzero once more as they swiveled back to the interloper.

Andery glanced at the governor to find himself being appraised: a long look up and down, weighing and ultimately discarding him as the governor bobbed his head in dismissal and swung back to square off with his brother.

Andery chuckled under his breath. *Fine by me. Your demise.*

The taut silence stretched for several long minutes, then Nicholas suddenly spoke. "Andery, the good planetary governor here would like to know by what right we have set up camp so close to *his* city?" He uncrossed his arms, then swung his right up, as though offering a hand to a dancing partner.

Only this partner won't appreciate the dance...or the finale.

"That's right, sir," the governor finally spoke. Much to Andery's surprise, the man's small build and portly size possessed a deep voice that shook the air almost as strongly as the hovercar he arrived in. "I was given my governorship of this colony by the Commanding General." He drew himself up as though to compensate for his small stature, and actually managed to deepen his voice further. "Since said deputization has not been revoked or remanded by the Commanding General, I ask by what right you claim dominion of this land? You did not even ask a by-your-leave when you began grounding in such numbers."

"Perhaps, Governor, you know of the troubles on the Pentagon Worlds? Surely, despite the distance, you know what has happened?"

"Sir," he began, chuckling lightly, as though at a joke. "You may think of us as a backwater, but we're well-aware of what's been going on there. War. And when there's war, there's refugees. We all know that, and I and my colony are already opening our arms to this flood you've unleashed." He shifted his weight, and raised his arm in return.

Ah, accepting the dance? The outcome couldn't be more predictable. *About like asking Samuel Helmer to admit to a mistake.* Andery almost smiled at the thought of his former belligerent student's antics.

"However, when there's war, there needs to be a commanding general. To him I would defer. From him I would expect commands of obedience and commitment, even from such a humble civil servant as myself." The governor inclined his head mockingly. "Perhaps you have paperwork from the Commanding General. A notification of such intent?"

Andery winced at the man's joviality and watched him falter, lower his arm and finally swallow loudly as Nicholas gutted him with those blue ice-pick eyes.

Long moments once again stretched, broken by a myriad of sounds: distant thumping of marching feet as thousands continued their migration off DropShips; shouts of master sergeants tongue-lashing troops into shape or moving dazed civilians along to their new quarters; guttural, air-pounding vibrations as their handful of diesel-engine-equipped IndustrialMechs worked to piece together prefabricated buildings for a more permanent base. The farther distant *thud* of heavy 'Mech feet circumnavigating a far perimeter—regardless of the supposed safety of Strana Mechty, too many friends and comrades lay dead for the vigilance of the current exiles to waver a micron.

Andery was on the verge of opening his mouth, but Nicholas beat him to the punch. "Do I have the Commanding General's orders with me?" he asked softly, as though contemplating what to have for lunch.

Andery sighed, well-aware of the violence that might erupt from such a deceptively calm exterior.

"Yes, sir." The governor looked on the brink of saying something more, but quailed under the merciless assault of his brother's gaze. Andery felt a smidgen of sympathy bubble to the surface. *Been there myself, Governor.*

Nicholas slowly moved around the holotable until he stood less than a meter from the man. Despite the almost visible waves of intensity cascading off Nicholas, Andery had to give the governor credit for not backing away.

"The Commanding General is dead," Nicholas said, as though invoking a ritual prayer.

The air left Andery in a *whoosh* as the pain he kept hiding from washed through his system; an arctic wind to plane away his defenses in thin slivers until nothing remained but memories and the pain they invoked. *Could it already have been a year?*

Father.

The other man jerked as though slapped full in the face, then shifted his gaze to the black band on Nicholas's arm; his eyes even swiveled enough to take in Andery as well.

A slight sheen appeared on his balding head as he opened his mouth, his deep voice subdued as he swept low a courtly bow. "I apologize, sir. I am well-aware that the Great General died a year ago this day," he finished the bow and straightened. "I did not mean my words to give offense or display ignorance. I simply asked whether you had orders from *a* commanding general. I sincerely apologize for any misunderstanding."

You only sound sincere 'cause Nicholas looks ready to gut you. Andery shook his head, liking the man less and less, despite his momentary sympathy.

"There is only *one* Commanding General," Nicholas stated emphatically, limning each word with power. You could only take one meaning from his statement.

"But sir, surely there must be leadership from the Star League Defense Force at such a time. Surely you must have a commanding general. Someone to stop this war. Someone to..." his voice drifted off at Nicholas's implacable look. He moved his gaze, almost bewildered now, toward Andery, but found no succor there and tried again. "How are you going to stop this war?"

"I'm not," Nicholas responded.

This time the governor did take a step back. "W-What?"

"This has been coming since the *Prinz Eugen* mutiny, Governor. There are elements of our society that will never live together peacefully. There are elements too wedded to our past. Not to our future. They must burn themselves out before we can reforge ourselves into a future we can call our own. A future that will truly accomplish the Great General's dream."

The governor's eyes darted away like a cornered animal's, his hands waving like sea fronds in an unruly tide. Uncertain, he took another step back and slammed his left leg into a folding chair, sending it crashing to the ground. The harsh *bang* broke the tableau enough to unstick his tongue, and once more Andery had to give the governor his due, despite his growing distaste for the man.

"You...you cannot mean that. The innocent citizens of our Star League-in-Exile. How can you let them be harmed?"

Nicholas took a single step forward, sending the governor back two more steps. "But I do, Governor. I watched your *innocent* citizens firebomb their own cities as I tried to evacuate them." He ground out his words. "The ashes of ten thousand dead coated my tongue and throat until I coughed up blood with every breath.

"I watched the finest of the Star League Defense Force crush civilians under their 'Mechs' feet and dip their hands in the blood of their enemies...who had been their fellow soldiers only weeks before. Sympathizers shot while asleep. Women raped. Children killed and left as garbage in refuse heaps of back alleys."

The governor finally moved to the edge of the tent flap and halted, desperation to flee in his every motion, but his political training too strong to allow him such a disgraceful exit.

"And Governor...I watched it *all*. And then rained down death to exterminate most of a regiment of those same SLDF troops—included some of my own." Nicholas leaned closer, his glacial gaze obliterating the last of the governor's naïveté. "Do you think that I would suffer all of that, and *not* feel I have the right to take Strana Mechty?"

The governor gulped air like a fish washed up on the bank, the sweat now running freely down his scalp to spot the lapels of his neo-suit. He tried three separate times to make words, but failed. Finally, he simply shook his head.

"Exactly, Governor. You may go."

Like a hound released from the hand of his master, the governor scurried through the tent flap and vanished. Andery winced at the brutality of the confrontation, but knew it could be no other way. The man's delusions were stupid and dangerous, and would only infect others. Better to squash them now. *But you know your master's leash now, don't you, Governor?*

"That one will not last."

Andery turned to find his brother contemplating the small spill of sunlight falling onto the rigid floor through the tent flap thrown askew by the governor's hasty departure.

"What?"

"That one will not last. The fires that burn the Pentagon Worlds must be wielded with an even finer hand here, Andery. Where the random conflagration sweeps aside the chaff, we must use laser precision to create what we need."

As always, Andery suffered an internal conflict; agreeing with his brother and yet terrified of the visions of brutality and bloodshed such talk evoked. Dreading the answer, yet he was forced to ask, "And what is it we need?"

"A new society, my brother. A new society to burn away our failures. A new society to return and remake the Star League."

Andery took that in, already knowing where this was all leading, but very unclear as to how his brother planned on getting from here to there. And how he fit in. He wanted to be done with all of it, wanted to just walk away, but the question pulled and pulled until it was nearly wrenched from his lips.

"And how do I fit in?"

Those cold, cold eyes penetrated him, as though weighing his soul on a colossal scale only Nicholas could see, much less understand. "You will continue teaching."

"*What*?!" Anger flared, painful in its intensity. "You sidelined me once, brother. And just after I've finally gotten a command, you're going to sideline me again. Why? *Why*!" What threat am I to you!" He just managed to keep the last from turning into a shout; despite his anger, he didn't want their disagreements to become common knowledge, and if a guard heard them...

The tableau held for painfully long, drawn-out heartbeats, before Nicholas finally responded. "You are no threat to me, my brother. Did you ever think that perhaps the reason I ensured you taught at the Academy last time is because I knew you would be more than competent at it? Perhaps even excel?"

"You mean having a Kerensky teaching is what's important. Especially now, as we have to start all over again!" Andery sucked in a ragged breath, trying to pull his anger under control. *All the years of piloting a BattleMech you stole from me, and now you're doing it* again!

"Must those two be mutually exclusive? Yes, having a Kerensky there was important. But you also excelled, becoming a superb teacher."

Andery's anger continued to climb; a fusion reactor trying to spin up out of control of damaged safety protocols. "Why must you always manipulate me?" he finally ground out.

Nicholas slowly cocked his head, as though struggling to explain it to him. *But you've never once had a problem with words. Or did the fever really damage you in ways we'll never know?* A shiver slowly worked its way up his spine as unease crept across his skin.

Nicholas slowly shook his head. "You assume I'm manipulating you. You assume malice where there is none, my brother. The Star League-in-Exile needed you to train a new generation of warriors. You did that admirably. Our new exile will need you even more. Will need you to teach new generations."

The calm, cool words—along with his own unease—began to bank Andery's anger, though it bubbled under the surface in a way that felt strange, unusual. Yet his brother's words were a siren song he found hard to resist. *As always.*

"Not to mention," Nicholas continued, "it will resonate better with the civilian leadership that their liaison with me is a teacher."

"What...?" Andery said again, poleaxed, anger momentarily deprived of oxygen at that explosive announcement.

Nicholas waved his hands. "I cannot possibly deal with civilian leadership, which will constantly demand my attention. Whether you like it or not, you will always be a Kerensky, Andery. And your good standing as a teacher, and your name, will allow you to quell the likes of him," he waved toward the retreated governor, "as well as all the others who will come. You'll bring reports to me only when you feel there is something you cannot handle."

There. That tone. Just a hint of a challenge. And the more I bring to you, the more disappointed you'll be? The anger swirled again, just below the surface. *Someday you will not have me. Someday my name will be mine and not yours!*

Part of Andery wanted to tell Nicholas that right now. To yell it in his face. But those cold, cold eyes cut through him and he was left hollow, simply nodding at yet another great weight shackled to him.

CHAPTER 3

ALPHA BIVOUAC, NEAR STRANA PRIME
NOVY TERRA
STRANA MECHTY
KERENSKY CLUSTER
17 JUNE 2802

"The Persian Empire. The Roman Empire. The Caliphate. The Mongol Empire. The Star League. These are the most powerful empires in the history of mankind," Lieutenant General Antonius Zalman said emphatically. As he had each of the last five days of meetings.

At least this time he didn't expound for twenty minutes concerning their military tactics and doctrine! Andery leaned back in his chair against the back wall of the large bivouac tent, and couldn't help his eye roll; managed to catch several around the large table unable to keep their own eye rolls in check. Major General Illya Ivaovitch—the oldest man in the group, and one with the most experienced—even yawned in Zalman's direction, causing the man to bristle. But you didn't call down a commander who'd fought through the entire Periphery and Liberation of Terra campaigns with one of the lowest casualty rates among his soldiers of any division.

Major General Absalom Truscott only nodded. "Your statements are too broad, Antonius," he said, firm and resolute, but each word filled with the respect due any commander within the SLDF.

Even this *band of SLDF, which is trying to figure out what the hell we're doing.* Andery surreptitiously took another bite of the locally-made fruit bars, trying to decide if he liked them. *They just taste so...alien.*

"We cannot just look at the strength of an empire," Truscott continued. Andery was fairly confident where Truscott was going. He'd also been making a similar argument for days, but at least he kept dividing and conquering; changing the tone and style of his pitch as he focused upon salient points with better effect. All in an effort to win more commanders—and Nicholas—to his way of thinking. "Just as an army—or empire, regardless of size—is only successful on the back of its logistics, the strength of an empire rests upon the back of its culture. China. India. Spain. Italy. While the culture and their empire are intrinsically linked, these are entities whose cultural footprint spanned millennia. Often their empires had utterly vanished, by any modern definition. And yet those same cultural roots are still the bedrock of the Great Houses thousands of years later, across thousands of star systems. Any emperor from the Han Dynasty would instantly recognize the Celestial Wisdom on the throne of the Capellan Confederation. That is a strength that binds billions together. That creates a foundation that strengthens and upholds any empire, even during times of turmoil."

He really is good at this. Andery continued looking around the large tent, filled with nearly two-dozen high-ranking commanders and a sprinkling of colonels. He'd shared a quick handshake earlier with Raymond, Windham, and Carson. Of course he knew Truscott (*did any not know the man?*), along with a handful of others, if even just to put a name to a face: Major General John Fletcher, Vice Admiral Rafe Kardaan (Stephen McKenna was still off exploring the Kerensky Cluster), and the aforementioned Major General Illya Ivaovitch and Lieutenant General Antonius Zalman.

Andery also saw a few others he recognized. His Dana sat quietly in the corner, eyes unfocused, as though she were opening herself to a vision that might help his brother (his thoughts skittered away from that). Elizabeth Hazen, who stood in an island of space, hand on her long braid of hair, eyes as hard as the will that forged the Ghosts of the Black Watch during the occupation; Andery quickly looked away before he made eye contact, the nightmares of the boarding action against the mutineers of the *Prinz Eugen* still surfacing now and then, all these years later.

He took another bite of his bar as he spied Karen Nagasawa in another corner; it was only in the last week that he'd discovered how his brother's nearly daily speeches for the four months of the crossing from the Pentagons to Mechty had improved so quickly (*somehow you found yourself a speech writer*). *And who's that?* While everyone in the tent couldn't avoid Nicholas completely, they still kept a respectful distance. Except for someone he'd not seen before. A woman, without any rank he could see, who seemed to purposefully intrude upon his brother's bubble of isolation; she sat within arm's length, reading the room as he did. He shook his head; Nicholas would ignore her, as he did most people around him.

A larger percentage of those present than on any previous day were nodding at Truscott's words, but the man still leaned forward, as though he was about to say something more and yet chose to drag out the moment. *Uh-oh. What are you about to say?*

"What," Truscott said, at just the right moment to instantly draw the attention of the whole room, "cultural footprint did the Star League establish? It is no more, and who will miss it? In a century, will there be anything to bind people to the Star League?"

Some faces around the room—particularly Zalman's—began to scowl at the perceived slight against the Star League, and hence the Star League Defense Force. *Against them. But you're not done yet. Are you going where I think you're going, General?*

"The mistake of General Kerensky was in trying to make a Star League-in-Exile built on the same faulty foundation."

Though braced for it, Andery couldn't help but wince as dozens of voices erupted into angry denials. His gaze darted to his brother, at the head of the table: his eyes unfocused, silent, as though he would let the men batter each other with their ideas. *You normally let no one disparage the Great General. What's your game, brother?*

"We cannot succeed here if we try that again," Truscott said more loudly, as he raised an arm and increased his volume to be heard over the angry din. "We must create something new. We cannot just look at empires and the power they wielded. We must build upon a foundation of all previous cultures alongside their empires, to find what is right for us here and now, if we are to survive."

Andery kept a close eye on Nicholas, who seemed almost oblivious to the shouting going around the table. *These, your most trusted commanders, Nicholas, and they're acting like schoolchildren!* And yet, Andery thought Truscott's words rang true as he mulled them over, ignoring the squabbling that washed over him.

Perhaps his father's mistake had been to try to recreate a past that you could not directly engineer. The original Star League was an organic construct, sculpted by the masterful hand of Ian Cameron, as an end result of centuries of development. *And if we're going to engineer something, we don't have those centuries of foundation. Truscott's right. Instead, we need to take the best of humanity's developments and purposefully mold a cultural fusion.*

"What did you say, Andery?"

He came back to himself to find the entire room of the most powerful men on the planet all staring at him, including his brother.

"What?" Andery responded lamely, caught completely flat-footed; feeling almost as dizzy as if he stood on a vertiginous cliffside, waiting for the room to laugh him off the edge.

"You said something," Nicholas prompted him. "What was it?"

Andery slowly looked around the room, at men who hammered their power past his shields and nearly stripped him of any sense of self. But his brother's words drew him into the conversation, and he finally realized he'd said his last thoughts out loud. He sought a few friendly eyes—Raymond, Windham, Carson, Dana—and found his tongue after a deep breath.

"A cultural fusion." He glanced at Truscott, nodded at him— received an inscrutable look back. "I believe General Truscott is right. Whatever it is we are building—what *you* are building,

Nicholas—it must include a cultural fusion of the best of mankind across the millennia. On such a bedrock maybe, just maybe, we can make this work."

What the hell? While there were still several hostile faces, including Hazen (she'd never forgive him for how badly his actions had gone during the mutiny) and Zalman (he was far too fanatical for Andery's tastes), the majority in the room were slowly nodding. *As though my words have weight?* He could barely fathom it.

And most strangely of all, as the meeting continued (and would continue for days or weeks, as they shared with Nicholas their thoughts of what they should be doing) and Andery sank back into his usual obscurity, he would've sworn on the soul of his beloved Dana that a smile flashed across Nicholas' face.

CHAPTER 4

The engine coughed, belched, then hacked a long throbbing beat until it awoke.

The mammoth internal combustion engine rattled the windows of those prefab buildings already completed with a final hammer-blow of sound, then fell into a hard purr, which spoke of power awaiting his call.

He adjusted the six-point safety harness, wiggled to settle himself better in the ancient and unfamiliar command couch, then laughed (voice lost to the high-pitched sound that spun up from the turbo diesel as he dead-tested the throttle) at the idea of *so much power* from an IndustrialMech. *More like a poodle compared to a timber wolf.*

He glanced over the controls one more time—practically tasting the mothballs from which the stored IndustrialMech so recently received a new lease on life (Senior Site Manager Sorren's acerbic voice almost materializing beside him with its biting commentary on his skills)—then moved the throttle forward slightly. The engine revved again, sending hot eddies swirling through the mostly open-air cockpit of the 'Mech, springing sweat up along grime-smeared arms and forehead, while he maneuvered the IndustrialMech into taking a thumping step forward.

Having set the machine into motion, Andery gave over the rudiments of the slow trundle to the state-of-the-art locomotion-neurohelmet interface that, among other things, tapped into his eyes' movements and focus to detect the direction for walking and when and where to stop.

It never ceased to amaze Andery that such an ancient machine could've survived and been so extensively upgraded, when the vast majority of such chassis—at least among Hegemony worlds—were decommissioned and recycled, replaced by fusion-powered IndustrialMechs. *A testament to how desperately we clung to any resource when we built our original Exodus fleet.* But when you've got to build a new city overnight, everything comes out. Even if the dearth of petrochemicals on any of the worlds they'd colonized so far meant it would be going back into mothballs all too soon. He smiled sadly, then chuckled at such empathy for a piece of hardware. *Not like you're a real 'Mech.*

Moving to secondary controls, he spun the 'Mech's arms up so giant, C-clamp vise-grips could grab a ten-by-fifteen-meter section of wall. With the ease of a child hefting a dollhouse, the ConstructionMech hoisted the load into the air. The keening of the internal gyro spoke of how it hungrily fed off Andery's own sense of balance through the ungainly neurohelmet (nearly twice as big as his 'Mech's), compensating for the shift in balance and the added, off-center weight.

Andery maneuvered joysticks and foot pedals in a choreographed dance that, despite his best efforts, still sent the machine stomping forward; unlike the simple movements through some sections, the current maelstrom of activity required he maneuver manually, overriding the automated system. He consoled himself with the knowledge that he wove through the veritable army of civilian contractors and builders, stockpiles of supplies and errant military vehicles traveling through the growing town without causing any damage. Or at least undue damage.

Katyusha.

Despite the cacophony of sound and visual stimulus spiraling around him, the word still managed to sigh through his mind; a soft autumn breeze through dappled leaves. Unlike his father and their unresolved issues, his mother's name did not usher in the hurt he expected. Despite the years of estrangement before her death, the echo of pain any mention of the Great General brought did not arise for her.

Instead, a soft melancholy of longing. As though remembering a long-ago summer day with brilliant colors, beautiful sounds and family and friends; ice cream and watermelon; cavorting kids and jovial, conversing adults: a happy memory softened in the distance like a rain-slicked boat receding on a pond. He managed to ignore that such events had never existed for him; these were invented memories pasted over a terrifying childhood under the Amaris Occupation, filled with hunger and loneliness and pain.

A particularly hard jolt pulled him from his reverie as the 'Mech set down one large pressure-padded foot into a depression. Slowing, Andery thumbed controllers and twisted joysticks—flipping on the automated movement system—sending actuators whining and raising the wall section. Andery closely watched the yellow flags of the construction workers directing his movement until he froze the section in place as their sticks crossed—the wall meshed with two previously raised sections—and momentarily locked down his machine. Andery tried to adjust a strap singlehandedly, threatening to dislocate his shoulder as the men set to work fastening the wall into place.

His eyes shifted to take in the rest of the area and the buildings sprouting from the soil like alien fauna run rampant. A city carved from the mostly barren plain of Novy Terra's southeastern region. Andery marveled at how fast the city was taking shape. *No, not a city. Still just a small town. A military outpost. But it's only been a month! What will it look like in six months? A year? Ten years?*

And just over those hills, not even fifteen kilometers away, the original settlement; a burgeoning colony city in its own right. Glancing around, his height in the cockpit allowing him to see all the bustling activity, Andery knew full well Nicholas had every intention of having his new "planned" city wipe away the existence of that settlement. *Is that your revenge against the governor, Niki? Your ultimate revenge for his audacity and stupidity?*

He shook his head. No, Nicholas was not petty. His plans were much grander than that, but if he pushed aside the governor along the way...so be it. Survival of the fittest. For as Nicholas took the first steps to forge a new society, he began by forging the ultimate city: a beacon to be the capital of Strana Mechty, the capital of the Kerensky Cluster, the capital of his new vision.

And named it after their mother. *And nothing for Father, Nicholas?*

A blaring horn snapped off his thoughts, telegraphing the crews were finished, and Andery unlocked the vise-grip arms, spun them open, then up and out of the way, while taking a careful step backward.

Weaving back through the same dance floor required just as much concentration; for once he wished he could engage the auto movement program. By the time he reached the staging area where the prefabricated sections were being off-loaded from recently landed DropShips, a dull headache thudded through his forebrain, matching the tempo of his 'Mech's footfalls.

Stepping into his assigned square chalked on the newly extruded ferrocrete, Andery began powering the machine down. A little early, but walking one of these machines around with a headache would be about as advisable as sticking your head into a *crana*'s nest. *If I have to watch one more safety video on the creature, I'll get sick on the spot.*

As he finished his checklist, fully locking down the machine's legs and cutting off the power to the engine—which struggled for life through several last coughs and belches of ghastly smoke—Andery noticed someone waiting for him. He couldn't quite make the person out through the deepening twilight; the nondescript orange jumpsuit didn't help.

Shucking off his neurohelmet, he stowed it behind the command couch, then unhitched the safety harness and heaved himself up and out. Muscles locked into a sitting position for long hours screamed at the unfair treatment and dull pain spidered out across a tired back. *What do you expect, Mr. Teacher Couch Potato? Do you good to get some exercise and feel what it's like to earn your living by the sweat of your brow.*

He almost fell the last few rungs of the metal ladder and stumbled before a strong hand grasped his shoulder.

"Easy there, Andery. Pushing yourself a little much, aren't you?"

Andery glanced up with a tired smile, taking in the large beard and even larger smile of Windham Khatib. "And you don't? How is it you've got only people working with you, no IndustrialMechs, and yet your church is almost finished."

Windham pulled himself into a pious pose, then spoke reverently. "With God's hands, anything is possible."

"Or several thousand tireless volunteers."

"What do you think God's hands are?"

They both laughed and Andery shook the kinks out of his legs, pinpricks of life skating down his flesh like ant bites, then began to slowly walk toward a distant Quonset and a desperately needed meal and bed.

"Why you here?" he said after they'd closed some of the distance.

"Was just wondering why you're not attending the staff meetings anymore. Nicholas has been using your word—the Fusion—like a sword to cut through discussions anytime they bog down."

Andery shrugged uncomfortably. "I do enough sitting around and discussing as I'm teaching. I felt like *doing* something was much better. Besides, you know that already."

"Can't I check up on an old friend?"

"Well, yeah. But that still doesn't tell me why you're here."

Windham shook his head, then ran fingers through the curly black hair under his chin. "You know, Andery, you're getting better."

"Hmm?"

"Can't fool you as often as I like."

"What," he responded with mock indignation. "You saying you fooled me on occasion?"

"Maybe once or twice."

They both chuckled again and Andery breathed in deep, taking in the alien smells that were quickly becoming home while reveling in the sparring conversation of such a longtime friend.

"You still avoided the question, though."

Less than a hundred meters from the Quonset, conversations and the scraping of utensils on metal plates drifted on the soft evening breeze. Windham stopped, then looked Andery square in the face. "What does Nicholas plan to do?"

Andery straightened, taken aback by the question. "What do you mean? He's building a city. What else?"

"No, what are his ultimate plans? This all has to be for something."

"To house all these refugees."

Windham's eyes grew determined, as he yanked hard on his beard. "Come on, Andery. Anyone can come up with that. It's not Nicholas." He held up his hands as Andery opened his mouth to protest. "I'm not trying to say Nicholas wouldn't build the city to help the refugees. But that's too simple. There's got to be more layers to it."

"You mean beyond also giving them something to do."

"Yeah, beyond giving them something to do. Which is fine. I know that all too well. Military and civilian alike, they all need something to keep them working and keep their minds off the horrors we just left, or the family members and friends still stuck there."

Andery shrugged, as though that said it all, uncomfortable with this line of questioning.

"But that's still not enough. I've seen the way he walks among the camps. Sure, he lends a hand here and there, speaks the words people need to hear. But I see his eyes, Andery. Remember, I've known you a long time, and your brother is not so far removed from you as you'd like to think. He's weighing everything. Everyone."

"Is that bad?"

"Of course not. But for what? It's as though he's weighing them for something to come."

"Even if I knew something, why would you feel you could ask me? He's your de facto military commander as well," Andery responded, suddenly defensive, angry and unsure why.

Windham actually wrung his hands, then yanked again on his beard (Andery couldn't remember when he'd adopted that mannerism). "I'm just trying to watch out for my flock, Andery. I've felt his eyes on me. On my congregation as we work. We never shirk our duties. We always do our job assignments first before we move to work on the church house. Yet his eyes...I simply want to know why I'm being judged. I know him well enough to realize he has plans for all of us. Fine. No problem. But do those plans include allowing us to worship as we see fit?"

Andery glanced toward the beckoning slip of white light of the Quonset, suddenly unwilling to answer his friend. Because he didn't know the answer, and that left him with the hollow feeling that always welled up when Nicholas and his plans for a new society were discussed.

Finally turning back, he looked at Windham's earnest face and truthful eyes and came to a decision. Despite anything Nicholas might do, Andery knew who his friends were. And he would treat them as such.

"I don't know everything. Yes, he has many ideas for a new society, but he's not shared much with me yet. And whether they include allowing you to continue your worship...I just can't say," he finished lamely, feeling guilty that he could not assure his friend more.

Windham looked aside, then raised his eyes to the brilliant, purple-tinged borealis lights stroking the firmament. Andery felt the breeze pick up to a slightly biting wind and hoped it was not an omen.

Finally, Windham met his eyes. "Okay, Andery. But please. I beg you, will you let me know when you do know something? Anything?"

Andery paused a moment, once more weighing what this might mean, balancing the consequences of what Nicholas might do if he found Andery sharing privileged information— Nicholas's personal punishment would be far worse than anything the military might mete out for "sharing secrets"— then nodded once firmly.

They exchanged a clasp of hands and a firm stare before going their separate ways. Come what may, regardless of any new societies, if friendships did not count, then perhaps Andery would want no part of Nicholas's new order.

CHAPTER 5

KATYUSHA
NOVY TERRA
STRANA MECHTY
KERENSKY CLUSTER
10 OCTOBER 2802

"*Aaaaaaahhhhhhhh!*"

The yell jolted Andery out of deep sleep; a 'Mech-size exhaustion weighed him down with all of the classes, construction work, and concerned-civilian committees he had to cram into a week. His brain refused to work, though adrenaline cascaded across his senses, and he breathed deeply, looking around from the chair he'd fallen asleep in for where that terrible yell had come from. Like beads lined up by a toddler taking their time, his brain finally pushed jumbled thoughts into order: *that was a yell; the bedroom; Dana!*

He surged out of the chair in their small, lightly-furnished apartment and ran down the short hallway from their kitchen/front room, past the bathroom, to the single bedroom to find Dana moaning, twisting and turning. He immediately turned on the light, fearful of what he might find. She was covered in sweat and twisted in the blankets: for just a moment, as sleep tried to keep a ruthless grip on his consciousness, it appeared as though the bed was trying to strangle her. He moved to her side, knelt down—aware of how to proceed, though still uncomfortable despite years of supporting her through these episodes.

"Dana," he said firmly, but not overly loudly. "It's Andery. It's time to come back," he continued with as much love as he could infuse into his voice (*ignore the disquiet and the fear!*). "I need you. You need to come back." He swallowed, tongue abruptly too big for his mouth as the last words he'd promised he would say to her at such times refused to be spoken. She thrashed again, letting out another yell as though in pain, smashing aside his own barriers. "Nicholas needs you," he finally managed; only his love for this amazing woman kept the words from tasting bitter enough to choke him.

He repeated the mantra several times, then reached out to take her cold, clammy hand as he continued. Her breathing eased as her muscles relaxed, and her eyes finally fluttered open. He cut off his recital and shivered at her blown pupils, which carried visions beyond his understanding, before she slowly blinked and abruptly her usual mysterious eyes took him in, and her loving smile melted away trepidation.

"Another vision?" he said.

"Yes," she said. She slowly sat up, the sheets damp as she untangled herself, leaving her disheveled in a sweat-stained pajama top.

He almost reached out to stop her, not wanting the guilt, as her eyes unfocused. *She always shares her visions with me, but refuses to share with anyone else. And yet I simply cannot believe. Why can't I believe?*

"There was a plain of endless, twisted columns," she began, head cocked, as though reciting from a script only she saw. "You moved among them, as did Nicholas. And shadows danced, while howls of pain filled the air until my eardrums burst. And stars fell from the skies, settling upon the columns, splitting them, until every step you and Nicholas took you nearly died, clawing and climbing over the destruction. And though you called and called to each other, the howls and the collapsing columns drowned out your cries, and the stars filled your eyes, and you walked for an eternity, always so close but always so far."

Despite his unbelief, in such moments, in the cathedral of their silent, nighttime communion and the strength of her conviction, he could almost...not believe, but almost feel *her* belief. And though he struggled mightily to understand—

especially as the visions had come more and more often since Mechty—her gift to him of her innermost self was precious beyond compare; he was always loathe to speak too quickly, a sacrilege of this shared moment that was as intimate as any coupling.

The minutes stretched, and though he took in every curve and line of her face, he knew her eyes were unseeing as she sprinted down dark paths to try to remember; to dredge up the feelings; to find the meanings the visions imparted.

She finally shook her head, abruptly *back*, breaking the spell. "I do not understand all this dream tells."

Andery smiled, getting up from the uncomfortable kneeling position by the bed, sitting beside her as he took her hand, always surprised it fit so perfectly in his. "I don't know," he began, always careful in these moments to not become the swine for her pearls (thanks Windham!). "Nicholas and I are always near and yet far from each other. And well, our entire universe has been torn to shreds. Twice. Seems pretty straightforward."

"Yes. But my visions are never so linear. If I believe I understand them too quickly, then often I have failed. I will continue to think on this."

He nodded, grateful for the moment to just quietly hold hands; she'd come home after he'd fallen asleep in the chair, and they all too often missed each other for days at a time with their work. Though luckily she was no longer on exploration expeditions among the stars.

She looked at the clock on the wall, then turned to Andery. "You meet soon with Nicholas. You should go."

The moment of companionable comfort evaporated in a surging fury, and he felt trapped, trying not to jerk his hand away, the love in her eyes straining against such hated words in this moment. *Even in my own bedroom, Nicholas! You reach into my own bedroom! This should be mine, and yet even here you will take and take and take!*

He nodded woodenly, not trusting his voice as he let her hand go, standing up and stepping away from her as headed down the hall. He couldn't seem to find the words. To explain how her love seemed undercut by her ever-growing devotion to his brother, alongside visions he didn't understand. And while he'd talked about it vaguely with Windham, discussing your relationship troubles with another man seemed foolhardy. *Who can I speak to? Perhaps...perhaps Sarah?* Ever since she'd saved his life getting off Eden, their friendship had grown. Perhaps he could ask her. That he even contemplated asking another woman questions he found he could not ask Dana hollowed him out until he wanted to weep.

He ignored his coat on the peg beside the door as the night enveloped him.

The sky wept a hard, cold rain, which slashed down brutal, uncaring.

As it hammered relentlessly, it cleansed the air of the pseudo-polyps pollen, which at this time of year—for only a short few weeks (or so the longtime colonists assured the uneasy newcomers)—bloomed in the air like endless, angry hives of wasps, practically blocking out the sun in their desperate desire to procreate before their short lives were annihilated by the burning sun that would follow the rainy season.

The strange symbiotic relationship between the polyps-like ground-based vegetation the colonists called pseudo-trees— they looked like a tree only if you squinted hard, in partial darkness—and the thriving schools of pseudo-polyps that populated the nearby oceans generally made Andery's head ache anytime Dana brought it up.

She, on the other hand, was endlessly fascinated by the alien fauna and for the last several weeks, after finishing her work assignments, had spent all her time with her holorecorder in a dangerously small dinghy, cruising among the pseudo-polyps as they breached the surface and ejected their pollen-like spoors from grotesquely swollen abdomens into the air. The spoors were then washed from the sky by the now standard-as-clockwork rains, pollinating the pseudo-trees (would he ever call them trees?), who returned the favor—as far as anyone could tell at this point—by releasing an enzyme in their root system, which trickled into the water table and made its way to the ocean, fertilizing the pseudo-polyps.

Unfortunately, the "pollen" dissolved in the rain—Andery supposed it made it easier for the pseudo-trees to absorb—turning any rainstorm into a golden-hued spectacle (for those into such things) and coating almost everything in a filmy residue. Which all led to a lot of cleaning duty this time of year.

Andery hunched his shoulders, moving quickly past the last few residential blocks, and almost slipped and fell on the newly laid ferrocrete. *Sky's weeping? Right! More like Mechty's pissing on us. And don't tell me we won't be having pseudo-polyp babies from drinking the damned enzymes.*

He paused for a moment in his rant, glancing down to find he'd stepped in a puddle; completely soaked his right pant leg, nearly to his knee! Finally taking a deep breath, knowing his anger should be directed at his blasted brother rather than the stupid polyps just trying to get laid, he moved on. *When the master calls, I come running! Even Dana knows that!*

He ignored the scathing commentary on his own apparent lack of willpower of late—or the feelings of being driven out of his own home—and finally crossed the remaining distance to the Star League Command Post. Of course, no one actually called it that to Nicholas's face, but that's what they called it nonetheless. Even Andery.

Reaching the double doors, he almost wrenched his arm out of his socket. *Locked!* "What the hell, Niki? You ask me here at this ungodly hour and then you don't even show!" He almost turned and left, but something caught his eye. Peering past the rain-slicked outer doors of the large, two-story building, a dim glow cast up refracting light through the glazed doors; a plethora of miniature rainbows, which looked touched by Midas's finger, their colors washed in gold tones through the polyp-saturated drops coating the glass. *Not that the rain is going to stop anytime soon. Why does every world we colonize seem to have a rainy season that lasts for months?!*

The cool, rain-splashed glass actually eased a burgeoning headache as he rested against it, trying to decide if he could get away with leaving. *Not likely.* He pulled his head away, rubbing the polyp film from his forehead, and began pounding on the glass.

Several minutes passed, then finally the light intensified as someone opened an interior door, then approached him down the nearly black corridor. At first, he thought it might be his brother, but the build was wrong. *Female? What's going on? Thought this was going to be one of our midnight chats.* More like rants, though, with Andery simply listening to his brother talk about every subject from the Bushido codes of ancient Japan, to twentieth-century China, to the Second Soviet Civil War, to the resurgence of nobility under the Camerons, to the events that led to the Amaris Occupation and downfall of the Star League; his flurry of thoughts and apparently random ideas were almost more than Andery could handle at times—especially at midnight, after a brutal, backbreaking day of work building the city, then leaving Dana on her own—bringing to mind an aphorism supposedly attributed to a McKenna: *"The line between genius and insanity is only contextual, for there is no line."*

He took a step back as Jennifer Winson let him in.

"Andery," she said. If possible, her tones were actually cooler than the outside.

"Jennifer," he responded politely. She'd been the first to do away with his rank and use his first name, as though that might demean him somehow. Of course he didn't mind. At least he kept telling himself that. *No, not getting to you at all, is she? And why's she here anyway?* Since he first spied her at the staff meetings after their groundings on Mechty, he'd thought for sure Nicholas would push her away. That he hadn't was just one more mystery he never seemed to penetrate concerning his brother.

"Nicholas sent for me."

She nodded, already walking away, as though Andery were some errant schoolboy to be brought to heel. It was not a sensation he relished, but he didn't know what to do about it.

Jennifer strode into the room before him, as though she owed the entire building. Despite his dislike of her, he had to admire her poise. *You could stand in rags and command more respect from your troops than half the commanders that came with us.* That admission stung.

Andery glanced around to once more notice how spare Nicholas kept his office. No personal tokens or images festooning either desk or wall, just a simple, utilitarian office—a place for everything and everything in its place. *Not much different from your tent, Niki. Afraid to get too attached?*

Nicholas glanced up from the holotable, which had his whole attention, stretching to relieve an obviously sore back. "Andery. I'm glad you came."

"Do we always have to meet so late?" he immediately responded, then silently cursed himself for sounding so childish in front of Jennifer. *Nothing like adding fuel to the fire.*

"Progress waits for no one, Andery." Jennifer spoke before Nicholas could open his mouth. Nicholas glanced toward her, and she matched his gaze. He could see not an iota's change on either face; twin glaciers staking out their terrain across continents and daring the other to touch a boulder without their permission. Yet Nicholas turned back to his brother without the tongue-lashing he most assuredly would've unleashed on anyone else.

Andery surreptitiously took in Jennifer one more time. *Where the hell did you come from, and where's my brother? Where did you put him? One moment you're simply one of his subcommanders, and suddenly you're coming to our brainstorming sessions?* If he didn't know any better, he might think Nicholas was in love with her. But the look they exchanged reminded Andery of no love he'd ever seen. *More like two ferroconcrete walls trying to... out-ferroconcrete each other?* It seemed something else was going on.

Something I intend to investigate. Just not now.

"The testing will begin January first."

As usual, Nicholas's mind seemed to work in some quantum-state, which fluctuated between this world and a hundred other mirror realities, allowing him to simply pull up conversations in mid-sentence, as though he'd already had the conversation with Andery in some other, mirrored reality, and was simply picking up where they'd left off at some point.

That McKenna aphorism once more struck him as appropriate.

Usually such a statement came after an intense brainstorming session. Andery tried and failed to keep his eyes from straying to Jennifer. *You taking my place there as well?*

"What testing?"

"The testing of our soldiers, Andery."

"Um, Nicholas. We did that already. On Eden. All of us. A million and a half soldiers were decommissioned after those six months of testing."

"And that worked oh *so* well," Jennifer jumped in.

"Why do we need to repeat it?" Andery continued, trying to ignore Jennifer's presence; she made it difficult.

"That failed, Andery. The General's tests relied too much on old forms and ways. We cannot simply test for the best warriors. We must test in new ways. In ways that will ensure that those who succeed will recognize the importance of what we do."

"I'm not sure I understand. How can we test differently than how we tested before? Our *father* made sure even MechWarriors had to test out using personal weapons." Memories surged of his failure in that exact test, that left him teaching cadets after his brother pulled some strings; he savagely thrust them aside. "What more do you want than what our own *father* did?" As usual he made sure to emphasis their father's connection; too often, it seemed even Nicholas fell into worship of the Great General.

"There are ways."

"Live-fire exercises are always good for bringing out the best and brightest," Jennifer interjected once more.

"What?"

Her short frame moved into his field of vision, until he couldn't help but meet her smoky eyes; short-cropped brunette hair framed pretty, freckled features. *Eyes too much like Nicholas's.* He almost shivered, angry that this upstart could confound him so quickly.

"Andery," Nicholas continued. "There are many ways to diverge from the past, one of which is live-fire exercises."

"You're not serious?"

Nicholas chin lowered fractionally.

Careful, Andery. Walk slowly. "How many wounded will this lead to? How many deaths? I know you plan on returning, Nicholas. I know you're looking to create a new society. I understand that. I even agree with it. But we've so few here compared to what's left in the Pentagon Worlds. Can we afford to lose troops like that? Just to test ourselves?"

"But Andery, you tested yourself in unusual ways, did you not?" Jennifer practically cooed.

He glanced at her again and was speared by her smoky eyes; he lost his train of thought, confusion welling. "What?"

"Come now, Andery. Your simulator battle with cadets. The one where you bribed the technicians for time to take on four cadets at once. Traumatized them quite badly, I hear?"

His mouth slowly fell open at her recitation. *How the hell did you find out about that?* A quick look at Nicholas and Andery found a knowing look on his brother's face.

"That was different. It was just a simulator battle." Memories of that event, long buried, rose and shame burned anew. A teacher doing that to his cadets, regardless of their egging him to it. "...And a terrible mistake," he finally got out, his words barely audible.

"I know how you feel, Andery," Nicholas said. "But regardless, it was a break with tradition. It showed brilliance. In handling four opponents so skillfully, with such little waste and terrible swiftness. Brilliance."

Nicholas moved around the holotable, his features losing their dark cast and coming into focus as he strode closer, the room's front fluorescent lighting his face to match the sudden intensity singing in his tone.

"The Star League army conquered through the use of maximum firepower at every turn. That all-or-nothing mentality permeated every level of the society the General tried to create. And now those civilians are using that same mentality as they annihilate one another. No, Andery, it's time to break completely from the past. Time to begin making a new society. And a new society needs warriors to accomplish its goals. We begin testing on January first."

Nicholas glanced at Jennifer, and they shared an inscrutable look before he turned back to the table. For a moment, Andery actually wondered why he'd been brought here, when Jennifer obviously would prefer he was dropped into a *burrock* nest and Nicholas had already made his decision.

Finally, a response slowly crept over him. "Nicholas," he said softly, bringing both their hard-as-'Mech-armor gazes to him. "As you break with the past, just remember that the past holds both bad and good. Don't forget the good our father did."

Jennifer's smoldering eyes cut deep, but Nicholas slowly nodded, which was all Andery could hope for.

CHAPTER 6

NEAR KATYUSHA
NOVY TERRA
STRANA MECHTY
KERENSKY CLUSTER
11 NOVEMBER 2802

"Jerome!" Andery yelled as he leaped out of the small jeep. He ignored the muddy ground, the crust of the first hard freeze broken by the constant loading and unloading of supplies on the grounded *Mule*-class DropShip that hunched in front of him like a mobile skyscraper.

"Andery!" Jerome Winson yelled back as they grabbed each other in a backslapping grip. Honks of horns from trawlers moving up and down the large DropShip ramp were ignored.

"Thanks for letting me know you were going to be on-world!" Andery broke away, looking at the man he hadn't seen in far too long. "Has it really been a decade?" The creep of grey hair and extra wrinkles around Jerome's eyes confirmed at least that many years had indeed passed.

Jerome shook his head as he motioned down the ramp—finally listening to the irate haulers—toward a set of chairs off to the side that someone had set up for breaks between long stretches of resupply work. "I think it's actually been twelve years, though how you continue to look so young I've no idea," he said, slapping Andery on the back one last time as they sat down. "It's hard keeping up with Stephen. And speaking of the McKenna devil..." He pointed as another man came down the ramp toward them. His open, smiling face, blue eyes, and thick, wheat-blond hair had been used on recruitment posters during the last years of the Star League; now nearing sixty, he looked half that age.

I feel older than he looks!

"Andery," the man said, reaching out to exchange a firm handshake.

Emotions swelled at seeing two people who had meant so much in his life over the years, even if such long stretches kept them apart. "Stephen," he finally got out. "I only heard Winson was coming here. Had no idea you would be here as well."

"And I'm not sure I realized you knew Winson," Stephen said as he grabbed a chair, pulling it close—dusting off some errant snow—and seating himself.

"I've known him since the end of the occupation," Andery said. "Father entrusted him with securing Mother, Nicholas, and I from Moscow during the Liberation." The usual pain of those years were kept at bay by the joy of seeing them both.

Winson chuckled softly, a knowing look in his eyes as he kept the conversation light. "Yup. Both pups when I first saw them; albeit more street mongrel than lap dog. I guess I became an older brother of sorts over the years while Aleksandr struggled to hold it all together. But when the Exodus came, and then our years on the Pentagon Worlds, well..." he paused, scratching his chin as he glanced at both of them, and shrugging uncomfortably as he looked at Andery. "There just is always so much to do."

"Aye," Stephen said—settling further in his chair, running his hands back through his somehow still-thick hair—at almost the exact same moment Andery responded identically.

"Seriously, Jerome," Andery continued, catching his eye. "You have absolutely nothing to apologize for. You were there when we needed you most. And we've all been busy. Besides, you've been off for how many years now trying to find additional star systems. How many more have you discovered?" he asked, honestly wanting to know, while simultaneously distracting Jerome from any perceived guilt. *If anything, I'm guilty of thinking of you too little myself. Sooo much work.* "I was a little shocked when Nicholas told me you were on your way back and would be leaving again soon. With all the work we have to do right here on Mechty, well, I was just surprised to find he was wholeheartedly supporting your continued exploration of the Kerensky Cluster."

Winson laughed and slapped his knee. "Ten systems so far have burgeoning colonies. We'll be heading back to our most recently colonized system, Brim, and continue coreward for the next two years. We've found plenty of systems not worth the effort. We're hopeful we might just get two more set up in that time frame. And luckily, your brother considers what we do part of his vision." He shrugged again, looking slightly off to the side.

You're uncomfortable, Winson. You've been gone for so many years; longer than Stephen. You're not sure if Nicholas's vision is something you can be a part of. But like the rest of us, you've no idea what to do differently.

"I know my brother recruited heavily among scientists when making the case for our second exodus," Andery continued, knowing he didn't want to bring up such uncomfortable discussions; he just wanted to be himself, talking among friends. *But how often does that really happen?* "Just didn't realize that extended into exploration as well."

"Your brother's visions are...impressive," Stephen said. "I believe he doesn't only see a year or two from now, or even a decade or two. Centuries stand before his eyes. And this new society he's building will eventually need every world we can discover."

Andery watched Stephen's face—his friend, a towering figure of the Star League Defense Force both before and after the Exodus—vacillate between the same uncomfortable look as Jerome, and the creeping awe of his brother Andery saw on far too many people. *Not you too, Stephen. Not you.*

"I turn around for a moment and you're all kicking back, lazy as usual," a new voice intruded on their conversation.

Andery looked over his shoulder as Major General James Carson extracted his massive frame from the jeep he'd been driving. "Carson!" he said, getting to his feet. This was the first time he'd seen the man since that moment back on Eden, nearly a year ago—the last time he'd seen Stephen, come to think of it—when they'd made the momentous decision to follow

Nicholas into this second exodus; a decision partially informed by Andery's own choice to follow his brother (he hastily pushed that volatile thought aside). "Um, should I salute? I mean, we are in public," he said, smiling as he raised his hand as though threatening to carry through.

Carson grinned in return, his receding hairline admitting—like several of them—that age was creeping up, even if just a shadow. "I believe the last time we saw each other, I told you we needed to relax a little more. Or everyone would start to think we're in the military."

Memories of days of teaching and civilian interactions threatened to overwhelm Andery. *Feels like I'm barely in the military.* He slapped down the pity-filled thought.

As Jerome had been an older brother of sorts prior to the start of the Exodus, Carson had later filled that role for Andery. *Because Nicholas has never been an older brother. He's just... Nicholas.*

Everyone laughed as Andery pointed at another chair, but Carson shook his head. "Sorry gents, but I'm actually here to personally hand some data to the ship's captain, and then I'm on duty."

Stephen's frown nearly matched Jerome's. "And that's not for me?"

Carson shrugged easily—if he was at all uncomfortable, he hid it well. "From Nicholas to the captain, who will be given charge of the data to hand to every colony's governor. I don't even know what this is," he said, patting a small satchel he was wearing. "Whether the captain decides to share with you, that's at their discretion." Carson did step forward, however, giving everyone a firm handshake, including Andery again, with a friendly smile that never failed to lift spirits, before walking up the ramp, timing it between vehicles still moving in and out of the cavernous hold.

What in the world is so secret that you don't trust it to any type of communication except physical copies? And why are you giving ship captains what seems preferential treatment over your own commanders? What are you up to, Nicholas? Andery wondered if there would ever come a day that such a question would not surface.

He breathed in, the smells of Mechty still unusual on his tongue, and turned to find Jerome and Stephen wearing their own troubled looks.

"I met your sister," Andery said to Jerome, trying to distract himself—and them—from dark thoughts. *I need to ask Carson about Jennifer, but it has to be the right moment. For now...let's see what Jerome has to say.*

"Yeah?" he responded, an odd look there and then gone from his eyes.

You're just as disturbed by that growing awe of Stephen as I am, not to mention what those messages might be. Andery just managed to keep a sigh from escaping. *Even here, even now, when it should just be the three of us, my brother casts a long, long shadow.*

"Yes," Andery continued. "She is...um...she's..." He was suddenly unsure what to say about the mysterious woman who seemed to be driving a wedge between him and his brother. *As if there could even be a wider chasm. But apparently...there can be.*

Jerome slapped his knee again. "She is something else, isn't she; been a pain for as long as I've known her!" He broke out laughing, apparently enjoying his own joke, the sound almost drowned out as a particularly large truck began making its way up the ramp, its diesel engine drowning out all talk for a moment with its gut-rumbling rhythm.

"Let me tell you about what she did to me as a kid," Jerome said, smiling easily, as the conversation became one of youthful pranks, and for a precious hour the men managed to not discuss the grandiose events inexorably grinding toward them.

CHAPTER 7

NEAR KATYUSHA
NOVY TERRA
STRANA MECHTY
KERENSKY CLUSTER
1 JANUARY 2803

The bitterness bit deep, hard.

A winter wonderland spread before Andery like a pristine sculpture cast in the most exquisite crystal. For kilometers into the distance, the wonders of nature were frozen in time. For this instant, this one single moment, the world seemed held fast against time's relentless wash.

The woods began almost immediately to his left. Hoarfrost thickly coated each pseudo-tree, and almost a meter of newly fallen snow finished the job, pushing spiny, tangled boughs low until the p-trees appeared to be ancient crones, shoulders hunched and backs bent to their heavy years and the burdens of a long life.

The nearest p-trees peeled away to his left at a hard angle, marching in an unbroken chain of old, green-and-white-wrapped women into the distance, while in front of him, a large valley slowly opened up. Like an endless field of transplanted pearl-wheat captured in a single instant of motion by a holophoto, the snow spread in a frozen, undulating wave for dozens of square kilometers. A line of low hills humped up along the far right; a mammoth, mythical giant, slumbering under the snow, its hips and shoulders just breaking free of winter's grasp and ringing the valley's right flank with its body.

Such a perfect scene should be on a holocard, bringing a mother news of her daughter's fun on her first trip off world, or love from a woman to her lover on her return home to visit her family. Not this.

Simultaneously, Andery's mind and the exterior world violated the pristine pastoral, rending it as Amaris had the Terran Hegemony. Blackness swirled; he fought the anger that followed on its heels like a ravenous predator sniffing prey.

Artillery goes there and there. Set up screens and pickets there, there and there. Lines of fire there and there, with overlapping lanes of fire along that line. Mines across that section, overlapping there and there. Infantry berms dug along lines there and there. Vehicles hull-down there and there. 'Mechs screened in the trees, lights back behind those hills for quick redeployment and final fallback there, there and there. Completely defensible. Could stave off an assaulting force three times the defender's size.

Snow shivered free from the nearest p-trees. As though the crones grew restless and tried to shake free of their slumber, preternatural senses awakening to coming danger, as the vibrations of heavy footfalls thudded metronomically to his militarily surgical analysis of the terrain.

The tableau broken, the cold stole over him once more, raising shivers as huge puffs of white trailed away on the light breeze and he coughed as numbing daggers of cold thrust blindly up his nose and down his throat and into lungs not built to breathe such frigid air.

Glancing behind him, Andery abruptly wondered if the mythical, slumbering giant had awoken. Yet in place of the pliable flesh it lay down with, the harsh winter had transformed its flesh into glistening ice-hard armor of a war avatar. Another shiver wormed up his spine and the fancy floated away like his breath as the reality of the twelve-meter-tall BattleMech stomped past him (the snow no impediment to its massive, myomer-driven legs), heading into the valley below.

Even through his cold gear and ear protection, the whine of actuators hung in his ears like an angry hornet as legs swung ponderously—but with incredible power and purpose—and arms matched rhythm. Sunlight glinted off weapon apertures on the torso and the mammoth particle projector cannon under-slung on the right arm, which held the promise of horrific energies soon to be unleashed.

Why did you have to be the first? Does it matter? Does any of it? He tried to keep the anger stoked and fueled, but too quickly it twisted into bitterness once more. *Is this all my fault? Don't I have enough demons? I don't have to carry this one as well.*

Some kilometers away—hard to tell at this distance, with the sun turning the entire valley into a burnished mirror— Andery could just make out the *Black Knight*'s opponents. He reached down, grabbed the rangefinder binoculars slung around his neck and raised them to his goggled eyes. A quick adjustment and the distant view leaped dizzyingly forward, bringing into sharp relief the *Knight*'s counterparts.

Lancelot. Night Hawk. Clint. *At least they're all lighter tonnages. At least Niki decided three was enough and didn't go for four.* Either thought didn't make him feel any better. "What are you thinking, Niki?" he said, using the demeaning nickname he usually only internalized.

"That winning a commission in his new military through real combat will create a fanatically loyal army."

Andery startled so badly he dropped the rangefinders and spun toward the voice. His body heat, despite the cold, had managed to soften the snow in the long minutes he'd stood there, just enough for his rapid movement to upset his balance, and he found himself landing hard on his hip, slamming his elbow painfully into the ground, despite the thick snow.

Leveraging into a better sitting position, he glanced up almost sheepishly—glad his gear hid his burning face—and found only an equally masked, swathed, and muffled individual. For all he knew, it could be Niki, or heaven forbid Winson, or anyone of the dozens of officers allowed to witness the first of what would be many seemingly endless combats. Just the idea of how many months would be involved; how much destroyed military equipment; how many casualties; how much work in fixing man and machine; how many deaths: too painful to contemplate for long. Especially when Andery knew this would only be the beginning of the transformations to come.

"Sorry about that," the figure over him said, extending a helping hand. Though Andery could not tell female from male in such clothing, the hand clasp *felt* female, as he was hoisted back to his feet. *Something about that voice.* Couldn't put his finger on it, though.

He laughed, despite the situation; surprised he could laugh. *Amazing what embarrassment can do.* "Don't worry about it. You just surprised me. My own stupid fault."

"In all this gear, a 'Mech could almost sneak up on you. Should've given you better warning."

"Like I said, no problem."

Large shoulders raised and resettled, as though the newcomer could care less as well. Already the victim once of his own embarrassment, Andery tried surreptitiously to discern who the person might be; *they knew my name, so why wouldn't I know theirs?*

"You were saying?" he finally said. *Perhaps if I get the person talking, I can figure it out.*

"That I think Nicholas knows exactly what he's doing."

"Yeah, but does he know what he wants?"

"Absolutely."

"And that is?"

"A fanatically loyal society."

"Huh?" Andery shifted his stance marginally, easing the slight ache in his hip. It dawned on him how uncomfortable he suddenly felt. *Why am I discussing this with a person I don't even recognize?* He tried to decide if he felt like a traitor to his brother, but found only curiosity that a person other than Windham or Raymond would evoke trust so quickly.

"Just what I said."

"Okay. What does that have to do with these trials?"

"It's not obvious?"

"Obviously not."

The person turned away from Andery as a series of echoing explosions suddenly rocked the morning. Guilt assailed him, and he almost fell on his back again, spinning toward the battle just starting to unfold. *How could I forget so quickly?* He shook his head at such denial. *Because I want to. Because I'm still upset* *and angry. Because if something happens...*he simply couldn't finish the thought.

Downrange, a withering fusillade of scintillating energy, pulsing darts and vomited streams of depleted uranium shells crisscrossed the sky in a horrific skein of latent death. Though the *Knight* weighed more than the other designs—the *Night Hawk*'s 35 tons and the *Clint*'s 40 tons matched the *Knight*'s own 75-ton weight—the combined armaments of the adversaries far exceeded the *Black Knight*'s.

Metal clasps snapped around his heart and squeezed until he couldn't breathe. Snatching up his rangefinders again, he brought the battle into exquisitely painful focus. A large laser from the *Night Hawk* and a PPC from the *Lancelot* almost merged into a unified energy stream before slamming into the right-leg armor of the *Knight*. A ton of armor sublimated instantaneously before clumping and hardening under the extreme temperatures into a rain of ill-shaped and misbegotten pellets, which peppered the snow, turning the idyllic white disease-ridden.

The *Black Knight* answered with unmatched precision, placing a PPC and paired medium lasers directly into the forward-thrusting torso-head assembly of the *Night Hawk*. The damage savaged the armor, ripping past its security, stabbing inward to wreak havoc on delicate controls. From a running lope, the *Hawk* suddenly stepped drunkenly and reeled away at an angle, with smoke billowing out of a gaping rent in its center torso.

Gyro hit, no doubt. Pride at the pilot's calm under fire and amazing marksmanship warred with paralyzing worry as another round of fire opened up. Man-made thunder echoed in the valley as a stream of shells from the *Clint*'s autocannon puffed a trough of white into the air before the rapidly moving machine's pilot could correct the aim and bring it into line with the *Black Knight*'s already damaged leg. The shells blasted armor away in huge flakes as the stream continued up and hammered into the lower chest before the shot spent itself. Meanwhile, a sun-bright trio of energy beams from the *Lancelot* almost obscured the entire upper torso as twin large lasers and a particle projector cannon snapped out from the 'Mech toward the *Black Knight*.

As though sensing the move, the *Knight* jinked hard out of line, causing the PPC to miss wide (steam boiled and flashed into vapor from the ice where the PPC caressed the ground), but the laser weapons still found their mark, one slamming hard into the cockpit; liquified armor ran in rivulets, but quickly froze into grotesque bas-reliefs in the cold.

"No!" He shouted at seeing the MechWarrior of the *Knight* so narrowly miss death's scythe. One more strike and it would all be over.

"Andery," the voice next to him interrupted, and despite everything, he turned away from the mesmerizing scene of violence. "She's brave, and fights like a demon."

"Yes," he said through a throat suddenly thick with emotion. "But stupid. So stupid. It's all so stupid."

"Is that what you really believe?"

Suddenly realizing how close he was to maligning his brother (his commanding officer!) to a total stranger, he shook himself, trying to clear away the cobwebs of fright and bitterness that seemed to shackle him. "Who are you?" Andery abruptly asked, no longer worried about being embarrassed.

The person slowly shook their head—a slight flush did prickle his skin, but Andery did his best to ignore it—then raised their hands to undo several straps, allowing the goggles and faceplate to be pulled to the side. A wash of hot air billowed white, completely obscuring the person momentarily, then clearing to reveal one of the most beautiful women he'd ever seen. Short brunette hair, small mouth, and flashing eyes came into view.

"Sarah!" he said. "Come out to watch the pain?"

"Of course. I heard you were out here, and decided to see what all the fun was about."

He chuckled despite the situation, then glanced back toward the fight as a new round of vicious weapon blows carved troughs and trenches into armor on all sides. For a moment he couldn't decide if his heart beat harder over anxiety for the MechWarrior, or for Sarah. Guilt, already piled high after the terrible fight several days ago, heaped higher. *Bastard. You're a sick, vile bastard. You don't deserve Dana.*

"Andery," Sarah spoke again, and he glanced over. "Dana made her own choice. She understands what Nicholas is trying to do, and has chosen to follow that path as best she can."

He swallowed past another lump, ignoring a previous conversation they'd had about Dana while also trying to ignore the constantly strobing lights in his peripheral vision and crump of weapons fire, as once more Star League Defense Force personnel tried to kill each other. "Why do we have to kill each other just to create a new society?"

"Is that what you think is happening?"

"Dammit, don't you? They're out there trying to kill each other. To kill Dana. And it's my damn fault."

She took a step forward and before he could register the movement, her gloved hand slammed his face. Though not nearly as painful as a bare-hand slap, his head bent to the side under the blow. Shock, more than pain, dropped his jaw open as he met her blazing eyes.

"Stop this. Nicholas would have found a way to achieve his ends regardless of what you might have done, Andery. Just because he mirrors some stupid event in your past doesn't mean it's your fault. Just as Dana out there fighting is not your fault. You need to stop putting burdens on your shoulders that do not belong to you."

The silence between them stretched as they looked at one another, Andery's thumping heart a counter-beat to the fighting still unfolding. Sudden silence descended, pulling their eyes.

Andery's guts clenched until he wanted to vomit as he saw the *Black Knight* fall to the ground in an avalanche of torn and scorched metal. Though he wanted to scream, he held his breath as the only standing 'Mech, the *Clint*, slowly moved closer. A pregnant half-minute passed before the *Clint* raised its arm, signaling the fight was over and all pilots were, at the minimum, alive.

But how alive? "See. She may not have managed your three kills, Andery, but she got two and no deaths. Good omen to begin the trials."

Aghast, he turned back to Sarah as though to a blasphemer. "But it can't last. You know there'll be deaths."

"Yeah, there will be. But everyone dies. I watched you kill my lancemates at the very end, just before we escaped off

Eden..." Her voice trailed off as she looked past his shoulder at horrors they both remembered all too well. "I killed my own when I switched to your side," she continued, voice husky with emotion as she brought her eyes back to his. "We all die. It's how we die that matters."

"No! Dammit, it can't just be that! There has to be more."

"Why?"

"Why?"

"Yeah, why?"

"I don't know. Just has to be."

"Well, when you know, you let me know."

Andery opened his mouth to reply, and realized he didn't have one, though he burned with the need to make her understand. Rummaging through his own feelings, he finally managed to draw up something that made sense, though it cut a little too deep for comfort.

Because there's no convincing Dana. Perhaps you can convince one person and make a difference. Convince one other person that though we walk a new path, we can still keep from sprinting down it without a thought for the precipices on all sides.

"You never answered my question," he finally said, realizing if he wanted to convince anyone, much less himself, it would take a lot longer than a single afternoon. Especially when Sarah already seemed in Dana's camp of blind devotion to Niki's dream.

"And what question would that be?"

"Why you felt this led to a new society."

Once more she shook her head and her expression reminded him too much of Nicholas's. Disappointment. She began to refasten her faceplate, and Andery realized her skin was bright red from the cold.

"Because," she began, her voice barely audible as the plate muffled her words, "a new society where the warrior stands at the top requires the warrior to know he stands at the top. And living when you should have died...nothing like it to bring on a sense of being touched by god."

But which god? The thought bubbled darkly, but Andery already knew.

Knew all too well.

CHAPTER 8

MECHTY BRIAN CACHE II
NOVY TERRA
STRANA MECHTY
KERENSKY CLUSTER
12 APRIL 2803

Finally, the mammoth doors yawned wide; teeth framing an insatiable gullet.

"That's it. Bring it back. Back!" the foreman yelled, frustrated at the lackluster way the ConstructionMech pilot finished opening the door to the Brian Cache. The foreman's face and posture went from embarrassed frustration to sheer terror in the blink of an eye as he suddenly raced forward, hands waving frantically as he shouted for the pilot to cease his activities.

Andery, just arrived from the hospital on a hoverbike, couldn't immediately see the problem. His mouth slowly opened into a large "O" as a hairline fracture in the giant stone doors hidden behind a false hillside abruptly fissured into a large fault, then a cleft, and rapidly escalated through several other descriptors he couldn't think of quickly enough as the right-side door literally broke in two. Dust and debris showered everywhere as a sonic boom blasted out from the epicenter where the door crashed to the ground. Easily several hundreds of tons, the shattering ferrocrete of the disguised door tumbled into the legs of the hapless IndustrialMech, toppling it as easily as a bowling ball striking pins.

Spitting grit and dust, Andery took off at a run—ignoring the ground still shaking from the collapse—as a small army of like-minded people raced toward the fallen 'Mech. Before he'd taken a dozen steps, his foot came down on a rolling chunk of ferrocrete and the world went topsy-turvy as he fell hard to the left. Blackness took him after an explosion of pain to his head, like a light bulb flaring, burning out.

He came to, pain rolling back like a soft, warm, tropic tide; the pain surged and receded and surged again, each time draining further away. He raised a hand to his forehead and hissed at the ache above his right temple. *No blood, but what a goose egg.* He sat up slowly and experimented with moving his head left and right, and found if he didn't move too quickly, he could deal with it.

As he looked around, he was surprised to see enough dust still hung in the air to obscure most everything, like a heavy morning fog near the ocean; evidence he hadn't been out long. As he cautiously regained his feet—ankle tender from rolling on the rock, but he could put weight on it—Andery noticed enough time had passed for the extraction of the ConstructionMech pilot. Moving gingerly, he began heading toward the downed 'Mech, then thought better of it as the rough terrain became more jumbled, and he realized his head and ankle wouldn't be up to climbing.

Shortly, Andery stood before the gaping hole of the Brian Cache and his initial impression once more surged to the fore.

Mouth of a beast.

He remembered, as a child, watching a holodocumentary on nearly extinct species—at the end of the era when mankind was trapped on its home world and the terribly resulting pollutions—that the long efforts of the Terran Alliance, Terran Hegemony, and Star League had brought back to abundance, along with immense restored forests, watersheds, and the oceans. The one that woke him with nightmares for many days following was the angler fish, which lived in the deep ocean. It had a phosphorescent appendage on its body that it dangled out in front to lure fish to its mouth; a mouth which, by the way, until man ran into some truly gruesome alien fauna, had been the largest known jaw-to-body ratio of any creature. This cache reminded Andery all too much of that animal, taunting them with its phosphorescent military hardware, but ultimately beckoning men and women to their deaths.

To the deaths we'll unleash on ourselves.

The crunch of footsteps behind him brought Andery's head around a little too quickly, and he bent over before he fell over.

"You alright?"

Andery slowly straightened to find Nicholas standing beside him. No emotions showed on his features or occupied his hard, ice-chip eyes. *As usual.* Andery shrugged, as much for his own thoughts as for Nicholas. "Just took a dumb spill trying to help the pilot."

"He was lazy and stupid."

"Sure, but that doesn't mean we shouldn't help him."

"It doesn't?" He quirked an eyebrow.

"Nicholas," Andery began, then decided to switch tacks. "Sir, should you leave a soldier in the field if he makes an honest mistake and is wounded?"

Nicholas actually quirked a small smile. "'Sir' doesn't work coming from you, Andery. As for that soldier, there *are* no 'honest mistakes.' Platitudes to excuse incompetence. I would hope no soldier in *my* army would be that lazy *or* stupid. And if they were, they would remedy it, immediately."

Andery noticed the subtle inflections, but decided to pass. *Of course it's his army, he's the commanding officer.* Though the shadings ran much deeper, Andery refused to fall into that trap. For now. *Plenty of fights to fight without that one.*

"You can't ever forget just plain bad dumb luck." Andery raised his hand to touch his goose egg. "Not to mention deliberate malfeasance. That was poured ferrocrete," he continued, sweeping his arm back up to the gaping wound in the false mountain. "No way a little manhandling should've done that. Our father may have been many things, but he was not superhuman, and with all the city building and the construction of these caches across the early years of the colonies, he simply couldn't monitor them all. Nor, obviously, could the supervisory board he established. Willing to bet some corners were cut, with some future trades and kickbacks stored up for the foreman in the bargain?" He returned his brother's eyebrow quirk.

"Touché."

Turning away from Andery, Nicholas hefted a heavy-duty flashlight and played the beam around the entrance. The light tried vainly to penetrate the dusty haze and inky darkness obscuring the long entryway beyond the doors. Andery tried to suppress a shiver at the idea of a long tongue waiting within, anxious and salivating to taste new meat.

Nicholas began walking forward.

With only a minor hesitation, Andery followed. "Is this safe?"

"Why wouldn't it be?"

Andery glanced around at the destroyed door, mangled IndustrialMech and general havoc. "Um, Nicholas..."

"Simply an error on his part. What, you think it sabotaged?" Nicholas didn't even deign to turn around, confident his voice carried sufficient scorn. It did. "Would the General really do that?"

Nice of you to ignore my explanation. Andery shook his head slowly and stepped around a chunk of rock, moving careful to keep dizziness at bay and ensure his hurting ankle didn't shift to something worse, covering his mouth and breathing shallowly as a particularly dense cloud of dust wafted by; stinging particles edging past his clamped fingers and finding their way down his nasal passages. As their footsteps began echoing, Andery sneezed, the sound a gunshot in the vast corridor, slapping around chaotically before falling away into the distance. He reeled for a moment, bending over until the spinning stopped.

"Sometimes I'm not sure what our father was capable of," he continued after straightening. "I do know he didn't want these caches falling into the wrong hands."

"And are our hands wrong?"

Andery paused before answering, again hoping Nicholas would turn and look in his direction, but once more he seemed more intent on what lay ahead than what lay behind. *But we have to learn from the past, don't we, Niki?*

"Anyone's hands can be the wrong hands if they're not careful."

A particularly noxious chill slithered across his spine, and Andery shivered and glanced behind him to find a diminutive figure silhouetted in the large entrance to the tunnel; a child entering the hall of a mountain king. As the figure began moving forward, Andery froze for a heartbeat, recognizing the gait. After so many years, his heart stuttered and his breath quickened as he braced for a view of sea-green eyes and hair the color of burning light, hating that any woman other than his beloved Dana could still affect him.

"Andery," she said, stepping close as a flashlight blazed to life, dazzling his eyes and momentarily crossing images in his head before he righted himself. *Not a holding cell and days of hunger and pain, but the here and now. And not Jes, but Jennifer.*

"Jennifer." Andery tried for the same cold, indifferent tone and failed utterly.

"A nasty rock fight?"

His brow furrowed for a moment before he glanced away, irritated, wondering what connection his brain was making between Jes and Jennifer. *Probably why I hate her so much.* He glanced back to find her slipping forward to Nicholas's side, a smile playing across his brother's lips.

"We found it," she said softly, but in the achingly quiet hall, the words were strong and firm in Andery's ears.

"You thought we wouldn't?" Nicholas responded.

"I thought it might prove more...difficult. It was purposefully hidden and the records destroyed, after all."

Nicholas bellowed loudly, a harsh sound Andery never could quite equate with laughter. "I would not call six months easy."

"It was more difficult to get here. And will only become more so."

Even Andery knew there was no response to that prediction, and finally picked up his own pace as the two of them continued farther into the long, 'Mech-size passageway. Andery glanced over his shoulder, expecting an army of curious soldiers and civilians, despite the possible dangers posed by this hidden Brian Cache. Then realized Jennifer likely had tossed around one of her famous "looks"—which could rival Nicholas's for icy—and without a word they would stay out until invited. The wrath of Nicholas was bad enough, but almost overnight (at least it seemed to Andery) Jennifer had carved out her own place and prominence in his regime.

How? Still can't figure out...

His thoughts trailed away like a leaf gently pulled on a night's soft breeze as they crossed from the long tunnel into the first of what must be many cavernous chambers. The enormous room seemed to mock their tiny stabs of light trying to penetrate the darkness. Like a 'Mech repair facility in stasis, a half-dozen giant cubicles marched away on either side into a gloom their beams could not pierce. Heavy webbing crisscrossed each opening, making it impossible to discern the contents... unless you knew what to expect. Beyond the spiderwebbing, caught and frozen in cocoons of decommissioning—'Mechs. A dozen, if not two dozen in this room alone. *How much more under your mountain kingdom?*

"How's the testing going?" Nicholas spoke.

Andery almost leaped out of his skin at the sacrilege of speech in this hallowed chamber dedicated to man's glorious war machines. He turned to Nicholas to find him a mere shadow, as his brother's light played against Andery and Jennifer began moving toward the nearest cubicle, a penitent believer on a quest to awaken slumbering gods.

"Another died yesterday, and three more are in the hospital. Just came from there. Scores have died so far."

"I know."

Previously kept at bay by his fascination, the cold of the place began to creep in. The cold and sterility. The pain in his head. He glanced around, clenched his fists and looked at Nicholas once more. "Then why ask?"

"You seem so interested."

"Interested in *your* soldiers. Of course I am. They're my comrades. Why wouldn't I be?"

"'The sole purpose of this army is to stand firmly with the people, who will then serve them wholeheartedly.'"

The change in tone always signaled a quote of some kind, but Andery found his brother once more outpacing his knowledge of ancient leaders. Andery wondered if this quote once again fell from the lips of the ancient Chinese leader of whom Nicholas seemed so fond of late. *Need to check on that.* He sniffed. *In my copious amounts of free time.*

"Your test nears?"

Andery felt whipped back and forth as Nicholas jumped from one topic to the next. *Are they all connected and I just don't see it yet, Niki?*

"Yes," he finally responded.

"We'll have your *Exterminator* fixed in time."

"I know," he said, then stopped as Jennifer trotted back to them. "With the supplies in this final, hidden cache, we'll be able to fix all of the machines."

"But what about the soldiers?"

Even in the semidarkness, he could feel her dagger-sharp eyes stabbing at him. "The women and men serve, as they are meant to serve. And in serving the people, they'll be cherished by them. As it should be. As it should've been."

As it was and yet failed, you want to say, but won't besmirch our father's name? Not in front of Niki? But this time, Andery knew the mailed fist their father had never used to enforce such "service" to the military would be openly exposed and unleashed by his brother, Jennifer or no Jennifer. A fist already starting to form in the endless testing; his stomach cramped at the idea of so many wounded, and the deaths as SLDF troops slowly killed each other in mere training.

A fist that would wear an armored gauntlet taken from the stores their father hid away.

And I'm next...

CHAPTER 9

"This, I must say, is not the pub," Raymond Sainze said, the usual taciturn look on his face as he came to a stop.

"What are you talking about, Raymond?" Windham Khatib said expansively, sweeping his arm around the dirt lot that had been staked out for a park someday, and the ramshackle table dragged into position and covered with take-out food. "This is some of the finest take-food credits can buy!"

Jason Everly grinned even wider than Windham, reached into the big bucket to pull out a large chicken leg—Andery desperately wanted to believe it was chicken—and took a big mouthful of the greasy meat. "PHeNomeNal!" he managed to get out without spitting too much food out.

Laughter swept the table, Andery joining in; winced slightly at the echo of pain on his head from his spill at the cache.

"I'm not sure about Jason's credentials to be a food critic," Stephen said, beaming his usual good looks around, "but the food actually isn't too bad."

"Agreed," Carson said, chewing on his own leg while standing just to the side of the table. "However, I'm not sure I'd trust that table," he said, giving it the stink eye.

"That's only because it can't handle your frame," Andery shot back. Laughter burst out as Raymond inclined his head and careful slid into the last available slot at the table; it only groaned slightly.

Several minutes passed in companionable silence, the never-ending construction sounds of the city washing over them and nearly forgotten.

After he finished off another leg—he was hungrier than he imagined—Andery wiped off his hands on a napkin, before scuffing his feet in the dirt. "This is great to get together—I can't believe we've not done it yet—but no substitute for the pub." He meant it as a good jest, but it fell somberly across the group. *Too close a reminder to all we've lost?* He mentally kicked himself for ruining the first chance he'd had to get together with so many of his friends since arriving on Mechty.

"Andery, your test is coming up, right?" Jason said, his grin still in place, despite the drop in the mood at the table.

Andery squinted as the sun abruptly moved past clouds, shining brightly, bringing warmth on a cool spring day. "Yeah. First of May. You?"

"May 15th?"

"We know you'll do well," Jason said. Confirming nods and grousing at the table made Andery feel uncomfortable. *Especially when any of them might die? And all because of me.*

Tightness clenched within at the specter that he could be at fault for any of their deaths. The confrontation with Nicholas and Jennifer months ago that had sparked the current training still gnawed at him. It wasn't often that he considered whether it might be better if Nicholas hadn't ever made it off Eden, but the thought struck in the moment, and he nearly laughed hysterically. *What, I'm going to replace him!* He barely kept it in check, and pushed such thoughts away as he struggled in the moment.

And yet, did he tell them any of it? Did he tell these, his best friends, anything at all? No? He shied away from it, rationalizing his indecision. *They could've said no. They could've backed out. They chose this!*

"Did any of you think to...to not participate in the test?" he finally managed to get the words out as a way to veer off his own internal thoughts.

There was an abrupt silence as Andery glanced around the table: Jason and Carson both immediately shook their heads. "Why would you even ask that?" Jason said, a nearly scandalized look on his face.

Because it's all so stupid! Andery shrugged even more uncomfortably, realizing how dumb it was to ask a question he didn't have an answer for. "Just wondering. You know I always ask questions." It was lame, but someone it seemed to calm Jason and the others took it in stride.

He realized Stephen, Raymond and Windham, hadn't responded, each of them taking a long moment to marshal his thoughts.

"I did think on it," Raymond finally said in his usual soft voice. "But I could think of no good reason not to. We have followed him this far. We have followed you this far, Andery. Why shouldn't we follow just a little while more?"

"You're asking us if we thought of not participating, knowing the thought never crossed your mind," Windham responded, his gaze deep and searching, as it so often was when his friend tried to dig past his walls. "You're getting all-new layers, Andery. As Raymond said. We followed your brother. We followed you. After all that's happened..." he continued glancing around, the glimmer of near-tears shimmering in his eyes, "...there is nothing but to move forward. To believe. To hold together no matter what may come."

Andery tried to squelch the rise of discomfort anytime his friends said such things. *If they came here for me—if—then they could die for me. Right here. Right now.* And they all seemed to understand that as the weight of the moment settled down upon them, and Windham's emotions engulfed the group. Knowing looks of bright eyes swept the table as years-long friends slowly reached out hands to grasp shoulders, bump fists, and even a punch from Jason.

The comradery a balm that almost kept Andery on an even keel as his mind raced and raced. *What is it you want, Andery? What do you want?* He hated that he had no answer. And in finding no answer, would continue as a leaf bouncing ever in the wake of his brother.

CHAPTER 10

JOTT GEYSER FOREST
NOVY TERRA
STRANA MECHTY
KERENSKY CLUSTER
1 MAY 2803

"You will do fine, Andery."

He didn't hear Dana at first, absorbed as he was in gazing up at the twelve-meter height of his *Exterminator*. *Why have I never named you?* The thought skipped across his consciousness—a stone skimming choppy waters—finally snagging on a particularly large thought-wave and sinking from view.

"Andery."

"Mmm..." The sun, just peeking through morning clouds, glinted on the forward-thrusting prow of the 'Mech, which ran straight from the lower torso all the way to the head, which knifed back from sleek shoulders. The small baffles that only a trained eye could see, nestled here and there about the *Exterminator*, indicated the inclusion of the experimental Chameleon Light Polarization Shield; Andery had never believed it lived up to its hype, and rarely used it because of the extreme overheating it caused.

He knew all the jokes. "Fat light 'Mech." "Overgrown medium." "Glorified IndustrialMech." He particularly liked that last one.

But they all missed the point. It was a design for finesse. For speed. And though it lacked the firepower of most heavies (even most mediums, he'd concede), a good warrior didn't need overmatched firepower. A good warrior needed a ride that suited him, made him feel he'd come home each time he strapped into the command couch. With that feeling, and the expertise to go with it, even light firepower could be devastating.

"Andery."

He finally turned aside from his newly repaired 'Mech to stare at his soul mate. The echo of pain in his thigh from his old wound as he gazed at his ride slowly faded, replaced by a new pain within.

"What is wrong, Andery?" As usual, her eyes saw more than most, and they seemed to reach inside him, to try to pull out what he hid.

"Just wondering how it will feel to pilot it in combat again," he dissembled, looking away. Sometimes it was easier that way. Like his questions about Jennifer that he'd avoided of late; he'd never once contemplated asking Dana about her.

"Are you sure?"

"Sure of what?"

"Sure that is all of it?

"What else could it be?"

"Nicholas?"

For a moment his stomach clenched, then he turned toward her, quirked his lips and shrugged sheepishly. Dissembling again. He was getting too good at it with Dana for his own liking.

"How often must you doubt your own abilities, Andery? How often must you compare yourself to your brother?"

As long as others do. As long as you do... "I know, just—falling back into bad habits, I guess." He looked down and massaged his thigh, feigning real pain. "Just a little nervous."

A hand rested on his shoulder, pulled him toward her. He let her strength pivot him around, then enfolded her in an embrace without looking into her eyes. Eyes that shone with all the love a man could possibly want. Eyes that shone just as bright for another. He didn't for a moment doubt her love. But something within him could not come to grips with her other dedication. A flame that burned as bright (brighter?) than her passion for him. *Am I so shallow?*

"It is time, Andery." She gave a final squeeze, then lightly stepped back. Though she never wore perfume, the scent of her skin lingered in the air and he sniffed; shivered at the idea of a man storing memories up of what he could no longer have.

He drank in her beauty to nourish his parched soul, than slowly turned away; the wrench it gave him was almost a physical manifestation of his unhappiness. He trudged across the pale blue spring scrub grass, uncaring of the dew slicking his boots. At the base of his 'Mech, he reached up to grasp the metal ladder and began the climb.

Halfway up, his mind totally occupied and boots slick and wet, his right foot slipped and suddenly he found himself falling slightly, white-knuckling the ladder as he swung out and down and then back in to bump hard against his 'Mech.

"Andery!"

The urgency in her voice seemed to calm him, to reach into the twisting knot of doubt and pain, bringing momentary release. He rested his head against the cool, aligned-crystal steel. *She loves me. She loves me.* Perhaps that was enough. For now.

"Alright," he managed to get out, his face flaming. "Wasn't watching my step."

"You watch your step on that battlefield, Andery Kerensky," she said, her voice letting him know what would happen if he didn't.

Despite everything, he smiled; the first true smile in far too long. "I will."

He slowly eased into the climb again, compartmentalizing his feelings and pushing them into a dark corner for now; if he died this day, no resolutions for anyone, much less himself.

Gaining the top rung, he stepped onto the shoulder of the 'Mech—mindful of his footing this time—then made his way to the back of the *Exterminator*'s head. There, he undogged the egress hatch and shimmied through. Once inside, he turned, dogged the hatch, then opened up the small compartment in the back of the command couch and pulled out several lightweight garments.

The first, a long-sleeved shirt, he quickly donned after wriggling off his utility jumpsuit in the tight confines; the synthetic heat-resistant cloth and its network of microtubes bunched and squirmed across his flesh, causing him to shiver. Then Andery pulled on the cooling jumpsuit (he ignored the gloves, always finding them too cumbersome). He had a bad habit of forgoing the cooling suit under normal circumstances, but he needed the reassurance now.

Finished suiting up, he stuffed the utility jumpsuit into the back of the chair, locked the compartment closed, then sidled around the front of his chair and settled into the command couch. A storm of visual and tactile senses assailed him; a cacophony of welcoming scents, sights, and touch.

Home.

He leaned back for a moment, squirming into the neo-leather, the squelching of flesh moving across the still cool and slightly hard material the final sign of coming home; he closed his eyes and rested his head against the back of the command couch, marshaling his thoughts one final time. *I'll confront Dana when this is done.*

He almost believed himself.

With a shrug to dislodge a mountain of burdens, he reached forward, grasped a large toggle and threw the switch, locking it in place. Beneath his feet, the fusion reactor hummed to life. The subtle vibrations sent tremors racing up and down his legs and arms, raising goosebumps.

Potential.

Andery always thought of it in such terms. Not in destructive might, or scientific know-how, or high technology. Simply potential. The potential for what he would do. What he could accomplish. Good or bad. *Always good or bad.*

And despite everything, despite all his arguments with Nicholas over the need for this testing and the unnecessary deaths and pain, a spot deep in his gut slowly flowered, radiating out, sending tendrils to every part of his body, finally ending with a shiver, which shook him with an energy almost as great as any orgasm he'd experienced.

MechWarrior.

He was a *MechWarrior*, about to stride forth in the most powerful machine ever created by mankind. A war machine unparalleled in three centuries of intergalactic warfare. An anthropomorphic tank set to dominate warfare for centuries to come.

Despite all his arguments, Andery was and would always be a MechWarrior. Regardless of his own doubts, nothing could ever change that—or the thrill of commanding such an awesome machine.

"*Voice authorization required.*" The electronic voice echoed in the confines of the cockpit as partial power cycled up through preliminary start-up, lighting a smorgasbord of tactical displays and systems readouts.

Toggling several switches, he responded, "Andery Kerensky." He could almost hear the *whir* of the computer as it ate the sound bite, processing it against stored data. He reached up, slightly behind and to the right, and pulled down the neurohelmet. Never liking this part, he slipped it onto his head, feeling it adhere to the shoulders of his cooling vest. He shrugged once or twice, settling the light helmet.

"*Voice authentication confirmed,*" the computer voice spoke. "*Authorization code.*"

"*Surkai.*" A small lump rose in his throat. Even after all the years separating him from the traumatic event, emotions still clogged his system each and every time he spoke that word. Twenty-four hours after the terrible revolt on the *Prinz Eugen* had been put down, a Lieutenant Colonel Surkai, with Asian features, intelligent eyes—and somehow, incredibly, a smile— in an airlock Andery was forced to use to execute the last of the mutineers; punishment for his unintended involvement that helped spark those awful events during the exodus. He might as well have made his authorization code "responsibility." For Andery, they were synonymous.

"*Welcome aboard, Andery Kerensky. Command is yours.*" Power rose to full and blank screens peeled back eyelids lit with digital fire to reveal readiness. Now and then, he believed he could almost feel the spirit of his 'Mech staring at him through the digital displays and tactical interfaces. How Windham would laugh at such spiritual ideas. But as he thought about that a bit more Andery changed his mind. *He'd probably think it completely appropriate.*

Andery clenched his jaw to open up a commline. "This is Andery Kerensky, ready for trial one." Suddenly, he couldn't remember the last time someone had used his rank. Or when he'd used a rank, beyond addressing Nicholas. He pondered that for a moment as he finished the start-up sequence, then it dawned on him and his jaw fell open.

Is it that easy, Niki? He knew the example must have come from Nicholas, or perhaps Jennifer. Just a few times is all it might have taken; a handful of important moments when Nicholas declined to use ranks, and others, so quick to follow his lead, took up the example. *A lifetime of military training swept aside so quickly? So easily?*

As he slowly closed his mouth and grasped the throttle with his left hand, easing it forward and sending the *Exterminator* into a determined step toward the detested testing, he marveled. *Perhaps it will be easier than I thought. Perhaps manipulating society and turning its course can be achieved quicker than I believed possible. If the pressures and the need are great enough...*

Elation and sorrow filled him in equal measure.

CHAPTER 11

JOTT GEYSER FOREST
NOVY TERRA
STRANA MECHTY
KERENSKY CLUSTER
1 MAY, 2803

A *Sentinel* raced between the glistening, fragile towers of salt and sediment.

When he'd first entered the columns, he felt a wash of familiarity, even though he'd never seen them before; the location had been randomly assigned to him. Only gradually had understanding dawned; it seemed a little too close for his comfort to a description of a vision Dana had shared with him more than a year and a half ago. But the frantic combat had quickly pushed aside such flights of fancy. *I can find any meaning in any of her visions*, he thought darkly.

The shockwave from the concussive blast of the Ultra autocannon shattered the delicate, almost artistic stalagmite-like structures nearest the *Sentinel*, shredding the last vestiges of such thoughts. Armor likewise exploded on the *Exterminator* under the hail of depleted uranium slugs, the fragments also slicing into the salt-encrusted sediment formations nearest Andery. Weakened by the bursts of shrapnel, several—two almost as tall as the *Exterminator*—wobbled, then toppled, knocking down additional columns.

The explosion of harsh mineral particles into the air, combined with a stiff breeze wafting a billowing wall of steam across his vision, cut off his visual senses as completely as a thrown light switch in a windowless room. Though his other sensors still screamed warnings of enemy proximity and target locks, his own internal siren blared louder, keeping him frozen: *Tominson. Tominson. Tominson.*

But there's no snow. And that's not Tominson. And this isn't a simulation and if you don't do something you're going to die!

Somehow, Andery dug deep and managed to dredge up a reserve; shook off his malaise like a dog shedding unwanted water. Grasped the throttles and with well-manipulated pedal strokes, got his *Exterminator* moving once more.

Almost without conscious thought, he danced his machine through the unique, ocher-colored forest of leftover salt and mud and unusual minerals (strange, almost iridescent hues that covered the gamut) that dried at unnatural speed after erupting out of the ground in scalding spews that carried steam and sprays of waters everywhere.

There were civilians pushing to protect the beautiful landscape. But the terrain made for spectacularly difficult maneuvering, making it a perfect venue for these tests. Anything Nicholas could do to make the tests more difficult, he would. *You'd send us out naked with sticks if you could get away with it, wouldn't you, Niki?*

Meanwhile, his mind pushed against the almost paralyzing déjà vu. Just over nine years ago, he'd been foolish enough to take on four cadets in a training simulation. A simulation that showed it was all too easy for Andery to lose control; a simulation that led directly to his final decision to cross the line with a student, Dana—his soul mate.

You're a paragon of virtue, Andery. Sleeping with a student and beating up on four more.

A bitter smile crept across his face while the stench of his own sweat and disgust curled and festered in his nostrils; despite the cooling suit, the bite of the harness into his shoulders felt more a straight-jacket built with his own hands across the years of his life, fashioned from his errors and mistakes, tying him down as surely as any insane asylum restraint.

Thunder rumbled nearby, picked up by the external mikes. *Autocannon fire? No. Not exactly right...* Andery's mind continued to wander until the ground shook as well—and he abruptly understood.

With desperate speed, he stomped down on the foot pedals, igniting the *Exterminator*'s jump jets. Plasma vented out magnetic baffles, launching the 65-ton machine into the air in a hard ballistic arc just as a geyser of searingly hot mud, alien minerals, and water exploded right next to him, bursting like an infected wound in Mechty's crust, exploding with pus, necrotic blood and bodily effluvium; the heat in the 'Mech spiked as a wave of the noxious, thick spew washed across the lower part of his left leg.

His eyes sought a safe landing zone while his hands automatically feathered the jump jets to bring him around and prepare for what was always a hard landing. He couldn't help but keep an eye on the geysering mass, which already had begun to harden in the middle as the exterior sloughed away in an ever-slowing torrent of runnels.

If not caught in this current fight for his life (or at least his position), Andery might have marveled at the unique qualities of this strange region. Instead, he adjusted his dropping trajectory, knowing there was no helping it, and braced for impact as the *Exterminator* slammed through the top portion of one towering structure, even as the roaring thrust from the jump jets bled off most of the remaining velocity. With an expertise learned years ago, Andery brought the *Exterminator* down, flexing the 'Mech's knees in a perfect touchdown.

Warning klaxons exploded in the cockpit, and like Mechty's aurora borealis across the night sky, the console lit up. *Incoming fire? Where?*

Already slamming the throttle full forward, Andery juked hard to the right, sliding the *Exterminator* down into a low crouch that swung up and around, pushing off the left foot and gaining its full height again on the right, as it spun in a new direction almost ninety degrees off its previous orientation.

Even with the fancy footwork—a move most MechWarriors could not duplicate—a barrage of missiles fell across his position; metal rain bringing destruction and chaos. His ride rattled under the heavy impacts as they tore into his 'Mech's lower extremities, flowering coppery brine in his mouth from a teeth-slashed cheek. Guiding the 'Mech between the pillars, Andery attempted to outrun the incoming fire while torso-twisting wildly to toss off a missile attack of his own.

As quickly as the reload could cycle and the weapon's display burn a cool green, he clenched his finger on the trigger and sent another barrage downrange toward what he believed to be the enemy position. Knowing his weapon discharges weren't likely to hit the target, he hoped the wildly flying missiles would slash into multiple structures, causing them to explode, sending dust and minerals into the air to confound visual, and hopefully some sensor, readings.

Suddenly a shadow loomed to his right, and the *Sentinel* literally pounced into a small clearing, its autocannon vomiting metal death in an arcing stream that ate into the *Exterminator*'s center torso armor like a rampaging virus.

Between one eyeblink and the next, Andery froze, the image of Tominson rising before him while his brain immediately plugged a red-haired Samuel into a *Thug*, which must be downrange, lobbing missiles...*except the* Thug *doesn't mount long-range missiles.*

Grinding his teeth until they ached and stars almost popped in front of his straining eyes, Andery's face lit with a furious grin. *I may not win this day, but I will not be defeated by my own hand!*

Like an Eden viper striking for food, his hands slashed across several keys, tying all of his weapons into a single targeting interlock circuit; his index finger curled around the trigger.

Though the *Exterminator* was not well armed for a 'Mech its size, Andery had never needed overmatched firepower. Instead, with preternatural ability, his targeting reticule lined up on the *Sentinel* as a quartet of medium lasers and a wash of long-range missiles speared into the target with unerring ease and devastating grace.

Andery's muscles froze as though overcome by rigor mortis as the armor shattered and boiled away from the bulbous, forward-thrusting cockpit. Like a beetle caught under a magnifying glass in a boy's hand, the carapace blackened, then split and shriveled, then caved in and pulled away, allowing the kilojoules of burning energy to stab straight into the cockpit; the running 'Mech fell as though poleaxed, slamming into the ground nose first, catching on a large rock and cartwheeling through two revolutions before coming to rest in a whirlwind of collapsing columns.

Long seconds drifted into minutes as the sand swirled and slithered at gravity's irresistible beckoning, quickly covering the entire 'Mech in a makeshift grave. His eyes began to itch from the strain of not blinking, but he refused to look away for a moment; look away from the possibility of movement. Of the MechWarrior climbing out of his entombment to give Andery a thumbs-up as he patted out a hot spot on his cooling suit.

Finally, with tears leaking onto his cheeks and his vision blurring from pain and strain, he slowly shut his eyes, just as a threat warning showed an incoming 'Mech. Dismissing the consequences, not even opening his eyes, Andery slowly began the shutdown sequence for his 'Mech. And all the while, Dana's vision haunted him. Of columns and lights shattered and destroyed, and the howls of pain—and this time he couldn't push them aside.

The pull of the restraining harness cut extra deep across his shoulders; a reminder of one more tie to bind. One more mistake that had cost a pilot his life. And for what? A new society he only partially believed in? *Must I always pay for your machinations, Niki? When will you pay?*

Cold blue eyes remained clear before him, even as the cockpit plunged into utter darkness and the silence of the grave took him.

CHAPTER 12

KATYUSHA CITY
NOVY TERRA
STRANA MECHTY
KERENSKY CLUSTER
15 JULY 2805

"Nicholas Kerensky recognizes the efforts of all the people of Strana Mechty to forge a bright tomorrow," Andery said loudly, voice carried to the crowd of hundreds via the microphone on the platform he stood upon, along with a bank of mobile speakers. "He knows, as we all do, that progress often requires destroying what has gone before, so something greater can take its place. This small power substation once allowed Strana Prime to flourish, employing dozens. Many of you good people here. But as we say goodbye to this edifice, know that it lays the foundation for a far greater substation. One that will employ hundreds, and help to feed the great city of Katyusha."

The pain of his mother's memory was no longer summoned by invoking her name.

"Thank you," he said, waving, then moving to the back of the platform. He passed Councilwoman Carlotta—all hard planes and chiseled features and ice—on her way to the podium, where she began her own speech.

He crouched to grab a bottle of water and took a swig, listening to her words and where she placed emphasis. Her speech patterns were not wrong. In fact, her speech was alright, except now and then when her emphasis was incorrect. She subtly changed the tone; nothing he could call her out on, of course. If he didn't know any better, he'd say she just wasn't that practiced at speaking. *Too bad I know better.*

"You're getting good at this," Carson said next to him as Andery placed the bottle at his feet and scanned the crowd.

Andery snorted. "Just goes to show how much you know."

"As always, you do yourself a disservice. There's a reason Nicholas handed the liaison task to you."

"To punish me." Andery couldn't help the automatic jab.

Carson shrugged, his massive frame always making Andery feel inadequate by comparison. "Perhaps. But that's between brothers. I've watched you here, as I've always done. And though you may hate it, you do it well. And you help all of us."

Andery wasn't sure how to respond—the warmth of a compliment from someone who very rarely handed them out versus his own antipathy for it all—and so he deflected as a new thought occurred.

"What do you know of Jennifer Winson?" He'd been incredibly circumspect in asking questions. There was power in play he knew would be dangerous to upset, especially as he continued to watch the relationship between her and Nicholas grow. Yet there was something about her he couldn't put his finger on. *I am not simply jealous.*

"She's a MechWarrior. Jerome's sister."

"Really. That's all you have?"

"Her and Nicholas appear to be...close."

Andery shook his head. "Yeah, not sure I understand what that's about either. But that still doesn't answer my question."

Carson shrugged again. "I don't know very much. She has Nicholas's ear. And I've seen her interacting with a lot of commanders, smoothing feathers here and bullying there. Whether Nicholas knows it or not, she is an incredibly powerful tool for him."

Oh, he knows. He always knows. "But...where did she come from? I've not found a single person who can remember her from before Strana Mechty."

Carson glanced at him quickly before resuming his scan of the crowd. "And why are you asking questions?"

And that's the rub. Why am *I asking?* He shrugged uncomfortably, always uneasy when he couldn't explain his actions. *Which happens all too often.* "Just something about her bugs me."

"Because she seems to hate you?"

He couldn't help but wince.

"She doesn't try to hide it. And that's got to be a tough thing to deal with. Brothers are already trouble, and then throw that into the mix?"

"It's not just that." Carson let the silence hang. "Yeah, okay. It's just that something doesn't feel right."

"I trust your judgment, Andery. If you want, I'll ask around. Carefully. But all I see is a hard, uncompromising woman working hand-in-hand with Nicholas to forge his vision. And I mean *hard.* I would not...want to cross her. I'm not sure I want to contemplate the punishments—from either of them—that might unfold if you're found digging into things they don't want uncovered. After all, your brother has a Pandora's box of secrets, and yet here you are."

Andery shrugged again, realizing he should let it drop. Carson would ask some questions, and that would need to be that. And he was right about Jennifer. But he couldn't help but jab back a little. "You're here as well."

"I'm here for security, and because Nicholas knew having a previous major general in attendance would increase the prestige and perhaps quell any problems. But in reality, any meat sack could fill this uniform and most civilians would've been happy." He paused, then chuckled dryly. "Though I imagine your brother is hoping my size will discourage any...unpleasantness."

Andery had no response at all to that statement, so he simply gazed out at the crowd.

There were several types of people. First were those with enthusiastic eyes and eager body language, as though they were at a rock concert of their favorite band; Dana had tried to get him to a local show, but he simply found the experience overwhelming, not understanding why you'd voluntarily try to harm your eardrums. He immediately discounted this group, always uncomfortable around unbridled adoration.

Next were those who were open to the changes; very little clapping and no pumping fists in the air, but engaged expressions, as though ready to see that the future might be better than the tension of the last few years as Nicholas continued his crunching, inexorable path forward.

The next group was the closed-minded, angry people, eyes blazing, staring around at anyone clapping as though they were traitors. It would be easy to consider such zealots dangerous. But you could see them a kilometer away; they were only dangerous to their relationships and their own mental health.

No, the truly dangerous ones were those who fell somewhere in the middle. Whose faces and body language seemed to indicate they were open to the new society Nicholas was building, but whose furtive and too-knowing eyes could be read, if you knew what to look for. Being too young, Andery hadn't experienced all the perils Nicholas had faced during the occupation. But he had still been old enough that his mother had taught him the skills he needed to spot these types among the scavengers during the worst of the years in Moscow. *Kept me alive, as it did Nicholas. And is still keeping me alive. Thank you, Mother.*

Beyond the busy work site—with the substation a half kilometer behind them—was one of the growing spokes of Katyusha City. The clean, new, incredibly large lines of the city were slowly demolishing the colonial city. *Is it any wonder some of them hate us? And we're here to blow up more of it!*

"There, northeast corner," Carson mumbled as a man approached from the far side, waving pamphlets in the air, apparently trying to yell loud enough to be heard. Andery was close enough to the speakers he couldn't hear the man's words, but anger limned every limb and gesture.

Despite the distance, Andery took in the whole scene, especially as Carson spoke into his concealed throat mic to discreetly deploy security personnel to move in that direction.

Andery slowly shook his head after a few heartbeats. "No," he mumbled back. "I don't see violence there. Take in the rest of the crowd. No one is cuing off the distraction. In fact, hardly anyone is paying attention to him."

Carson responded after his eyes carved a careful circuit, while the security guards continued closing in on the man. "You may be right, but I'm not about to take any chances. I'm not sure how long I might live if I allowed you to come to harm."

Andery almost expected a laugh to follow such an absurd statement, but grew cold at Carson's deadly seriousness. *Nicholas would never do that, would he?*

"And now Andery *Kerensky* will assist me in initiating this demolition," Councilwoman Carlotta said loudly, pulling him back with a wave of her hands; they both approached a fancy setup that was still just a big plunger for making things go boom. *Was your careful emphasis for scorn or sycophancy?* He contemplated the woman and her smile, and decided it might be a bit of both. *You may dislike me, you may even hate me, but I can still be a back door to Nicholas for you. At least that's what you'd love to get, right?*

He smiled in return—he was a tough dog to teach new tricks, but he *could* learn—and placed his hands on the plunger while a large electronic clock started a countdown at thirty seconds, which the crowd enthusiastically picked up. He opened his mouth to say something to the councilwoman during the chanting, but realized they'd bumped heads several times before, and would likely do so again. What else was there to say right now?

Instead, he kept an eye on the pamphleteer, who was now angrily trying to push past several security personnel who'd reached him.

"Five, four, three, two, one!"

They pushed the plunger together; several seconds passed before the concussive blast and the tremors surging through the ground hammered another shot across the bow of the old and heralded the coming of the new.

Andery shrugged and shared a small, last smile with the councilwoman before waving at the crowds—people just loved to see anything blown up—and turned to find Carson moving quickly off the stage. He glanced back over his shoulder, in the direction of that pamphleteer, and his hackles rose: a half-dozen security guards were pushing the crowd away from the area, and there was someone down on the ground.

What?! Was I wrong? Andery immediately jogged down and caught up with Carson. "What happened?"

Carson stopped, momentarily placing an arm across Andery's chest—he'd be more likely to lift his *Exterminator* than move that arm—as he checked with his guards. "Is the area secure?" he asked softly, while his gaze pushed anyone and everyone away from their immediate vicinity. The crowd's previously good feelings fell away as the last sounds of the blast echoed to silence and they became aware of the downed man and the guards surrounding him. And then looks of concern stole over too many faces as they glanced at Andery, then backed away.

He'd seen it before and still it stung. *They love having a Kerensky in their midst, but when there's danger, they fear what Nicholas might do if I was harmed, and suddenly I'm a plague carrier.* Nauseatingly, now Carson's earlier comment didn't seem so far-fetched. A soul-weary sigh escaped his lips as Carson nodded his head, dropped his arm and kept moving.

"Not sure yet, Andery. Looks like the man tried to pull something during the bedlam of the demolition, and he was shot." They reached the outer cordon of guards and slipped inside. "Kia, report," Carson barked.

A small, diminutive woman—it might take six or seven of her to equal Carson's volume—snapped a salute. "We tried to calm him, sir. He was told several times to step back. That once the demolition was completed, he could talk to anyone he wanted. Even the two of you," she said, nodding at Carson, but never breaking eye contact.

While the report continued, Andery glanced down and saw a completely unremarkable, middle-aged man. *This is a killer?*

"When the blast occurred, he reached into his pocket as he tried to push past us in the confusion. Considering the distance to the podium, and the two of you...well, sir, I made the call to use lethal force to stop him."

"Was a weapon found?"

"No sir. Nothing."

Carson stared at her as Andery scraped dry lips with his tongue, bile rising. *Did we just kill a man who only wanted to talk?*

"You are on administrative duty effective immediately, Lieutenant. You are to report to your superior, who will instruct you on the report you are to compile."

Before she'd even saluted, Carson turned to another guard. "Jinx, I want every single holovid of these events—including all civilian recording devices; I don't care about the outcry—on my desk at 0800 tomorrow morning."

"Yes sir."

As they moved away, Carson muttered words only Andery managed to hear: "Gods, not another one. We have to keep it together."

Feeling numb, Andery glanced at one of the pamphlets the man had been handing out before it had all gone wrong. He reached down and picked up the paper, its garish colors eye-catching, and he read the words.

Life, Liberty, and the Pursuit of Happiness.

Those were once the rights the Star League guaranteed us all. But now, it is survival of the fittest and the rest be damned.

This is a peaceful civilian colony world, or at least it was before Kerensky's sons showed up. Who gets the lion's share of the food? The military. Who takes the resources they want and leaves us the scraps? The military. Who has been tearing down our city to build their own, and forcing us to do their work for them or arrest us for treason? And who is censoring every word written or broadcast in the once-free press?

We are living under a military dictatorship. Oppression in all forms must be crushed, lest freedom be banished in favor of slavery!

One of Nicholas's latest statements echoed in his ears: "*Anything new grows over the death of what's come before. Out of the pain of the past.*"

Andery slowly clenched his fist, wadding up the paper: the demolition of the substation seemed a poetic signature and exclamation point.

Will it always need to be so painful? So full of death? He hated the whisper that seemed to batter him from all directions with the same answer.

CHAPTER 13

The wind cut straight through him.

Andery pushed harder, breath ragged, heart a staccato of pressure, exhilaration: fleeing. His tough-soled boots—khaki pants tucked in tight (shirt and coat matching)—scrabbled through scree, shattered remains of the mountain's young bones discarded like a deer's unneeded antlers. It was the only month in which the last of winter's coat sloughed off the upper reaches of Mount Simon before a new cloak settled white and imperious, and Andery struggled for the top, ignoring the demands of his body to halt. Focused with laser precision, sight tunneled until the final outcropping of Simon's crown became the end of existence.

The beginning of another. He shied away from such thoughts, knowing the futility of dreams.

Yet *some* dreams remained within reach; Andery collapsed into a kneeling huddle, dumping the backpack without a thought for its contents. Finally, after long minutes, as the heaving subsided, pinpricks in oxygen-starved eyes faded, and his burning throat was quenched under several manna-like mouthfuls of water, Andery gazed in triumph, startled to realize how much this solo accomplishment meant.

Why do all my accomplishments have to be alone and all my failures public? He let the idea pass without further investigation (ignoring the pain once more), instead drinking in the scene.

The mountain dropped away like a fall of frozen stone, tumultuous waters ridged and humped as though giant bones were attempting to thrust up from the mountain's flank in unusual formations. Millennia of erosion bared the mountain's ancient skeleton to clawing winds year-round and monstrous cold during the harsh winter months. Almost a full kilometer below his current position, the last of anything that could respectably be called a tree halted, as though an invisible line had slashed away all significant life. With the tenacity of desperation, a myriad of moss and lichen canvassed the lee of every stone as far as the eye could see, from his location to that tree line.

Beyond the immediate vista, a chain of smaller mountains marched along in a straight-as-an-arrow line northeast, neatly bisecting the continent; lesser mounds kneeling in supplication to the grandeur of Simon. The folds of land spread to either side of the divide into hazy, unseen distances like soft butter thickly spread by God's own loving hand onto the bedrock crust of creation.

Now why did I think of God? Andery laughed softly, with only a hint of rancor. *Windham would be proud. Then again, perhaps even an atheist might revise their stance at such scenery.*

Not the largest mountain on Strana Mechty, Simon was the tallest that one could scale without cybernetic enhancement—not that that was an option in their current situation—or external breathing apparatus. And the view...yeah, Sarah had been right. Worth the effort. The blistering sun stripped the "oh, how beautiful" exclamation such a vista might normally elicit. In its place, the stark reality of nature's implacable will could and would put life's circumstances into perspective with the arrogance of an adult expecting a child to follow commands without question.

Against such a canvas, the painting of his own weighty concerns seemed to lessen, to fall into proportion. The ending of a life, after all, couldn't be the end of existence. *Could it?*

"Captain Johann Keyes." The words came softly, with a pain still trying to find its place amid the scarred internal landscape, even after two years.

Andery turned slowly, pulled the pack he'd toted up the entire mountain to his side (disregarding the ache permeating his knees from the jagged rocks and cold dirt; even during high summer, the ground never truly lost its permafrost), and retrieved a small package wrapped in bubble-foam to stave off damage. With deliberate yet delicate movements, he slowly stripped the packaging away to reveal a plain and graceless jar.

Memories of a stupid, needless death at his hands battered him as fresh and new as the day they were born, regardless of distance, until the thin air and internal demons made him lightheaded. And another stupid, needless death also introduced itself, as though he would have his time in the sun as well. *Why did I never learn that pamphleteer's name?* Through shimmering walls of pain, Andery looked out upon the magnificence and once more began to find equilibrium. Slowly, he unstopped the bottle, stood and carefully tipped it. As the incessant wind grasped with greedy fingers at the bottle's contents, Andery found his voice and spoke.

"To this world where you followed leaders you believed in..." The words died off momentarily as a hitch in his breath squeezed his throat. *What is expected of us. Of us!* His mind heaved as though sick at his own failures and arrogance. *Enough of me! This is not my time!* "...I consign your ashes, Captain Johann Keyes. As you have no family I could find and few friendships, none will remember you, or what you sacrificed for the creation of Niki's grand dream."

As the bottle continued to turn, the ashes tumbled free and spun away in a vortex. For a moment, Andery imagined he almost could see in the streaming remains the face of the man he'd never met in life. *A face I'll never meet. No matter what I do, a face I'll never meet.*

For a moment, something seemed to settle a reassuring hand on his heaving chest. His anguish did not diminish; nothing accomplished that (at least not anymore; he jerked again away from that train of thought). But whether a conjuring of his own besieged conscience or an actual visitation from a departed spirit (*how's* that, *Windham, for starting to believe?*), something tweaked him. Something brought assurance that if he did not forget and if he forged ahead to try to make it better...it just might be.

Despite the past year of once more falling into the persona of a teacher for accelerated classes, it was hard to believe. So hard...

He swallowed with a dry throat, chapped lips stretching and splitting; the physical pain, and this second-year anniversary pilgrimage to try to set things right within, a burden and benediction for his heart. *Yes. As ever, I can go on...and remember;* he engraved one more name onto his soul.

"I will remember. I will."

INTERLUDE ONE

UNITY CITY
PUGET SOUND
TERRA
TERRAN HEGEMONY
18 OCTOBER 2780

Aaron DeChavilier strode into the room, a noteputer under his arm, closing the door firmly behind him. Wearing the full, resplendent uniform of the acting head of the Star League Defense Force, even as he nodded at Nicholas he had a look in his eye like he'd stolen a cookie from his mother's jar and knew he'd get away with it.

Nicholas nodded back, fidgeting in his new cadet's uniform. Ignored the name on the tag he'd been issued upon entering the building: *Koyla. Will I ever be called by my given name, Father?* His hands fluttered in time with the unanswered questions bouncing around. Plucked at the uniform's buttons. *I don't really deserve this...*

"Alex," Aaron said, dropping all formality when they were alone, "you need to see this."

His father (*I'm actually here with my father!*), Aleksandr Kerensky, Protector of the Realm, stood ramrod straight in the corner. Looking out at the water and the swaths of trees of the Puget Sound area beyond Unity City, beautiful despite the visible blackened scars of combat trenches from the Liberation of Terra.

Nicholas had silently stood beside his father, looking out that same window for some time, before he became impatient and began pacing. He'd tried several times to engage his father, but the man's growing impatience with the Great House lords—especially after the morning's council session—were coming to the surface, and he was in no mood for small talk.

"Alex," Aaron repeated, raising his voice. "Look, I know you're annoyed with those twits. But you need to see this."

The solemn-faced man turned, murmuring "respect" as he moved away from the single window of the small room—one of many such rooms alongside the massive council chambers of the Star League—and came to stand beside his longtime friend.

Aaron snorted. "I'll give them respect when they've earned it."

His father opened his mouth to speak, and Aaron forestalled him by raising his hand. "Seriously, Alex, leave off. I've heard all your arguments concerning the respect the military must have for government, or we simply become dictators. But I don't care, not when they can barely keep the drool off their chins at how weak the Hegemony is, and how they can prosper from it."

Nicholas drew in a breath, expecting at least a stern look for Aaron—what would've been an explosive outburst from anyone else—but instead he returned a small smile. *I forget how long these two have served together. How long they have served this Star League. Can it really be saved?*

"Apparently our discussions were not long enough. We can save the League yet," Alexsandr finished, voice strong, his features the resolute general who had saved trillions of people.

"Speaking of which," Aaron continued, tapping on the noteputer for a moment, angling it for his father to see.

Not wishing to interrupt the two, Nicholas sidled around the edge of the room until he could see the video as well. It shifted to a news channel—he couldn't see the icon to know which one—and the video began to play. He immediately recognized the sharp, dour features of Nadia Salvic, the new Director Consulate of Moscow.

"Director-General Laghari is mere months in office, and yet already he has moved with lightning speed to disregard the wishes of Commanding General Kerensky by enacting the Berlin Protocols legislation. He has declared a pogrom against literally millions of

citizens of the Terran Hegemony, whose only crime was trying to live their lives under the brutal dictatorship of Amaris."

She paused, her short, blond hair blowing in a gust of wind, causing a harsh sound on the recording even through the soft tip of the mic the reporter held in front of her face. Nicholas nodded as discussions with his father bubbled up: she was the loudest political voice against the director-general, leader of the Terran Hegemony since he was voted into office on his anti-Amaris platform earlier in the year.

"Now let me be absolutely clear. Those truly responsible are already undergoing their trials. And other trials will follow. Those responsible will be held accountable. But Laghari's protocols go too far. They bar anyone who served in office or as a soldier or in the police from ever serving again. Lest our esteemed Laghari forgets, Amaris was duly and legally elected director-general, whether we wish to admit it or not. Which means the lowliest planetary government clerk on far-off New Rhodes III is now barred from service in perpetuity! He is eviscerating the Hegemony's ability to govern itself, tossing out every capable person and replacing them with his own incompetent cronies."

A cheer could be heard over the video, as she smiled and waved to off-screen supporters. But against such cheers angry yells calling for her removal were equally loud.

She raised her voice to continue, *"Not only does this recklessness endanger our ability to rebuild our beloved Hegemony, but it embraces the worst of our natures, harkening back to the very monsters we say we are fighting. My beloved city has seen all too many bone-fish signs daubed on houses who residents find themselves ostracized or beaten. And yes, even killed as collaborators."*

Nicholas, though he could only see his father in profile, could see the wrinkles around his eyes tighten and lips draw thin; sure anger at her words. His stomach dropped, sourness on his tongue, as the words pulled up memories of his own hand at justice. He closed his eyes, thinking of the years he and Andery and their mother had survived. He gritted his teeth and kept listening. *We were right. We were right in what we did.*

"By all accounts, a hundred million citizens were killed under despotic rule. How many more need to die before we realize we

are still under despotic rule!" The cheers and jeers exploded, overpowering her words as she tried raising her voice, but something (a can?) was tossed at her, and she ducked before reaching out to grab the mic and pull it close, eyes seething with intensity.

"There is only one solution. I call on our savior, the Protector of the Realm, Aleksandr Kerensky. Please. Save us. Take control of the Hegemony. Take control of the Star League. There is no other path forward but by your hand. Only you—"

The last was cut off as a crowd of people stormed into view, pushing Nadia away, causing the camera to sway and jerk before it finally cut out.

Nicholas waited with bated breath while Aaron stared hard at his father.

"Is she okay?" he asked softly, head bowed, but shoulders still tense.

"Yes. This was two days ago. There's another interview video, her with a bandage on her face from yesterday, but inside, with numerous security guards in the background. The news hasn't actually been broadcast here, yet. This was flown in by confederates that knew we needed to see it. It would seem the director-general is trying to squelch this."

Nicholas could hear only his heartbeat as the silence stretched.

"Well?" Aaron finally spoke.

"Well what?" his father responded.

Aaron heaved a heavy sigh. "You're going to make me say it, aren't you?" His father refused to look at his friend, and Aaron finally threw up his hands before slapping the table, causing the noteputer to jump.

"Alex. You are my friend. The most noble man I have ever known. And also the most obstinate. In fact, I dare say we stand here, trying to reassemble the shambles of the Hegemony from that monster's grip precisely because you are as obstinate as a mountain. But she...is...*right*. The director-general is a ham-fisted moron. He and his party are letting their hatred of the past destroy our future. All while the Great House lords—" he stabbed his right hand back toward the chambers they'd been ensconced in for days, "—lope along the fence, wondering if they should wait a respectable while to gnaw at our bones, or perhaps start...right...*now*. And you know, you *know* our own soldiers are upset with things; morale is low and only getting worse. You cannot avoid this. If you want to save the League, if you want to save your troops, you must take control!"

Nicholas had had less than a year to get to know Aaron, but he'd always enjoyed his devil-may-care attitude. Yet none of that was apparent at this moment as he directed his full anger and rage at Aleksandr. Nicholas could barely breathe for the tension binding the room as Aaron's anger echoed slowly away.

His father stood with eyes closed, and the long minutes stretched and stretched until Nicholas thought he might explode—confident Aaron would—before finally the Protector of the Realm opened his eyes, stood straight and looked directly at his friend.

"I love you, my friend," he said, shocking Nicholas with such an intimate response; a stab of jealousy wormed into the moment, as he'd never heard those words himself. But it was quickly squelched in recognition of these momentous events.

"You have been as faithful a friend as any man can hope for. But you still do not see." He plucked at the flowing robes of his office. "If I do as you ask, this means nothing. If I do as you ask, all of our years of service mean nothing. If I do as you ask, I'm no better than Amaris, simply taking what he wanted. If I do as you ask, then the League is already dead."

"It already *is* dead!" Aaron yelled, face animated with anger. "The Camerons are dead! The genie is out of the bottle! The Great House lords have their armies, and are just looking for a good excuse for a war. Do you honestly believe the genie can be put back?"

The two old soldiers glared at each other, sparks nearly flying visibly.

His father slowly shook his head. "I gave up my honor once to kill the devil. I cannot do it again. I will see the League die before I betray it." He looked at his watch, noticing the time, and placed a firm, comforting hand on Aaron's shoulder. "It's time for the afternoon session to start." He finally glanced back at Nicholas, as though just remembering his son was there. "Are you coming?" He opened the door and swept out.

"Yes, sir!" Nicholas called out, striding past Aaron, whose shoulders had slumped. He leaned against the table, eyes closed, mumbling words Nicholas barely heard as he walked out after his father.

"Then the Star League *is* already dead."

"And who exactly will back your emergency funding for the Hegemony worlds?" Chancellor Barbara Liao, leader of the Capellan Confederation said, her dark eyes flashing contempt at First Prince John Davion, leader of the Federated Suns. The two lords of the Great Houses stared daggers across the council chamber floor, each on their respective chairs—nearly as large as thrones.

"So, you are willing to condemn billions to starve?" he shot back.

"Please," she said, her jade headdress swaying with a jerk of her perfectly coiffed black air, the white gloves on her hands slashing the air. "My realm has already provided immense funding. You're simply looking to draw more funds and ensure it doesn't come from your own resources."

"And yet," John shot back, his own eyes bright with anger, the sunburst on his shirt sparkling with its own light as the man thrust his chest out, "all of that funding has gone only to worlds that border your Confederation. I'm sure the billions you say are deprived of food are so glad you're willing to help only those with ancient ties to your realm."

Despite the fact that she was sitting down, and her small stature, she somehow managed to gain height as she drew in breath, and launched into an antagonistic rejoinder.

Nicholas stopped listening after the second hour began. *Are these the leaders of star empires? They squabble like schoolkids. I would beat the lot of them until they couldn't sit down.*

Standing in the very corner of the council chamber, he watched as the five lords bickered and seemed to say so much without saying anything. At the edge of the half-circle dais that included the large chairs for the lords, a table had been erected. And sitting at the table were his father as Protector of the

Realm—unmoving, stoic—Aaron DeChavilier, as acting head of the SLDF, and Jens Pinera, head of the Hegemony Congress.

Beyond the dais, three other chairs were conspicuously empty after the Periphery Uprising and the secession of the Outworlds Alliance, Taurian Concordant, and Magistracy of Canopus. The fourth chair, where once sat the leader of the Rim Worlds Republic, Stefan Amaris, had been completely removed, as though it were a stain none could bear to look upon.

He could see just his father's profile, and knew the tensed shoulders and that flat look spoke of contained anger, which was muted compared to Aaron and Jens, who sat next to him. A morning spent trying to direct the important conversation of this council—of trying to get them to deal with the emergencies within the Hegemony and the Star League at large—had left his father silent this afternoon, only listening to the endless haranguing back and forth.

Nicholas' own anger surged and beat strong. Not that long ago, he'd been the one starving, living on the streets. And these lords had never experienced a fraction of such deprivation in their lives. And cared even less for anything that didn't advance their own power.

On the verge of tuning it all out, he caught a particularly smug look on the face of Archon Robert Steiner, ruler of the Lyran Commonwealth. *Uh-oh. Wait...he's not said much yet. What's going on?*

As though suddenly back on the bad streets of Moscow, wary of scavengers lurking where he couldn't see them, he watched as the Archon swept that smug expression past all the lords then stared at his father for long minutes, until he slowly stood, causing the arguments to sputter to a halt.

"My fellow great lords," he began, tone as obsequious as anything Nicholas had heard on the streets when a lowlife was trying to avoid a beating, "I know our time is precious. And what we have been discussing is *very* important," he said, waving his hand languidly in the air.

Nicholas bristled further as he noted even Chancellor Liao could not keep a slight smile from her face. If possible, his father's shoulders grew more tense, while Aaron's gaze seemed to move around the room, likely delivering his own dagger stares.

The Archon reached back to his large chair, pulling out a legislative tube. "However, I have here a proclamation that I believe we all can agree upon. One that will unite us as we continue to work together in undoing the terrible crimes perpetrated by Amaris." He took off the top and pulled out a formal sheet that included numerous ribbons.

Even Nicholas knew this was ready to be signed by the House lords, once they voted.

First Prince John Davion waved his hand. "Fine, fine. Please, read how you'll unite us."

"Of course, my fellow House Lord." He placed the empty tube back behind him, stood straight, cleared his throat, and began to read:

"I, Archon Robert Steiner, ruler of the Lyran Commonwealth and duly anointed Lord of the Star League, do hereby declare that the state of emergency that allowed for the full mobilization of the Star League Defense Force is no longer in effect. And as such, hereby declare that the demilitarization of the SLDF to a pre-war, peacetime configuration, must begin forthwith, immediately upon the council's ratification of this proclamation."

Nicholas's fists clenched until they started to ache. *What are they doing? What are they doing? They cannot do this!* His eyes stayed laser-focused on his father, whose statue-like frame didn't move a muscle, until Aaron pushed back his chair, angrily standing, and his father carefully raised a hand, cutting him off before he could say anything. Aaron slowly sat back down. The smiles on the lords' faces infuriated Nicholas. *They think Aaron's been put on a leash. They've no idea...*

"Furthermore," Robert continued, the glee in his voice barely contained, "with the council once more in session and the cessation of the state of emergency, I declare that this council should forthwith strip Aleksandr Sergeyevich Kerensky of his title of Protector of the Realm."

Aaron surged forward again, but his father's hand kept his friend in his seat and silent, though Nicholas could see Aaron's shoulders shaking from anger.

"That title, with all its rights, privileges and responsibilities, is a usurpation of the rights and privileges of this council. It served a necessary purpose, enabling the Star League Defense Force to put down a rabid dog. But it is past time to return to peace and prosperity. A Protector of the Realm is no longer needed. Thus saith the united Star League Council."

The Archon finished with a flourish and smoothly sat down amid total silence, until voices erupted from all the leaders. But it was all braying asses to Nicholas, whose fingernails had begun to cut into his palms. A fugue turned the voices into a cacophony he simply couldn't understand as they continued yapping, the arguments dragging on and on. And all the while, his father remained immobile. *How can they do this? After a lifetime of service, Father. After all you gave them. After all we sacrificed. How can they do this?*

Nicholas had no idea how much time had passed, but he came back to himself when he realized that First Prince John Davion was standing, and the room was silent. *He's going to declare the deliberations.*

At least, unlike the Archon, there was no apparent glee on his face as the First Prince began to speak. "After deliberation, this council is unanimous in its support of the proclamation put forth by the Archon of the Lyran Commonwealth. This august body—"

Aleksandr Kerensky slowly pushed back his chair and stood. The sheer power of his presence cut off the First Prince's speech, and he stumbled to a halt, looking nervously at the other House Lords, and then back at Nicholas's father. Silence gripped the room, and Nicholas wondered if he'd start feeling blood dripping down from his palms for the force of his clenched fists. For so many years, he'd dreamed of the day his father would return. Dreamed of the day he would take his place beside his father as a MechWarrior in the Star League Defense Force, as the Star League once again returned to the golden age of human history. Dreamed of the day he would don the uniform—though he felt unworthy to wear it.

The dream cracked and wavered and began to crumble as his father slowly reached up to his shoulders, unfastening the robes of his office, bringing them reverently in front of him.

He carefully kissed the robes, then with a jerk tore the fabric apart in a sound that echoed harshly through the room, causing several of the leaders to gasp.

Aleksandr Kerensky, the man who had led the greatest military campaign in human history to save the cradle of humanity, slowly stripped off every medal from his uniform, tossing them onto the table; not with anger, but with the casual carelessness with which one tosses a worthless item into the garbage.

After dropping the last medal, he looked every lord directly in the eyes before turning and marching from the room. Aaron slowly stood, nearly bursting with fury, but somehow managed to keep a leash on his anger and stalked away, following Aleksandr's lead, leaving old man Pena slumped in shock at the table.

Nicholas, knowing he couldn't possibly stay, sidled toward the door, taking one last look before he stepped out. Finding indifference on most faces; the Archon's filled with smugness, of course; but strangely, Chancellor Liao looked sad. As though perhaps only she understood what had just happened, even as she'd voted for it and even if it might yet take years to come to fruition.

Aaron's words haunted Nicholas as he left the council chamber for the last time.

"...the Star League is *already dead.*"

BOOK TWO

"Fearing no insult, asking for no crown, receive with indifference both flattery and slander, and do not argue with a fool."

—ALEXANDER PUSHKIN

CHAPTER 14

ALEKSANDR BETA TRAINING GROUNDS
NOVY TERRA
STRANA MECHTY
KERENSKY CLUSTER
29 JANUARY 2807

"No, not like that. I told you," Andery spoke, voice muffled slightly by his cold-weather headgear, frustration plain to all. "Hold the stock firmly against your shoulder. Take two deep breaths, a third, and hold, and squeeze the trigger. Soft, but firm and smooth. The shot that surprises you will always hit the target. You jerk that gun one more time and you'll be jerking nothing but yourself for the next thirty days, you hear me?!"

"Yes, sir," the young man said, his flushing face visible even through the goggles and matching white headgear that swathed his face into a camouflaged, indistinct form in the endless tundra stretching in all directions.

As the young man (more a boy) returned to target practice, joining the thirty other boys and girls desperately trying to please a Kerensky, Andery stamped his feet against the cold and ground his teeth at these accelerated classes.

You'd think we'd be past putting children into harm's way. But no, Niki wants them younger and younger. Can't train them early enough! Swear this damn kid isn't even fourteen. What's next, Niki, get them before they hit puberty? Rob the cradle. Make it so they have a gun in the womb!

He tried smiling, but it turned sickly with the realization he might not be too far off the mark. After all, when it came to Niki and his grand dream, nothing would stand in his way. Nothing.

"Some people tell me you never used to lose your temper. Not sure I'd recognize that Andery."

Startled, Andery turned to find flashing eyes and a small, beaming mouth that brought a warmth that still shamed him, though he was getting better and better at ignoring it. He smiled in return. "Not sure *I* would recognize that Andery."

Sarah McEvedy tilted her head slightly, finding the hint of bitterness despite Andery's best efforts to conceal it. In so many ways, she was like Dana. And yet in so many others, nothing like her. Yet of late, when he could not find the words with his beloved, he could with Sarah. *Perhaps that explains the warmth. Perhaps.*

She opened her mouth, paused as though shifting gears, then spoke. "How is the training coming along?"

"Don't you mean, how do I like endlessly training new kids in small-arms combat? How many years have I been a teacher? At least on Eden, they were proper students," he said, lowering his voice, "not these children. And aren't you cold?" he finished, changing the subject as he realized she wore no head protection beyond a light hood.

Her smile turned even bigger. "I'm only cold if I let myself be cold."

"And that actually works?"

"Do I look cold to you?"

As though invited to peer closer, he looked and saw her face flushed, cheeks red and lips a deep burgundy that almost glistened in the harsh early dawn light. But no overt shivering. A deep look into her eyes showed resolute control, and something else that compelled Andery to turn away quickly, scanning his cadets as though his life suddenly depended upon their instant grasp of small-arms fire; something that would require years for some of them—and likely never occur for a few.

"I suppose not," he finally responded.

"I didn't think so."

Was that a smile in her voice? His skin burned with shame, and he was glad to be facing mostly away.

"As for you training kids, no, that's not what I meant at all. Come on, Andery, we all have jobs to do that we might not like."

He turned back. "And what, Sarah, might be the terrible job *you're* stuck with?"

"Well, for one thing, coming and visiting your sorry self." Her smile brought soft laughter to them both.

"Seriously?"

"Seriously. Have you been on 'civilian guidance' duty yet?"

He shook his head. "No, but I've heard rumors."

"Well, whatever you've heard, it's all true. And likely not even close."

Andery glanced away and concentrated on young Bryant, glad to see the boy finally putting endless weeks of classroom study and more than a month of field trials into actual practice; turned back. "That bad?"

"Worse. The civilians who came with us...they're not the problem. It's the on-world colonists. Doesn't matter how many times we tell them, or show them, with the legion of holovids we've got. They just didn't experience the fighting like we did. It's not as immediate. As intimate. And so some of Nicholas' changes...the more the years pass, the more we sweep away everything they've ever known...it's not going over well." Her eyes held a look of distaste, as the breath from her longish talk wreathed her head in steam before shredding away.

"Well, that's understandable."

Her eyes refocused, a hawk to its prey. "You agree with them."

He shied away from those snapping eyes, thumping his hands together in an exaggeration of trying to warm himself; not too much of an exaggeration. "I didn't say that," he continued, eyes once more roving over the young cadets to make sure they weren't about to kill themselves or each other. Of course, he would never have allowed them to this point if they didn't have *some* safety measures pounded thoroughly into their skulls, but some of them just seemed too young to truly grasp what they were doing or the consequences of screwing up. *After all, you're immortal when you're this age. You grow out of that all too quickly with just a few more years under the belt or a few times in a real combat zone. At least most people do.* Samuel Helmer came to mind, and he wondered if the arrogant student ever found his mortality.

"All I'm saying is that it can't be easy to accept what Nik... Nicholas is doing." He coughed slightly, amazed that he had almost slipped and used his nickname for his brother in Sarah's presence.

"Nothing's ever easy. And it's not just us. I might expect them to distrust the military, especially with how we failed to stop the civil war in the first place. But they ignore the accounts from other civilians. Like we brought along a hundred thousand spies, all ready to convert them to some diabolical scheme of a madman."

Andery decided not to respond as her words settled a little too close to the mark. Instead, he held Sarah's eyes until she finally turned away. *Do you feel it, too? Do you also sense how easily this can all end in disaster? We left chaos, and we could spiral back down into it so easily. I may agree with Niki and Jennifer in principle, but in practice? It can all go so wrong, so quickly.*

A new thought surfaced. *Jennifer.* He'd spent so long ignoring the questions that still lurked in corners. And Carson hadn't brought anything to light. *Do I ask Sarah?* Before he realized what he was doing, the words were coming out. "What do you know about Jennifer?"

She seemed caught off guard. "What? Where did that come from?"

Andery took in a deep, cold breath. "Just...she's still such a mystery. I've been asking around—"

"Wait, you've been asking around," she cut in, tone sobering even more. "About Jennifer?"

He shrugged, uncomfortable with her tone.

"You're asking questions about a powerful woman you don't like who stands by your brother's side?"

"It's not like that. I'm just trying to find out where she came from."

"Who cares? Do you realize how many lost people came with us? A million people followed Nicholas. A *million*! And I bet every tenth person you'd struggle to find a hint of their background before our Exodus. There are plenty of people who seem to have leaped out of the ground with outstanding MechWarrior skills!"

"I don't think the dripping sarcasm is needed," he said sullenly, despite his best efforts otherwise.

"I think it is. She's a hard woman, in her own way every bit as hard as Nicholas. You've found out firsthand what happens when you try to directly face off against your brother. This can only end badly."

Andery was already regretting bringing it up, realizing he would find no ally here. A sound he'd been waiting for penetrated his thoughts, whipping his head around just as Bryant fell, weapon discharging. Andery pelted forward the five meters to his side, wrenching the weapon away even as the boy attempted to use it to regain his feet. His temper boiled until it threatened to burst loose. Yet remembering Sarah's comments about not recognizing him angry, he managed to hold his tongue, instead bludgeoning the boy with silence and a razor-hot look of disgust and disappointment.

"Cadet Bryant," he began, voice pitched to carry to the entire class, which now looked in their direction, but calm and collected, as devoid of emotion as the grave. "You will report to the stockade, where you will spend the next five days thinking about the twenty rules you have just violated, as well as the death you might have caused. You will then report for latrine duty for the next twenty-five, after which you will return to me, with a written report of no less than five thousand words regarding what happened here and why it will never happen again." He raised his voice louder. "Resume your exercise. The next cadet to break a rule today will find themself in the stockade for sixty days and out of this program."

Without a backward glance he stalked back to Sarah, ignoring the new snowfall just starting as if his anger could wash it away, their conversation prior to his Jennifer question surging to the fore once more. "You see, Sarah," he began in a whipcord-tight voice, but low so as not to carry. "This is what we are pushed to. Kids carrying guns. Is this what we want? Is this our new society?"

She simply looked back, her inability to answer plain on her face. But what spiked his fury was always the same, his own lack as well.

CHAPTER 15

Thunder rolled.

Andery continued his Saturday morning ritual, begun with the new year. A New Year's resolution. Up before dawn, walking the circuit of the new city until duty called.

When is thunder not *rolling in Katyusha City?* He hunched his shoulders against winter's last gasp, burrowed balled fists deeper into his light jacket, and continued down the straight-as-an-arrow boulevard. Eyes tasting every sight, the old and the new, he dug out an energy bar, eating the honey-dried nuts and dates as he ignored the reason he began the walking ritual; after all, he jogged every other morning now, why should he need to walk to keep fit?

How am I in my forties? He swallowed roughly, coughing on the nuts. As he continued walking, he tried to ignore the thought as he had been ignoring so much lately. Tried to simply enjoy the early morning stroll in the brisk dawn and forget that he was forty and that it seemed his whole life had been spent at others' beck and call, and never on his own agenda.

But try as he might to find his peace, he couldn't ignore the constant thrum of low-level thunder. Not the earth-shattering crackle of true thunder, but the subsonic beat of construction work thrumming through the air and rippling the very earth. *How many years now? How many years and it never seems to end. Just how big do you want this city, Niki?*

A soft disturbance that gained speed turned his head to the left, as the small hanging monorail extension sped by on the way to the central quarter. The faces of civilians and military alike gazed out, their thoughts as masked as his own.

He could also see the faces of several earnest children; some bright-eyed with curiosity, others darkened with fear. *On the way to your first fostering.* One of the few changes implemented on a grand scale that Andery absolutely supported. First begun on the exodus from the Inner Sphere over twenty years ago, but expanded in breadth and scope by Nicholas, young children were fostered to other families and mentors to begin training for their future occupations. Too much to do to allow them a childhood; he had never examined the lack of his own childhood during the Amaris years and whether that might color his perceptions.

He did note, however, how young the faces were becoming, knowing all too well that that was one of the sorest points of contention with the civilians, but especially the original colonists. Cries of attempting to destroy the family unit, and them along with it, found outlets in rallies and graffiti on equipment and new buildings. He laughed ironically that he could support his brother's program while hating the fact that he himself was a mentor to those same young kids, training them to shoot and kill. *But you can't be halfway, can you, Andery? Either you support it or you don't. Teaching them to carry a gun doesn't change the fact that the kid running errands for a scientist he hopes to one day replace is only seven.*

He shrugged it off, one more thing not to think about, as the train sped away. Yet he couldn't help notice one final bit of information: the small gaps left around the military personnel in the monorail cars. Try as he might, he couldn't help but come to the same conclusion Sarah had months ago. The original civilians were not happy. Not happy at all.

Especially as we demolish their city to make room for this monstrosity.

One foot after another, Andery continued moving, small hovercars and larger truck transports beginning to break the low-key volumes of early dawn. The sun cracked upon the horizon, shedding its night's cloak and bathing the city in the harshness devoid of dreams. *Or small dreams. There's only room for one Dream here.*

Reaching the central square, he paused at the junction of several mammoth streets. Four total: one running back the direction he came from; the first point of what would eventually be a gargantuan five-pointed star. *Or was it six points?* Andery could never remember, used to his mind wandering as Niki waxed eloquent about his dream of the perfect city.

The next boulevard shot off at almost a ninety-degree angle toward the nearly completed new DropPoint, some twenty-five kilometers distant; that segment of the monorail was already finished. The other two streets moved off at flat angles to the points of the star facing away from the central square, the roads also a pentagonal border to the central quarter. Which was ten kilometers on a side.

Ten kilometers, Niki. Ten kilometers! Andery slowly cocked his head. *Except you would've made it twenty, or fifty, if we had the resources, but this is stretching us as it is; even the civilians we brought with us are not exactly crowing about the work you put them to.*

He stared at the central region, mostly devoid of life. What had been the central part of the original city was now gone. Wiped away as thoroughly as though by an orbital bombardment. *How can you be surprised they dislike you, Niki? That they fear you. You come in and demolish their city. Then you leave the central region bare, waiting for who knows what...*

His thoughts trailed off as his eyes found something in the center. A towering, lonely figure amid a barren landscape.

Feet dragging, he shuffled forward as though yanked by invisible chains.

In an effort to distract himself, he gazed beyond the square, as he walked slowly toward the center. The other three eventual (*or was that four?*) star points were hardly even begun. But the official notices had been posted, and despite protests and almost daily removal of citizens chaining themselves to buildings to stop the IndustrialMechs, the construction would move ahead. In his own way, Niki was as inexorable as any force of nature.

The sun was now well above the horizon and despite the late winter, the heat began to make him sweat; the energy bar sat heavy in his belly, and he swallowed several times to work moisture back into his mouth.

His mind wandered and worked itself into a near-frenzy of dithering and excuse-making until he yanked himself out of the cesspool of never-ending doubts and malaise. "Damn it, Andery. Must it always be like this? Get ahold of yourself."

The furious words seemed to help. Yet he could almost hear their echo fall across the kilometers of emptiness. As though he moved into a no-man's-land, a place where the proverbial "abandon hope all ye who enter" would be found hammered into the ground with a skeleton's femur, blood still slicking its surface.

A cool hand seemed to touch his forehead and Andery almost jumped as he came to a stop and glanced up, heart fluttering, blood pounding noisily in ears red with shame. He breathed deeply as he moved into the shadow and his eyes grew accustomed to the bright flare of the sun.

Eyes suddenly itching, he took in the towering, twelve-meter-tall statue. Though many found comfort in the proud, thoughtful pose imparted by the artist—as it gazed down the point of the star he'd just walked, toward the distant point where Nicholas had first made planetfall—the look seemed incongruous. Once or twice he'd even witnessed shed tears as people were overcome, with what emotion he couldn't tell.

But his tears that threatened to fall were not of pride. Or passion. Or dedication. The itchiness wormed up from a deeper well until they pushed silent drops down a weary face.

Sorrow.

A sudden memory ballooned, and the tears now flowed. A blank pedestal in Cameron Park on lost Eden. *I knew what would happen. I knew it then, I just never imagined I would be on another world, finding what I knew would come to pass.*

The tears continued unabated, as they did every Saturday, demons he couldn't seem to wrestle with anywhere else, coming clean, expunged in the shadow of the greatest general in the history of the human race.

"I'm sorry for what they've done to you, Father."

CHAPTER 16

NICHOLAS JUNGLE
MCKENNA
STRANA MECHTY
KERENSKY CLUSTER
18 MARCH 2807

Something moved in the dense foliage.

Andery tried not to wiggle, but found he'd put the sneak suit on improperly; an itch, which had been only a light twinge a half-hour ago, was quickly working toward a burning that demanded immediate attention. But he knew if he moved, whatever was about to appear would bolt, trapped lamb or no. *And Niki would hate that, wouldn't you? After all, this is your show. Whatever show it might be.*

The oppressive heat of the jungle sat heavy, slicking his face despite the almost completely sealed sneak suit; the better to hide his and Nicholas's scent. Moisture seemed to coat every surface, as the equator-straddling McKenna continent made this thousands-of-kilometer-long jungle as impenetrable as nature could make it.

After going "feet dry" on McKenna for over an hour, Andery thought Nicholas must be nuts. The Cobra Transport VTOL, though a venerable workhorse of the SLDF for over two centuries, still required a rather large footprint to land, with its large wingspan; a footprint that simply didn't exist in the endless vegetation girdling the continent like an overly large, warm blanket clutched to its bosom.

But another three hours had brought an unexpected airstrip and an outbuilding. And upon landing, an entire complex of hidden buildings stretching away under the canopy of twisted trees and ropy strains of vegetation that sat like exposed intestines. And then a two-and-a-half-hour hike through the jungle to this remote location, where another hour of solitude brought the sun close to the horizon and shadows dappled the already dark jungle into a playground for early nocturnal predators.

Despite the pistol in his hand, laser rifle across his back, the sneak suit and the squad of men deployed behind, the subtle movement of shadows and light in the direction Nicholas slowly pointed put Andery on edge. The itch burned with greater urgency, and he swallowed several times against the heat and sudden suffocating, enveloping feeling, as though he were buried in a pile of soft loam; nothing he couldn't get out of, but with his mobility bound to Nicholas's desires...he almost panicked.

Trying to keep the fear at bay, Andery peered closer, concentrating on a particular patch of darkness. A patch he swore had just moved. Not just something within the darkness, but the entire patch itself. He tried to write it off as his tired eyes betraying him, but after almost a minute, he became more convinced there was something occupying that spot.

As a long minute stretched into five, what he originally assumed were two bioluminescent toadstools festooning the side of a tree slowly blinked out, then reappeared. The twin milky white orbs seemed to hang for a moment before repeating the cycle. It took another full minute before what he was looking at finally registered, and Andery almost gasped just as a pair of ghostly white eyes moved into view, sprouting a snout and a gaping jaw hovering below, whiskers a-twitch, pink tongue tasting the air.

Andery caught his breath and held it, afraid even the recycled breathing would be heard at this distance. By increments, the magnificent beast flowed out of the shadows as though pulling them along in its wake. As though it *were* shadows come to life in rippling muscles and taut pelt stretched across the sinewy grace of a full-size, four-legged feline. The mottled gray fur appeared smoke-like, to the point that Andery wondered if the beast sported some type of mimetic fur; each time it cautiously stepped into a shadow, it seemed to simply vanish.

Never good at guesstimating size, the beast nonetheless appeared huge, bringing Andery's apprehension to the boiling point; he breathed shallowly, almost afraid his lips might spout a scream of internal pressure.

A moment later, Andery almost did scream. Unexpectedly, the big cat slunk forward, then sprang several meters over fallen logs and a small pool of putrid water, bearing the lamb to the ground with its great weight, jaws already latched onto the neck, tearing the prey's head almost completely off its body. With a roar that sent pinpricks of fear stabbing down the length of Andery's back, the cat announced its victory then set about demolishing its feast, tearing off chunks of flesh and eagerly slurping them down.

A signal from Nicholas broke the terrible tableau, and they very carefully backed away from the feeding. Retracing their steps, they met up with their screen of guards and started the trek back to the airstrip. Andery scratched vigorously at the itch, relief (both physical and psychological) almost making him faint. The heat, long day, and extreme violence of the alien fauna seemed to sap Andery's energy. Always uneasy with the *alienness* of the worlds they colonized despite decades of living on them, the eeriness of strange colors and unearthly sights and sounds in the jungle slowed him down until Nicholas vanished far ahead, into the verdant undergrowth.

Finally, as darkness smothered all light, Andery seemed to find a type of equilibrium and increased his pace. It was as if the coming darkness hid the flora and fauna his senses found so wrong, until he could once more move at something approaching a normal pace. Soon harsh, actinic light bit into the gloom, announcing man-made structures, as he abruptly swept from the dense jungle into a small clearing of several buildings.

Without a word, his guide led him to a structure on the side of one of the larger buildings, where he opened the door solicitously, as though Andery were enfeebled, before saluting smartly and departing.

Well, considering the pace I set, I guess he just might think that.

Stepping through the door into the small room filled with a single table, several noteputers and four chairs, he found Nicholas standing before a large chalkboard on the opposite wall, which contained literally hundreds of names, most of them crossed out. Andery stopped, nonplussed for a moment at the incongruity of the obviously technologically advanced facility and the *shk-shk* of dry chalk on the board, as Nicholas added a new name to the huge list. He slowly set the chalk down, then casually dusted his hands as he stepped back.

Andery hesitated a moment before squaring his shoulders and moving forward. As he neared Nicholas, he stopped as the names became readable: *Fire Mandrill, Ghost Bear, Eden Beaver, Jade Falcon, Ice Hellion, Steel Viper, Sphinx Raptor, Snow Raven, Surat, Thunderbird, Chimera Hawk, Coyote, Wolverine, Wolf, Cobalt Kite*—the list went on and on with no apparent rhyme or reason, names of a myriad of animals spanning the Pentagon Worlds and those of the Kerensky Cluster. Most Andery recognized, while a few jumped out as nothing he'd ever heard of: *Hell's Horse? Crimson Shade?* And now the name Nicholas had just added—*Smoke Jaguar.*

"What in the world?" Andery finally spoke, voice hoarse after so many tense hours of not speaking.

Nicholas turned to his brother, a slight curve to his lips dissolving the appearance of anger.

Then again, perhaps you're always angry, or at least frustrated, aren't you? Frustrated by the lack of others knowing what you know. Seeing what you know...like me? Andery shivered at the momentary idea of two sides of a coin, Andery on one, Nicholas on the other. Forever so close, forever separated.

That shiver turned into ghostly fingers caressing his spine as he remembered a vision from Dana, years in the past, of the two of them so close and yet so far. Could that possibly be what she meant? *Does that vision than apply here somehow?* He shook himself, setting such unknowables aside.

"Just something I'm working on."

Andery turned away, glad of the chance to avoid Nicholas's eyes and once more scanned the endless list of animal names. "Creating a zoo?" He raised his hand, pointing at one at random that had been crossed off. "Sphinx Raptor not good enough for your zoo? Then again, no idea how you'd hold something like that; mothers wouldn't take too kindly to having their children eaten after the bugger escapes the bars."

Nicholas turned back to the chalkboard as well, giving Andery nothing in return for his hard work at a jibe. After all, kidding a brother like Nicholas was never easy.

"Not a zoo, exactly. Though I'm sure it will seem that way at first. You like my pet?" Nicholas nodded toward his latest entry, changing subjects in his usual liquid-silver manner.

Zoo? Seem like...what? "Terrifying," he responded, trying to nudge his thoughts into following his brother's erratic discussion.

"Isn't it? Genetically designed."

"What?!" Andery whipped his head to look at Nicholas, only to find two pools of implacable blue; shields against any battering ram Andery had been able to raise in long, long years. "I know we've been genetically modifying Terran stock for years, but I've never seen anything like this...Smoke Jaguar."

"That's because it's not genetically modified. It's a whole new species."

Andery's mind reeled at the possibilities. "I didn't think that was possible."

"It wasn't. Until now."

"But, how can you..."

Nicholas quirked an eyebrow. "How can I what? Play god?"
I wasn't going to say it...

"Andery, we've been genetically modifying creatures for decades to adapt them to these worlds. The Star Adder. The Strana Mechty Wolf. The Jade Falcon. We started light and have moved further down the line of 'playing god.' Much further than anything the Star League accomplished. But when your toe is in the pool, isn't it hypocritical to ignore you're wet, claiming it's only a toe?

"The next step was logical. Design one from the ground up. Synthetic biology, as it were." He paused and cocked his head with a smile, as though a boy suddenly invited to talk about his favorite toy. "Well, they tell me it's not *true* synthetic biology, as we borrowed heavily from several genomes, but it's as close as anyone has ever come."

"But why?"

"A test."

"A test?"

"Of course. Isn't everything?"

Andery couldn't find a response, and foundered; the image of the coin rose sharply. *We'll forever be separated, Niki, even if just by the thickness of a coin.* "A test. Just to see if you could? Just because? Couldn't you have come up with a better reason?"

Something moved in Nicholas's eyes, as though he had been on the verge of sharing something, but Andery's comments shut a door. "I have *never* done anything 'just because,'" he answered, voice suddenly as cold as his perpetually frozen eyes.

Andery looked away, shame burning his ears despite his distaste for the idea of designing an animal. *No, you never do. Not even when we were kids. But you already play god with your men, Niki. Must you play god with genetics as well?*

"As with everything I do, this was a test. And so far, despite a few irregularities, is a complete success."

"And what does success mean?" Andery responded, trying to marshal composure and mollify his brother. Silence greeted his question, until he finally glanced over to find Nicholas staring at the board again. It slowly dawned on Andery that he'd been dismissed. He raised a hand as though to lay it on Nicholas's shoulder, then let it fall and headed back out into the sultry night, head and heart heavy.

I must have failed whatever test you set for me, Niki. Because this obviously was a test. With that thought, another popped to the surface right behind it; an answer to the question Nicholas refused to answer. An answer that only sparked more questions.

The next test.

CHAPTER 17

"It's been too long," Windham said, teeth flashing from a face full of fur.

"Yeah, too long," Andery replied, almost sheepishly.

Despite the stares of a few individuals on the street, they gave each other the bear hug of old friends meeting after too long apart. Windham released first, then pulled back and gripped Andery on either arm, staring hard into his face, as though searching for something.

Andery squirmed a little, trying not to meet his eyes too directly, then asked—hoping words would break Windham's concentration—"How's your congregation?"

For a moment Windham's brow furrowed, and his eyes told Andery he knew exactly what was going on, then shrugged lightly as he let him go after one final squeeze and turned to lead him into the small church house. "They're doing fine."

He ushered Andery into the building, leaving the hustle and bustle of the street outside. Windham opened his mouth to speak again, then paused as the tram trundled by, noise drowning out all ability to speak and even shaking the building.

The church house, built by willing hands near the original site where Nicholas's primary command had made planetfall, already felt like a relic among a towering metropolis. The single-story wood structure reminded Andery of nothing so much as holovids he'd seen of London, on Terra, before the occupation, with its mix of truly ancient structures of stone speaking of an earlier, simpler time, next to the towering edifices of high technology and the monolithic entities representing the Star League and its horrifyingly huge bureaucracy.

So much love in this building. Despite its small size, the devotion of its adherents could be seen in the meticulous wood paneling along the walls, the bas-relief scrolls on the pews, the amazingly intricate stained-glass window behind the raised podium: dedication and love in equal measure.

Despite their endless discussions of theology and god, Andery had never felt comfortable with the subject, much less setting foot in a church, best friend or no. As such, he walked lightly between the two rows of pews after Windham, as though to hide his footfalls from a deity he did not believe in. After all, in his own mind, it was never God with a capital *"G"...but you should always be careful.*

Reaching the front of the room (had he called it a nave?), Windham led Andery into a small office off to the right; barely more than a closet, with a small desk, two chairs and a makeshift filing cabinet, overflowing as though the paperwork were alive and trying to explode out of its confinement; the lack of a computer terminal or even a noteputer was almost conspicuous. He motioned for Andery to take a chair while he moved around the desk and plopped down heavily, chair protesting with a loud squeak as a heavy sigh shook his frame.

"That bad, huh?" Andery spoke, trying for levity, but missing the mark.

"No, not *that* bad. But bad enough."

"Well, how do you expect to get anything done without a computer?" Andery smiled.

Windham smiled tiredly in return. "Our lives are beyond complicated. Even though it may take extra time, I find the scratch of pencil actually soothes me. Not to mention, not as much paperwork of late." He shrugged, as though it was not important, but the pain rode large in his eyes.

"Numbers down?" Andery spoke.

"Yeah."

"What about refugees from the Pentagon Worlds? If memory serves, each time a group of them find their way here, you and your congregation are the first to meet them. Not only incredibly gracious of you and yours, but that generosity almost always left some joining your church."

Windham shrugged. "The last such group was nearly a year ago. And the spacing between the refugee groups grows longer and longer. I'm convinced we'll not see any more. Not after this much time. We've no idea what's going on there, but whatever it is, I think our last connections are finally severed for good."

"So then what's up? After such growth, your numbers are that far down? Why?"

Windham held his eyes without speaking. Andery finally nodded slowly, knowing the answer. "Nicholas."

"Of course, Nicholas.

"What has he done now?"

"Nothing. Of course. Never directly says anything against me or my church."

"But..."

"But he doesn't have to. The vast majority of my congregation were warriors. And despite what faith they may have found, when you fail Nicholas's tests, you can only stand to be in a room for so long with those who have stepped beyond you. For far too many, not even the faith I have to offer is salve enough for that pain, despite all my best efforts. And it certainly doesn't help that I'm still riding a 'Mech, trying to succor those without. Which even I realize feels a little...hollow."

Andery shivered, memories of his own time as a dispossessed flaring. *Bad enough to lose your ride for a while, but to know you'll never be in a 'Mech again...* He shivered once more and Windham shared a knowing look of agreement, filled with sadness.

"Then, toss in him dismantling Strana Prime's original church to clear space for his unfinished central park, and the message seems loud and clear enough for any to see."

Andery shook his head, knowing that would come up. "Still not sure about that."

"Not sure, Andery? He *dismantled* it. And be damned his promises of reassembling it, he never will. And you know it."

Andery glanced away, no answer beyond affirmation on his tongue.

"And so we sit here, waiting for the hand of god to smite us. And still the numbers dwindle."

Andery caught Windham's eyes at the unusual statement. "Don't you mean protecting you?"

"That would be God, not god."

They stared at one another for a full thirty seconds before they both broke up laughing, the inflections very clear in Windham's voice. It felt so good to laugh, even at such a topic.

Eventually, Windham's face sobered. "Seriously, though, Andery. Why are you here? Are you bringing me *the* news?"

Andery shook his head, trying to allay any concerns. "Not of Nicholas's impending arrival at your doorstep to burn down your church. No. But I do sense something big is coming to a head. Something."

Windham nodded. "So do I. So do I. Extra tension in the air, especially with the final segment of the latest tests underway. He's pared us down to a nub, it seems."

Andery shrugged, as though he didn't care, but the unease of his strange visit with Nicholas, the continuing tension in the cities, his own problems with Dana: the weight seemed to sink in claws he could not dislodge. He shifted in the small wooden chair, accidentally scraping it across the hardwood floor. He glanced down to find a new mark, looked up sheepishly.

"Churches are to be used, Andery. Reverently, of course, but used."

Andery nodded, then responded to the previous statement. "He has pared us down. But something is happening. And Windham..." he paused, placing a hand on the desk as though to steady himself, preparing to say what he'd come to say. "If you want to protect your congregation, do it from the inside. Do not fail in whatever tests Nicholas has coming."

Windham smiled as though Andery were joking, before it wilted under his intense stare. He finally cleared his throat and answered. "I have. Every test Nicholas has thrown at me, I've passed, as have those of my congregation. At least, those who are left." You could hardly hear the bitterness.

"I know. But the testing will never end, Windham. And at any step of the way, if you falter, there will be no forgiveness." He thought back to the test he must have failed so recently with Nicholas and realized he dreaded the eventual response from his brother; licked his lips nervously, then pressed on. "You'll be cast aside as quickly as you lose your usefulness in his grand schemes. And if you're cast off, you'll have no protection at all. He'll swat this church house and your congregation aside as thoroughly as he used the *Minotaur* to scour away the final resistance to our exodus from Eden."

Windham stared at him hard, as though he'd sprouted horns and a tail, before finally nodding. He cracked a slight smile and spoke. "*Aff.* Isn't that what you say in a time like this. *Aff?*"

Andery shook his head at Windham's attempts to lighten the mood, slightly embarrassed. "I'll never live that down, will I?"

"Of course you won't. Not when you've got an entire segment of the military saying it. And Andery."

"What?"

"It's especially true when you see the numbers from Nicholas's tests of who have passed and who haven't."

Andery sat back heavily, rubbing his fingers roughly together while looking away, slightly ashamed once more. "I stopped following it. Couldn't handle it."

"You may hate it, Andery, but your cadets have a much higher survival rate than any other instructor's. Whether you like being a teacher or not, you're good at it. *Very* good."

Andery glanced up just as Windham dropped the inevitable conclusion squarely in his lap. "Which means you'll be hearing your '*aff*' everywhere you go in your brother's new military."

Windham's laugh boomed out, until Andery couldn't help but laugh in return, despite wincing internally at the very idea.

CHAPTER 18

The man fiddled with the contraption as hell exploded around him.

Andery continued gazing intently through the high-image binoculars, ignoring the acerbic taste of cordite smoke on his tongue, simply unable to believe the combat engineer still lived, much less was still out there, working away. "Unbelievable."

"Magnificent, isn't it?" Sarah responded next to him, their shoulders almost rubbing.

"Sure it is," he said without taking his eyes away from the unfolding train wreck. "So magnificent he's dumb enough to try to take on a 'Mech on foot."

"But the courage."

"But the stupidity."

"Courage does count, Andery. Nicholas has that right."

He began to shake his head as a sigh escaped him, but he stopped, not wanting to miss the spectacle, regardless of the only possible outcome. "Of course courage is important. I've never said otherwise. But how many deaths, Sarah? How many deaths? Not to mention the injured. And all for what? Nicholas's image of a new army?"

"You do seem to repeat yourself, Andery. Often."

"Because no one seems to take my words at face value the first time around. Seems like I've got to ram it down your throats, or everybody ignores me."

A flight of missiles from the approaching *Kintaro* washed across the man's position, detonations violently twisting the landscape into a new, distorted reality, the thumps reaching their ears several moments after their eyes took them in. The wall of dust and thrown dirt obscured the scene as a lance of vehicles tried desperately to stave off the assault of the 'Mech, flashes of autocannons and PPC fire illuminating the cloud from within, as though a thunderhead hovered right on the ground during a massive storm. Miraculously, when the dirt-curtain cleared, the man still worked at his contrivance, unruffled by the chaos unleashed around him.

"Magnificent," Sarah breathed.

"Stupid."

Another ten seconds ticked by, counted down by several blinks, as Andery kept his eyes glued on the madman trying to prove a point. As the *Kintaro* blasted through a final vehicle and rounded the bend of the slight hill, the madman seemed to finally have cajoled his machine into working and he dodged away. Ducking behind boulders and zigzagging, as though a salvo from the *Kintaro*'s weapons wouldn't obliterate the man and everything around him for meters.

Andery was concentrating so hard on the running figure he almost missed the device deploying. With a light puff of smoke, a strange ball shot from the mouth of the mortar-like contraption and immediately began to expand and stretch into a weblike structure, albeit longer through the middle than it was tall. It rushed toward the *Kintaro*, which had continued to advance, expanding until it slammed into both legs below the knees. Nodules of adhesive (taken from almost thirty grapple rods, if one believed the rumors) adhered both sides of the myomer-mesh webbing, sealing the net to the legs. A flash of energy expanded from some type of module at the center of the web and engulfed the entire apparatus.

From one moment to the next, the electric jolt through the myomer webbing jerked it back into as small a space as the adhering nodules allowed, yanking the legs of the ponderous titan together with terrible force. Though most of the nodules tore free under the horrific contraction, enough remained adhered to pull the legs sharply together—the ear-piercing screech of servos damaged in the forced movement cut the air—and the *Kintaro* toppled like a felled oak; 55 tons of metal hitting the ground at speed could be felt even at this distance.

Andery's mouth slowly dropped open as an ancient child's story ran through his head. *I don't believe it.*

"Ah, Jack, you felled the giant."

Startled, Andery pulled the binoculars away to find Sarah smiling at him; her eyes and smile lit up her face like Mechty's aurora borealis, taking his breath away. *How could you also be thinking of Jack and the Beanstalk?*

"It would seem he won."

Andery shook his head, trying to dislodge the uneasy feelings that always sprouted around Sarah and glanced back to the battlefield, where the *Kintaro* slowly maneuvered to its feet; the legs jerked for a moment, then tore the webbing apart. The unsteadiness of the act meant a damaged hip actuator, or the pilot took the fall hard. "But he didn't destroy the 'Mech. He didn't pass the test."

"Who says the test was to destroy the 'Mech? You scoffed at the idea that his contraption would even work. As did most people. But it did."

"Doesn't mean it's worthwhile."

"No, it doesn't. But he proved he could make it plausibly work."

"So?"

"Come on, Andery. He was thinking outside the box. Isn't that what you keep harping on?"

He finally looked back at Sarah, frustrated that he never seemed to reach her. Pulled the binocular strap over his head and set it casually on the hoverjeep behind them. "No, that's Nicholas talking. 'Think outside of what has gone before.'" He shook his head. "Not that that's bad. But what makes it bad, what could make it very bad, is the idea that thinking outside the box allows us to do whatever we want." Images of the smoke jaguar rose with a pounding snarl, echoing its victory yowl. *A roar you want to emulate, Niki?*

"So, just because our goodly combat engineer, Cyrus something or other, showed that under the right circumstances, even a noncombatant can bring down a 'Mech, we're now all going to become murders? Drink babies' blood? Kick puppies?"

Though he was still angry, her soothing smile and last comment flattened his temper somewhat. "Cyrus Elam."

"What?"

"The combat engineer. Cyrus Elam. And I'd hardly consider him a noncombatant. Not after all the training he's passed. He's almost as good a marksman as I am."

"And *that*, of course, is saying *so* much."

"Hey, it is," he responded, finally sloughing off most of his anger as he fell into an easy camaraderie of joking. Almost. "I happen to be one of the finest marksmen in Nicholas's entire new military." He puffed up, as though to demonstrate his point with a bigger chest.

"You are," she responded, nodding at him, despite her larger grin at his antics. "And if Cyrus can almost match you, he's got to be good. But he's still a combat engineer at heart, and for him to display this type of talent, that says something."

"You don't actually believe this will allow him to pass? He failed. He didn't take the 'Mech down, at least not for good." Memories of his own failure with Nicholas, despite purging his feelings with Windham, still rode a little too high.

"You never know with Nicholas. But that was a pretty spectacular way to modify some grapple rods and a mortar. And that's only the latest and greatest of what he's done all through the trials. And any 'Mech takes damage getting knocked down. And if you've got something to follow that up with? Specially trained infantry or something? That could be very useful in the end. Might just take that knocked-down 'Mech and keep it down."

"I doubt it. He should've been wiped out by the missile strikes. Sheer dumb luck. Not to mention the 'Mech has to be right on top of it."

She shrugged his comment away. "So it never works. Never is practical. It's still an amazing feat of ingenuity. And don't forget the courage. Nicholas is all about courage."

I know.

"And you never did explain how you think we'll all turn into murderers."

He sighed heavily, frustrated at how many times they'd had this conversation. *Then again, at least Sarah will have it. Dana won't even allow the topic to be brought up.* He shied away from that thought and its implications like a moth trying desperately to resist the siren call of the bright death-light in the darkness.

"We're not going to turn into monsters overnight. But the mores of society are built across generations upon generations. Mores that have helped sustain society and kept it from devolving into utter chaos and complete destruction."

"We have war," she interjected, hopping up to sit on the hood of the hoverjeep now that the action was over. "The wars that have probably wiped out the Inner Sphere. The horrible Pentagon Wars."

"Of course we do. And we always will. But war is one thing. Murder, rape, and genocide are something completely different. Whether I like it or not—whether any of us like it—war is accepted as a moral possibility by humanity as a whole. But we try, however badly, to draw the line at those others."

"So."

"So?" Andery scratched his head rapidly, as though trying to dig for the right words, while he began pacing. "So, when you strip a society down to the ground—a society millennia in the making—then try to rebuild it almost overnight...you're going to lose the backbone of what makes humanity...human."

"What makes a human a human?" she countered easily, the grin evident without him looking directly at her.

"I'm not talking esoterics. Nor do I want to get into the origins of man, or spirituality. You want that, go to Windham. I'm also not talking about the individual, but the whole. Nicholas is systematically stripping our culture to the bones, whether everyone is aware of it or not."

"Well, not sure how you *can't* be aware of it, after all the changes since we grounded."

"Yes. But are they aware of the more subtle bonds being broken? I'm not talking about just the military, though that's big enough. But he's breaking down the family."

She shrugged again, her perennial favorite pastime it seemed. "So. He's just sending kids to live with other families. Sponsorship. Apprenticeship. That's all. That's old-school talk."

"But it's more than that. Much more." The smoke jaguar yowled again, as did memories of his last talk with Sarah, and the students getting younger and younger in his classes. "Mark my words, he'll do away with the family entirely." He couldn't bring himself, even with Sarah, to voice his concerns of where he suspected Nicholas would ultimately take his genetic manipulations.

"So what if he does? It'll only make us stronger."

"How can we know? He's stripping society down and he'll build it back up. Him. One man. How can you know we'll survive? How can you know this new military-centered life he's heading toward will not lead to the enslavement of civilians? Genocides and mass subjugations?"

"What are you talking about?" she said, confusion creasing her eyebrows. "All he talks about is service."

"Come on! Wake up, Sarah! Look past what he says to what's really happening. Service, yes. But *his* service. Service with an iron fist. Service that says we'll make it better for all civilians— whether they want it or not."

For perhaps the first time in all their discussions, real confusion seemed to war on her face; her obvious devotion to Nicholas's dream—a devotion she had paid for in blood by killing her own troops on Eden—against Andery's arguments and her own intelligence. "I don't know if I agree with you, Andery. But we have to go in some direction. Don't we? If not Nicholas's way, then where?"

She shook her head. "You rail, Andery. You rail against what Nicholas is doing, and yet I don't see you standing up with a new way. With a different answer." Her chin rose, as though casting a gauntlet to the ground, trying to regain her equilibrium, her sense of self.

Andery stopped his endless pacing and collapsed inward, shoulders slumping; he felt hollowed out, as though an endless sirocco swept him clean. He tried to meet her eyes, but could not answer her demand, as there was nothing inside him to contradict her.

*And that's what eats at me most, Sarah. I have no answers...
because the only answers I can find is for me to take his place. And
that wouldn't work. I cannot do the hard things. Not like Nicholas.
I didn't survive Moscow like he did. I didn't stand beside our father
as it all crashed down in the end. I would fail.*

I...would...fail.

CHAPTER 19

KATYUSHA CITY
NOVY TERRA
STRANA MECHTY
KERENSKY CLUSTER
11 JUNE 2807

"*It is time.*

"*The past has been a stain of pains and memories we refuse to allow ourselves to forget. Memories that bow us down with the weight of our sorrows and grief over past mistakes and failures.*

"*Over past losses.*

"*We, all of us, have lost so many precious to us. Those who have left their indelible mark upon who we are. Who we can become, due to their unselfish love and sacrifice.*

"*But should we dwell on that loss? Is that a fitting epitaph to the memories of those we were forced to leave behind? Or, as the sun burns away the darkness of a terrible night filled with horrors, should we not look to the future? Should we not raise our faces and drink in the warmth of hope? Is hope not what brought us this distance?*

"*Is this not what our cherished lost would desire?*"

The dramatic words flared out of the giant holoprojection in the central plaza, rolling out and away into the distance as the sun set dramatically, flaring a halo behind the icon. Nicholas, eyes conveying not warmth (never that), but a sense of inclusiveness Andery only saw when he gave such speeches, towered above the tens-of-thousands-strong congregation in three-dimensional glory until his image filled the eyes of all those present to the same height as their father's statue.

Too bad those seeing it broadcast to the entire Kerensky Cluster will miss that fine piece of showmanship. Glancing away from the towering personage to the stage where Nicholas spoke, which was almost miniscule by comparison, Andery knew even at this distance his brother would likely pick him out. *He probably wants me on the dais with him. But I'm sure his beloved Jennifer will likely spin it for him,* he thought bitterly. *"It's best to have Andery among the common folk. After all, he's so common."* He wallowed in his intense dislike of Jennifer, gritting his teeth in frustration, as Nicholas continued.

"During the first year of our Exodus, the Great General was forced by small-minded men to take a firm hand and issue General Order 137. Though some considered this move harsh, with the clear sight and perspective of history, we now know his decisive hand saved our nascent Star League-in-Exile.

"Just as we all took drastic measures to adapt to life on the Pentagon Worlds.

"Just as we took drastic measures to survive the war that those who forgot the General's dream—our dream—are waging even now. A war that has ravaged not simply our bodies and our minds and our spirits, but the very foundation upon which we placed ourselves, in the Great General's hands."

Andery watched numerous heads move to take in his father's towering statue to their right, most nodding subconsciously as though unable to disagree while in the shadow of the Great General.

Ah Niki, I see Nagasawa's hand all over this speech. You can be eloquent, dear brother, but your pocket reporter has a preternatural way with words. Andery smiled suddenly, enjoying the thought, despite its pettiness. *Must have pissed Jen off something fierce, 'cause I'm sure she tried to write this speech for you.* He smiled a little more at his first use of the diminutive, liking how it belittled; ignored the slight guilt at such sulkiness.

"Now is the time for our future.

"A time to nurture the hopes of the cherished lost, who lent us their helping hand. Of those whose memories we must never let go, but whom we must honor by living each day to the fullest.

"You have all heard the words of General Order 137 many times, but I would speak them again on this day, of all days."

Nicholas looked down and paused, as if marshaling his words, and when he gazed back up, the entire crowed seemed to vibrate. Despite the obvious distaste of many in the crowd for Nicholas and his "regime," his voice and the look on his face spoke to many more, reeking as they did of the departed General; surreptitious glances toward the statue swept the crowd. *You can wear that mantle so easily, can't you, Niki? Does it ever hurt?*

Nicholas began to speak, and for a heartbeat, even Andery was taken in by his timbre, as though the statue itself had begun to speak.

"'Return to the Inner Sphere is impossible for us. Our heritage and our convictions are different from those we left behind. The greed of the five Great Houses and the Council Lords is a disease that can only be burned away by the passing of decades, even centuries. And though the fighting may seem to slow, or even cease, it will erupt again as long as there are powerful men to covet one another's wealth. We shall live apart, conserving all the good of the Star League and ridding ourselves of the bad, so that we can return—and return we shall—our shining moral character will be as much our shield as our BattleMechs and fighters.'"

The years were stripped away, the words drawn up in memory, as though heard only yesterday, echoing down the long corridors of thousands of ships in deep space. Nicholas looked down, as though pained to accept that mantle, and Andery shivered. *You've kept me out of the loop, Niki, but I can feel what's coming. Where you will take this?*

Nicholas glanced up once more, eyes again his own. But though the sense of inclusiveness remained, Andery could begin to make out the winter landscape just below the surface; the mailed fist ready for the velvet glove to be removed.

"Though almost twenty-two years have passed since the Great General decreed those fateful words, they are more relevant today than ever before. For they not only speak of a far distant future our grandchildren's grandchildren will march toward, but they speak of a more immediate future all of us will and must participate in.

"The fires of corruption and greed have been ignited, and as the Great General foresaw so clearly, they must be allowed to burn themselves out. To burn every last trace of their evil from the Pentagon Worlds, whether it take a year or ten or twenty. And while that cauterization is underway, we must prepare for a return. We will return to save the Pentagon Worlds.

"These words from our Great Father shall forever more be our Hidden Hope of returning first to the Pentagon Worlds, and then to the Inner Sphere. To save them from themselves."

Great Father. Hidden Hope. Bitterness swelled. *Not enough for you to build a monstrous statue of Father, Niki. But now you've laid the foundations to transform him into the messianic figure who led us here. While you, his prophet, leads us to a promised land only you can see.* If it wasn't all so terribly effective—and, despite his hateful denials, perhaps needed—he'd salute another masterstroke. *Nagasawa indeed.*

As the speech continued, confirming Andery's assessment of where it would lead, his eyes wandered the stage as he tried to mellow his bitterness. Though he couldn't see details at this distance—the holoprojector only showed Nicholas, to the point of excising any background—he easily picked out Jennifer's arrogant stance, along with the venerable presence of Truscott, Hazen, Zalman, and McKenna. He noted a few new faces, including one, next to Antonius Zalman, that even at this distance seemed to have an even more-than-usual avid look on her young features.

He casually leaned over and whispered, "Who's the young woman on the far right? By Zalman."

Dana gave him a scathing look, as though he were violating some ceremony, before whispering, "Ellie Kinnison." She turned back to Nicholas with a resolute shake of her head, which promised trouble if he broke her concentration again.

Once more, despite all his best efforts, he couldn't help the pang of jealousy that reared its head. *If I'm your soul mate, Dana, if I am your beloved, then why do your eyes burn brighter for my brother than me?* Through the years, as the question continued to haunt him, inexorably pushing him away from the only person who seemed to really understand him, no amount of rationalizations about "she loves you, but is dedicated to his vision" could completely ease his pain.

He ached, as his eyes fell away from those on the stage, no longer interested in who they might be or why Nicholas honored them with inclusion at this monumental announcement. He slowly rubbed calloused fingers together, the too-dry skin rasping as angrily as his thoughts, while his mind found the thread of Nicholas's words once more, almost against his will.

"Yet we cannot return as we are. The Great General believed in all of us. Believed we all held the potential to set aside our differences and our old prejudices to make a thriving Star League-in-Exile.

"But behold an ingot of iron. It holds the potential to become a gleaming blade, wielded by a stalwart soul in defense of the Star League. Yet to achieve such a worthy goal, it must be hammered and heated. And reheated and hammered again. Quenched.

"It...must...be...forged.

"It must be taken from latency and, through trials, forged into a useful weapon. So must we all. Like the Great General, I see the latent potential in all of us. The potential for great things. But it is a potential that must be crafted to reach fruition.

"'The sole purpose of the army is to stand firmly with the people.' This ancient adage is truer today than when it was spoken more than half a millennia ago on our birth world."

Andery winced, then automatically tried to hide it from Dana. He breathed with relief after a quick glance to assure himself she didn't notice; now the growing stink of too many people in one location for too long was almost curling his tongue.

Except that's not the real quote, is it, Nicholas? Not what you quoted me: 'The sole purpose of the army is to stand firmly with the people, who will then serve them wholeheartedly.' And more importantly, not the original quote at all. He remembered his brother catching him off guard in the past, and he'd done his research on Mao since. 'The sole purpose of this army is to stand firmly with the Chinese people and to serve them wholeheartedly.'

As ever, my brother, you may be right in the end, but I cannot condone all you do along that path. You've taken father's love of ancient literature and wisdom and dishonored it. He prided himself on getting a quote exactly right, every time. He practically *considered it a sin to misquote accidentally, much less deliberately, as you do. The specific misappropriation and malicious violation of a quote to suit your needs.* His previous chastisements to his brother for quoting monstrous figures of history continued to fall on deaf ears.

Andery gripped his hands together angrily, knowing he couldn't stop what was already unfolding, and continued listening.

"Almost from the moment our feet touched Strana Mechty, the military under my command has endured this forging, in the knowledge they shall lead the way in service. With each hammer blow, we are forging a stronger future. A future that will allow us to grasp the hopes our departed loved ones left with us. Yet it is now time for the next step.

"The quenching.

"The Star League Defense Force served an honorable, and pivotal, role in all of our lives. And like our lost loved ones, will never be replaced. But like our lost kin, it is time to set the past behind, and move into a future that will allow us to rekindle the bright flame of the League's Golden Age.

"For four long years, the men and women of the military have pared themselves down to an elite cadre of MechWarriors. A number not only to serve, but a number our current resources and manpower can sustain. More importantly, through that forging, the only number we will need to reclaim the Pentagon Worlds for all those who have gone before."

For the first time in long minutes, Nicholas paused, as the usual hard shell on his face rose to the surface, a shark fin breaching warm waters, sending a shiver of thrill and fear in equal measure into everyone who saw it. The thrum of the crowed ratcheted up another level.

Andery took in the multitude, waiting to see disgust at such a transformation, but found none. Only rapt eyes, drinking in the spectacle. Andery shook his head, glancing carefully toward Dana and away as quickly, as he found on her face the same enraptured expression as on the majority of those present. *How can it be so easy, Niki? How?*

When he resumed speaking, Nicholas's voice held a power and passion that seemed to make the crowd sway back, as though the doors of an endless blast furnace were revealing the passions within for the first time in a public setting. A passion of the vision Nicholas held, which he began to unveil, if only a little, to those who would participate in his reshaping of history.

"Eight hundred warriors.

"They shall be my Clans. They shall be your Clans. Twenty Clans to represent the twenty colonized worlds of the Kerensky Cluster. For though Strana Mechty is the heart, those worlds are the body: the future belongs to all of us. We all shall share in the bright dream to come, as we all work toward a common future.

"So many of us found despair taking hold when the Great Father left us in the hour of our greatest need. But his memory lives on. And on this day, the anniversary of when he was stolen from us by those who would tread upon a dream we all hold precious, we shall look forward, knowing we are ready and willing to do what we must to create a new society. To seize the day.

"Selah."

Stunned silence met the end of the speech, as the giant holovid fizzled into static and then finally blinked out. As though unstoppered, the crowd exploded into a flurry of conversations, while Nicholas and all those on the stage made a stately but expertly executed withdrawal under the watchful eyes of two BattleMechs at the edges of the plaza; evidence that, despite his flowery words, might would make Nicholas's dream happen if words failed.

As Andery allowed the excited and worried and angry voices to wash over him, and as Dana clutched his arm and began pulling him away, talking almost feverishly about one of her visions and that the time was at hand when Nicholas would come into his own, all Andery could think about was his mother.

Selah.

The word their mother spoke at the end of her prayers when they were little children. Before the Amaris Civil War and before Katyusha abandoned saying her prayers with her kids. *What signal are you sending, Nicholas? What were you saying? Was that for me? For the people? Or only for you? A prayer to Mother and Father that you were right all along.*

He followed Dana's rough pull, oblivious to her babbling as his mind wandered, unable (as ever) to find an answer, or a place to rest.

CHAPTER 20

KATYUSHA CITY
NOVY TERRA
STRANA MECHTY
KERENSKY CLUSTER
13 JUNE, 2807

Andery tried, but could no more ignore her than he could the sun breaking through cloud cover.

But he tried anyway, while the command room slowly filled with the eight hundred warriors of Nicholas's new army. Friendly faces and not. The spartan room, containing the ubiquitous holotable at the center and a smattering of computer terminals—along with the microfiber poly-myomer woven flooring, charged to rigidity—seemed like a corral more than a military command center. *Corralling cattle? No, a zoo. I should've seen it coming. Should have...so many should-haves.*

"What are you saying?"

The unkind thought skittered across the surface of his mind like a reentry turned bad. He tried to blank his mind, but found her voice could and would shatter any concentration; a blazing sun burning away cloud cover, rolling back endless banks of gray-white until a searing blue sky left no shade; a molecule on the slide, bared for bright eyes.

Without turning, he responded, "What I always say."

"You would say that? Here?" Her voice sounded scandalized. As though he threatened to urinate on the altar of Strana Prime's principal church.

Oh, that's right. Strana Prime's *church was dismantled. After all, it stood in what would be the central square of mystical Katyusha, eh Niki?* The sarcasm almost carried him away on a wave of bitterness he never seemed able to hold off for too long. *And you promised to rebuild it, just like Windham said, better than ever, didn't you? Or wait...no, you didn't. Jennifer promised. And I'd accept her promise as quickly as enter a* burrock *hole. So you'll keep delaying. After all, we're resource-strapped, and you're just trying to find homes for all of us refugees, and what can you do about it, right? I mean, you've only got so much men and materials, and infrastructure is so important right now...and making sure that we have a good defense against any possible incursion from the Pentagon Worlds.*

But you'll never rebuild it. Because religion has no place in your society, does it, Niki? No place at all. There can be only one God before Me. And that God is you, isn't it, Niki? Oh, if push came to shove, you'd probably say our God is now one of stone, twelve meters tall and standing in the central plaza. You might even go so far as to say you're simply a spokesperson, though they treat you more like a prophet. But isn't a prophet supposed to listen to the words of his God? But you don't listen to anyone, do you? The old god, Father, is dead and you intend to remake humanity in your own image.

But what image is that, Niki? What are these Clans? What image?

"Andery."

The voice seemed to jar something loose, as though a circuit dislodged from the endless loop of his thoughts gyrating madly, and he physically jerked, turning to meet Dana's eyes. Those powerful, soul-mirroring eyes...that now held a shadow. Nothing she ever said. Likely nothing she even realized. But the eyes that mirrored his soul so completely seemed to have...a fog on them. A light tracing of moisture from an unknown source, turning his image into a wan simulacrum of the previous robust picture.

Like our relationship.

He fought off a heavy sigh, running his hands through hair that seemed to be thinning of late. (Imagination, or the stress of life?) "What?"

"This is what I talk of, Andery. You no longer listen to the words I speak."

And you never listen to me. Wouldn't even talk with me when Niki made his big announcement, would you?! Only at *me.* "I'm just tired. The long classes and field exercises. Preparing each class at breakneck speed for preliminary trials. It's all...taxing."

Her face bordered on rebuke. "We are all taxed. What right does that give you to talk like you do, especially here in his presence?"

Eyes slewed away to take in the crowd, stomach clenching. *Almost a capital H, there, Dana. We committed ourselves to following Niki's dream...but I never imagined you would become a sycophant, following blindly. So blindly...*

"Andery," she said.

His eyes found Carson's at some distance, and the two shared a brief nod before his good friend resumed talking to one of his subcommanders. Andery used the moment to continue to hide from her tone; it almost verged on the caress to his ears he first heard the night they had became one...a tone not heard in so long.

He sought others he might know in the room, some seen recently and some not in long months. Windham and Sainze. Sandra Tseng and Hans Jorgensson standing close together (his eyes skipped over them, forever reminders of the *Prinz Eugen*). Karen Nagasawa. John Fletcher talking with Stephen McKenna. Samuel Helmer, his former student, now a full adult—he looked for his ever-present companion, Tominson, but did not see him, which was odd—standing within the orbit of Elizabeth Hazen (eyes skipping again to avoid memories he wished to forget).

Just when he knew he must turn back to Dana or risk sparking a situation he could not control, a commotion by the main door saved him, as most of those present turned to see one of the last to arrive.

General Absalom Truscott swept into the room (no matter how much Niki changed his military, Truscott would *always* be "General"), hard eyes and firm expression stripping away pretenses and digging for the absolute truth of the matter.

He watched as Truscott moved steadily toward the center of the room, passing Carson with an almost condescending look;

Andery stiffened as Carson broke eye contact with Truscott and looked down. Even though Nicholas effectively made Truscott commanding general in charge of all forces in the second Exodus, the man refused to give up proprietary leanings toward the 149th. Never mind that Carson had commanded the division for years now. Even as it was pared down to a mere ghost of its previous size. And though Andery might be able to face down his brother now and then, the few times he spoke with Truscott, he was always left feeling twisted, wrung out and tossed to the wind; a limp, useless rag.

Truscott was a man who had *learned* at the feet of the Great General.

Don't you have enough worries, Andery? Can't just leave things be. It's what Carson wants. Doesn't want to buck the bronco. Especially with how easy it is to find yourself on the outs of late. So much tension...

Truscott arrived at the front of the room and fell into an easy waiting stance. The tension grew as the warriors continued to speculate in low-key whispers and sharp hand gestures about Nicholas's grand announcement a few days prior. Andery tried to quiet his mind, but found Dana's silence as loud as the roar of a thousand voices.

Finally, Nicholas entered alone, drawing all eyes. While some of the warriors present had gone so far as to stop wearing rank insignias, all still wore the olive-drab uniforms of the Star League Defense Force. Nicholas, in a plain white jumpsuit, with a strange red version of the Star League symbol at his collar—it was hard to see, but it appeared as though the extended point swept down and not to the right—the sigil stuck out like a blood drop on a pristine, snowy landscape. Andery reluctantly pulled his eyes away to take the pulse of the room. His heart wavered, as almost every pair of eyes centered avidly upon their leader.

No. Not just their leader. Their cult of personality. Andery rubbed sweaty palms on his pant legs, uncaring of the stains, knowing the uniform would be hung in a closet at the end of this day, never to be worn again. Sadness welled.

Father had a cult of personality, Nicholas. But it occurred naturally. You forced this. You manipulated it until there could be no other outcome. But what happens now, Niki? What happens if you don't survive this? No cult survives the death of its leader.

Nicholas moved to the front, receiving endless salutes, but returning none. He nodded to Jennifer Winson then turned to take in each warrior before speaking.

"Warriors," he began, voice low, forcing all into absolute silence to hear. "I have ordered you assembled this day to take the next step. More so than any military in history, you have passed test after test, whittling your ranks down to an elite cadre. You will no longer need to pass a test to determine whether you will still be warriors."

"*You* are my military."

He slowly made a circuit, taking in every soldier present with the fierce pride of a parent for children who have reached adulthood. "But," he continued, "it is now time for you to finally cast off the cloak of the Star League Defense Force and take on a new mantle. But we do not do this with malice. Or with any thought to diminish the SLDF name. We do this because there *is no* Star League. We do this because, in the absence of the Star League and thus in the absence of a true Star League Defense Force, we take on a new name and a new calling. We warriors will become the Clans. The calling of the Star League Defense Force was to defend the Star League. Our calling is to return to the Pentagon Worlds. And from there, to produce a society ready and willing to spend all our energy, all our devotion, in making the Great Father's dream a reality. To return to the Inner Sphere at the appropriate time, and to rebuild the Star League *they* destroyed."

The room seethed with energy. With power. With a mission.

Even Andery, swathed in the cocoon of knowledge of his brother and the heart-wrenching potential for devastating consequences if Nicholas's dream went astray, felt the call. The gathered warriors demanded he fully embrace this goal. This identity. This need to follow their leader, no matter where he led.

"My Clans," he finally continued, weaving the spell tighter. "Now is the time for a new series of tests to begin. Not the testing of warriors, for you have all proven yourselves a hundred times over. No, now is the time to prove your desire for this transformation." He pointed toward the central holotable, which flared to life as the room darkened, throwing an ethereal halo around him.

I can feel the pull, Niki. But I know it's staged. You may embrace everything you say, but you never do anything without a plan. Isn't that what you said? What you always say? Every action, every body movement, a stage to manipulate? As you've manipulated me for so many years? Hell, I should be used to it by now...but I'm not...

An icon blazed to life in the holovid. A stylized white star on a bloodred teardrop, set against a gold shield, words riding proudly above the emblem: *Clan Blood Spirit.* It faded away to resolve into another icon of a spiraling burrock, with its own label: *Clan Burrock.* Then a tangle of a snake, in purple and blue against a shield: *Clan Cloud Cobra.* Then a fierce coyote head— with that same strange symbol as on Nicholas's collar imposed on its forehead—against an inverted triangle: *Clan Coyote.* The symbols and words progressed slowly, as everyone present hung on the revelations as though they were holy writ unveiled from newly found scripture: *Fire Mandrill, Ghost Bear, Goliath Scorpion, Hell's Horses, Ice Hellion, Jade Falcon, Mongoose, Nova Cat, Sea Fox, Smoke Jaguar, Snow Raven, Star Adder,* Steel Viper, *Widowmaker, Wolf,* and *Wolverine.*

"Twenty Clans, of forty warriors each. I have tracked your progress through every test and have determined which of you are to be assigned to each new Clan. Each Clan has been assigned a parcel of land to the north of Katyusha City, from this moment forth called Svoboda Zemylya. On this new land, you will all start from scratch. You will take on the namesake of your Clan as totem and make it your own. From working the very ground to building facilities, you will begin the job of forging your Clan into a new, unified whole. And we will all work together in the construction of a central Hall of Khans. And in the end, the twenty Clans will create a sum greater than their parts."

He swept his hands toward the holoprojection and stepped to the side. "Step forward and seize your destiny."

Without conscious volition, the warriors surged forward toward the list. Dana grabbed his hand and pulled him with her, eager to view their names.

A terrible, gibbering fear crawled out from the corner of Andery's mind. That damn cat howled again, and he knew failure. Could feel it looming over him. Knew it was about to be revealed for all to see. Most terrifying of all, knew it was about to be revealed to Dana.

The holoprojection loomed like a terrifying white cliff of endless possibilities stretching away in all directions, while hundreds of voices talked excitedly about that future they would share.

His eyes skittering across the projection, catching glimpses of familiar names.

Clan Jade Falcon: Khan Elizabeth Hazen
Clan Star Adder: Khan Absalom Truscott
Clan Snow Raven: Khan Stephen McKenna
Clan Wolf: Khan Jerome Winson
Clan Mongoose: James Carson

Those were to be expected (*why no Khanship for Carson?*). But others cut more powerfully.

Clan Cloud Cobra: Khan Windham Khatib
Clan Fire Mandrill: Khan Raymond Sainze
Clan Wolverine: Khan Sarah McEvedy

Not because they didn't deserve such accolades; they all were brilliant people. Yet every person he would call a close friend had risen to the top of Nicholas's wild experiment, while he—

Dana gasped next to him. He slowly turned to find her animated face and out-stretched arm pinpointing her name. He tried to focus on her words, but couldn't quite manage it. The best he could do was allow his eyes to follow her finger.

Clan Coyote: Khan Dana Kufahl

The strange words seemed to brand him; a painful searing, and a stench of burning flesh that paralyzed him. His eyes finally pushed past the holoprojection, finding his brother against a back wall, his companion Jen (the diminutive failed to bring its usual satisfaction) at his side. Despite the distance and the harsh light, while his brother sat in darkness, he could easily read Niki's eyes. Knew what was coming.

"Andery, your name's not on the list."

No. I wouldn't be.

"Andery, why isn't your name on the list? You're here." Her confusion and insistent voice, along with a pull on his hand, tried to rob him of his concentration on Nicholas, but nothing could do that.

You found some pride in me, Nicholas. You found something in me. And yet you fail me now? You cannot cast me aside and besmirch our name, but I failed your test.

"Why, Andery? Why are you..." her voice trailed off, before resuming, the momentary confusion dashed away with newfound awe. "Nicholas is not on the list. Of course. The Kerensky name stands apart. Now I understand."

Of everything, even knowing nearly all his friends were now Khans while his name didn't make the list, that stabbed hardest, until a sob threatened to tear loose. He stared his hatred across the room, hoping his brother might finally see what his manipulations had wrought. For Andery to hear his name used that way by Dana. To hear her so easily accept some benevolent plan by Nicholas, when it was simply one more machination in an endless series, forced his eyes shut.

In a room of strident enthusiasm and overwhelming joy for the future, Andery stood within his own circle of sorrow, lamenting the shattering of a past he alone seemed to miss.

CHAPTER 21

KATYUSHA CITY
NOVY TERRA
STRANA MECHTY
KERENSKY CLUSTER
13 JUNE, 2807

As he knew would happen, Andery waited and waited, and soon the rest of the warriors slid away in small groups to discuss their own burgeoning Clans. Dana had pulled on his arm several times, but he'd refused to budge, his mind locked in an immovable need to speak with his brother; one moment she was there, the next gone.

He had a memory of Nicholas looking at Jennifer, the last to leave them alone, before she also departed; if he had not been so caught up in his own grief, he might have exulted in the dismissal.

And then, it was only the two of them. Andery tried to open his mouth and speak, but nothing came out. The silence stretched, and finally Andery dared to look at his brother, and almost took a step back, as the icy frost that always rimed Nicholas' gaze was missing this time. The usual depths of dismissal and disdain. Instead, for once...he looked like just an...older brother. *Are you even that to me?*

The shock of it unstoppered his lips, and the only question he could possibly ask spilled out. "Why?"

"Why what?"

"Stop it, Nicholas. You always do that. You always force me to pry it out of you. Please. Not this time. Not...this...time. Why? You've forced me to be apart my whole life. And now, when you have crafted a culture from the ground up, you could do anything you want. Anything. And yet you still chose to leave...me...out."

Nicholas closed the distance, and shocked Andery further by reaching out to squeeze his shoulder. "Andery, Andery. Others may think I can do anything. And yet, I know you know better. You know, having listened to father all those years. Leadership is anything but 'whatever you want.' And the more power you have, the more careful you must be in how you use it."

"But...why...?" was all Andery could get out past his hurt and the anger. He didn't want platitudes and explanations. Those were for another day. Now, he just needed an answer.

Nicholas slowly nodded, that calm look in his eyes again catching Andery off guard. *Perhaps after finally reaching this point, he doesn't need to continually use me? Ha!* The bitter laugh echoed hollowly in his head.

"I understand your disappointment—I truly do," Nicholas said at the grimace that rose to Andery's face. "Nothing would please me more than to give you a Clan, Andery, as a reward for your tireless service to what we are building here. But I could not do so, for two reasons.

"First, your liaison with the civilians is too important to our plans. You're already a warrior, and that puts some distance between you and those you watch; enough to keep them off their guard. But you are also in a unique position: of the Clans, but not of the Clans. This will allow you to continue in that position. If we are ever to realize the full vision of what we must do, if we are ever to succeed in bringing that vision to reality, the civilians *must* be at our side."

Andery hated the knocking of that logic against his emotions. Even so, he dreaded the next point even more, for he thought he knew what it would be.

"Second," Nicholas continued in that strangely becalmed voice. "We are building a meritocracy, where anyone can rise as high as their intelligence, skill, and courage can take them. And whether you like it or not, you are still a Kerensky. I cannot simply hand you anything, for it would undermine everything we've built. Whatever comes to you, you must earn, Andery. Always, you must earn whatever you possess. I hope you understand that?"

His brother's logic was unfailing. Both arguments sound. The becalmed moment almost...brotherly. *Is this the true you, finally, Niki? Or is this you just manipulating me all over again?*

Ultimately, Andery realized he couldn't know in the moment. And he was too emotionally drained to cared. As always, he felt the inexorable pull of Nicholas' vision, and almost without realizing he was doing it, found himself nodding in agreement as he drifted in the vortices of his brother's passage.

CHAPTER 22

SVOBODA ZEMYLYA
NOVY TERRA
STRANA MECHTY
KERENSKY CLUSTER
15 JUNE 2807

Andery trudged through the growing darkness.

The sun set, and he quickly lost the ability to see more than a half-dozen steps in front of him, despite the purple aurora borealis sparking overhead. Yet he didn't falter; he'd moved through the last two days in darkness more absolute than any planetary nightfall.

Night continued to creep across the land as Andery and his two companions headed farther into the prairie-like lands, some thirty kilometers directly north of Katyusha City. A soft hint of a breeze stirred hidden leaves in the distance, and sent fronds of some alien heather wafting against their pant legs like the soft nudge of a kitten's nose. Crickets (or their alien counterparts, Andery had never cared to learn which) sang their cacophony, as though a dirge to the loss of light, and the smells of night tickled noses and garnished tongues.

He ignored it all, too far inside his head to notice the beauty nature so freely spread before eyes overshadowed with his own memories.

He jerked as a man-made *click* clashed against the soft sounds of nature and a piercing light sprang into existence;

his companion waved the flashlight around momentarily, as though reorienting, and they continued.

He trudged on, mind a molasses trap out of which he could not break. His companion waved the light again erratically, causing Andery to shift his eyes momentarily before resuming his zombie-like forward shuffle; he'd not spoken a word to either of them since they'd rousted him from an early slumber and calmly tucked him into a ground car, which sped into the evening sun.

Now, despite his apathy, Andery made out a wavering light source ahead that soon broke into multiple dancing torches, surrounding a roaring bonfire. The size of it pierced the night like a 'Mech-sized fist of defiance against the darkness, causing him to lose all his night vision; he shielded his eyes until they'd adjusted. By the time he reached the circle of torches, his brain finally registered the small ring of troopers he'd passed through (the guard signaling with the flashlight), and that his companions had dropped away to join the protective cordon.

His feet moved from the soft grass to a sudden barren stretch of dirt, causing him to stumble to a stop and glance down somewhat stupidly, before he took in the entire circle of dirt, perhaps ten meters across, bereft of all vegetation. Around the circle, twenty long shafts of wood stood equidistant, each topped by a flickering torch. Within the circle, a giant conflagration voraciously consumed wood, and two individuals stood arm's distance apart, closer than must be comfortable to the main blaze. The heat eddies made it momentarily impossible to identify either one, but a metronome, first started when the warriors pulled him from bed, stamped out the beat of a name in his head.

Niki. What now? Have you not done enough? Can't you let me wallow in self-pity for even a few hours? He blinked rapidly against the searing light and heat, tears squeezing onto cheeks already growing warm.

Finally able to penetrate the blazing radiance, he saw Nicholas and Jennifer in pristine white jumpsuits, the lurid flames painting their clothing an angry red, as though a reflection of the fire's rage.

"Andery. Come." Nicholas's voice, almost lost amid the roaring fire, drew Andery forward, despite his resentment. The heat, now a physical wall, beat at him, as though to tear down barricades and bare his soul.

"Come, Andery." Jennifer's voice joined the siren song of Nicholas's, and for the first time in long memory, he could find no condescension in her expression. But as he took in her face turned to his, he changed his mind.

No condescension, perhaps. But you don't need that now, do you? You've won. You've helped forge Nicholas on his current path. The Clans have been born, and you'll be the mother to see them raised right, won't you? And my careful questions have netted me nothing. You're an enigma I should ignore. But somehow I cannot...

Her eyes sparkled, as though she knew his thoughts and answered with a knowing look.

But how? I've known my brother since birth, yet you manage to work your way into his life in such a short time. He never lets anyone in. What makes you so special? His mind tackled unanswerable questions, ignoring his own love of Dana and that his brother just might truly *be* in love (seemed too...human, for him), while still reeling with his brother's final sprint in forging his Clans.

He'd heard of some warriors not included on Nicholas' list that had confronted him, demanding inclusion. One of Samuel's cohorts (of course!), Daniel Mattlov, had practically shouted into Nicholas face. And the audacity paid off, with some given a chance to prove themselves in the comings months to see if they could join the already hallowed names. Yet even the thought of coming to the table to beg Nicholas for a spot left him ill and dazed. That could never be a route for him, especially after their confrontation.

"Andery, the time has come."

Eyes moved from Jennifer to Nicholas, where he found... something. Despite the wicked heat reddening skin to an almost sunburn, Nicholas's eyes retained most of their ice-chip temperament. But behind that another emotion lurked, as though tasting a freedom Nicholas rarely allowed.

"Time for what?" Andery finally responded, pulling in a lungful of air so hot it almost seared; the size of the blaze actually ejected the smoke and soot above their heads, making it surprisingly easy to breathe if you ignored the sizzle of your hair on the verge of smoldering.

"We have given birth to the Clans, Andery. Now it is time to give birth to something else. Something that has been long in coming."

While he noticed it before, Andery's mind momentarily latched onto the slightly strange phrasing of Nicholas's words. But the next instant swept that thought away in a new torrent of emotions.

"It is time for Nicholas and I to wed, Andery." Jennifer casually lobbed the bombshell, as though discussing paperclip orders.

Andery's mouth slowly slid open, as the momentary calm within roiled to a new emotion, churning his malaise into froth; he glanced between the two several times, finally understanding Nicholas's look and the power shining beacon-bright beyond Jennifer's serene façade.

"When?" He felt a simpleton, but couldn't cough up more.

Jennifer smiled, and the condescension she reserved for Andery broke through, as she quirked a smile. "Why do you think we roused you from sleep? Or why you're the only one here?"

"Now?"

"Were you struck on the head?" Her smile changed, as though shifting shadows from the fire adjusted the emphasis, laugh lines turning harsh; Andery didn't believe for a moment that shadows created the change. *Why do you hate me so?*

"Jen..." Nicholas began, the warning tone soft but distinct.

Andery almost jerked, as though goosed. Not only was this the first time he'd ever heard Nicholas refer to her as anything other than Jennifer, but to know they had the same diminutive for her...shame flooded at the idea that his belittling name was obviously one of endearment and who knew what else between them; he thanked whatever gods might be watching that his skin already looked as red as a basted ham at this point.

"We wed tonight, Andery."

"Why tonight?"

"Why not tonight?"

He opened his mouth for the flood of refusals, only to come up short. Because there was no reason. They'd been together for five years now, if his math was right. Almost a common-law marriage by any definition of the word. And they were adults, fully capable of making their own decisions.

Then why did he hear alarms ringing?

"Where's your preacher?" he spoke, tossing out the first thing to come to mind.

Nicholas cocked a quizzical eyebrow, but Jennifer beat him to the answer.

"A pastor, Andery? A preacher? I didn't realize you'd become so religious. Has your friend Khatib rubbed off so much on you?"

He slowly shook his head. "No. It's just...well..." he shrugged, as though unable to find a good answer.

"Because that's how it's done, right? *Aff.*" Now the condescension reached her voice.

"Yes."

"Well, you of all people should know about doing things differently. And we have never done things any other way."

"Andery." Nicholas drew his attention, nodding toward Jennifer. "Andery, if there is a God, then he will respect the vows we exchange no matter if they are witnessed by a preacher, or no one at all. If there is a God, then as Mother taught us at her knee, what matters is what is within. We have been dedicated to one other for so long, we are already married in our eyes, Andery. But as there came a time to formally announce to the world the formation of the Clans, regardless of how long they were nurtured in my breast, there comes a time to formally announce our marriage to the world."

Andery looked deep into his brother's eyes, trying to find something. Trying to find...he wasn't sure. But whatever he wanted, he swam back up from Nicholas's icy depths without resolution, and he spoke the first thing to come to mind. "Then why here? Why not in the central square, where all can see?"

Nicholas's face closed even more, if possible, the dancing shades of light casting liquid shadows to darken his countenance further. "Because this is a private matter, Andery. A sacred moment for myself, and Jen. And you." The last came cold and deliberate, as though a rebuke. A reminder that Nicholas could reconsider.

Then what about the warriors, Nicholas? Why do you need them? Are they so easily included in this sacred ceremony? Or do you need their protection from those who would do you harm? Is that really how you wish to live? His brain finally seemed to be casting off the webs strapping it down for the last two days, and he abruptly wondered who these warriors were. *You've got eight hundred warriors fanatically devoted to you. Who among them has dedication that warrants this?*

His neck muscles strained to look around, but just as he thanked his lucky stars he'd failed to voice those questions, he kept his face and eyes firmly pegged to his brother. There were times for questions and times to shut up and move with the flow, and the obviousness of the course of action in this scenario spoke as loudly as the snapping fire.

"Then I'm honored, Nicholas. Jennifer." He turned to nod to her as well.

While he tried to avoid her eyes, their stare scorched almost hotter than the flames. "As you should be, Andery."

He nodded again, afraid any further response would only worsen the situation. He closed his eyes and could swear he felt the dryness of his eyeballs scrape roughly against the inside of his eyelids; even closed, the light pierced easily, providing no relief. Abruptly he realized what they wanted and stepped back two full steps; even that little distance brought a momentary reprieve from the heat.

Nicholas and Jennifer stepped toward each other until they could grasp hands. Raising their entwined fingers, they gazed at one another. Nicholas spoke first, then Jennifer. The words were not audible over the sound of the blaze, and at first Andery began to lean forward, as though they'd forgotten to speak up. Suddenly he straightened, as it dawned on him that they may have brought him to bear witness to this moment, but the intimacies would be for them alone.

Gazing at the two white-clothed figures wrapped in the heat eddies, on the verge of being swallowed by flames, memories of mythological entities sprang to mind, as though unfolding from the pages of a textbook lost many decades ago. With sudden insight, Andery surreptitiously glanced right and left and found the guards, mere shadows in the darkness outside the light of the bonfire, but each a statue of attention, gazing raptly on the scene before him.

And glancing back on the nascent gods, he knew exactly why these warriors were chosen. He knew there would be at least two from each Clan; two as a witness to this event; two to spread the rumors of their mystical marriage among the flames; to intentionally expand on reality and create another level of mythos to bind the Clans to Nicholas and Jennifer, his wife.

Andery's tears evaporated before they could trace a track down reddened cheeks.

CHAPTER 23

"What did you expect?" Andery, flabbergasted by his brother, couldn't stop the anger and turned away.

"I expected them to follow orders." Nicholas's voice might as well have been an open window to the frigid temperatures blowing down from the Antarctic Circle.

Andery continued to stare at the wall, digging his fingernails into his palms to keep his anger in check. *Always anger. Always.*

"Nicholas, we're not talking about following orders. You're talking about moving beyond their service to the military." He paused for a moment, "to you" hovering on his lips, but managed to restrain the comment. "You're talking about their personal lives. They're married. Happily. And you tried to interfere in that!"

"Can we divide personal and Clan anymore?"

Andery's fists involuntarily clenched hard while he swallowed convulsively; Jen's voice always did that to him. Always.

He slowly turned to find her in the entryway to Niki's office. One of the few who could just walk in without announcing themselves. *And even I get the ice-stare now and then. But not Jen. Why? All this time, and I still don't know how you managed to slip under my brother's skin.*

"What do you mean?" He knew perfectly well what she meant. She'd been surreptitiously suggesting it for years. *But is it wholly your idea, Jen, or did Niki put you up to it, to try to slowly wear people down? Wear me down?* Though Andery had fought long and hard for the current modicum of respect Nicholas showed him, the endless years of manipulations still sat heavy on his shoulders, and the ghostly sensations of marionette strings softly tugging limbs never seemed too far from his perception.

"Exactly what I said, Andery. Can we separate the two anymore?"

"Of course we can."

"We can?" She cocked her head in that infuriating way that denigrated his every word. "Did the Great Father's dream die in the Pentagon Worlds?"

He glanced toward Nicholas, sensing a trap but not seeing it, and found his brother examining an actual hardbound volume on his desk, as though leaving his wife to batter down the gates for him. Affronted by Nicholas's attitude, he almost turned away before noticing the delicate way in which Nicholas turned the pages. As though it were an ancient text. And precious. He peered closer for a moment, and realization dawned for what it must be. Andery had dug into the volume on his noteputer, but found it to be a jumble of incomprehensible blowhard quotes and self-aggrandizing offerings that seemed as silly as they were pretentious. *Mao's* Little Red Book, *eh Niki. Is that what you curl up with at night? You quote it often enough. But like I told you, Niki, you pervert what you find. Even the Usurper probably spoke truths now and then, but it didn't make him any less of a madman.* He'd given up trying to stop Niki from using quotes from monsters.

"Andery?"

He jerked back to Jen, finding her eyeing him as though he were daft. "What?"

Her fiery eyes cast scorn (something that always sparked memories of nightmares best left in the past), as she quirked an eyebrow. He remembered the question, and responded before he could contain it, slightly embarrassed to be caught so flat-footed. "Yes."

"Then we have to find new ways. Isn't that what we've been doing?"

"Haven't we had this conversation before?"

"Obviously not often enough, Andery. We've broken the military and are reshaping it. Do you think it can really stop there? Do you honestly think that only the military must be scoured from the past that almost destroyed us?"

Now he saw the trap. Saw it, and realized there was nothing he could do about. He shrugged, trying to accept her reasons without admitting defeat.

"Do you, Andery?" she responded. Her voice didn't rise in volume, but the edge grated across nerve endings like a hot branding iron.

"No."

"No. As the military moves toward our new destiny, the civilians must follow. And to do that, we must break all bonds."

Andery sighed, feeling the breaking of his own bindings one by one, as the Jennifer/Nicholas tag team wore him down. An image of stone worn down to a brittle mockery of a once-robust statue saturated him until the howling wind outside threatened to metaphorically knock him down. He grasped around for straws, and came back to the start of this conversation. "Then what are you going to do about Sandra and Hans?"

"You're going to find them." Nicholas spoke, looking up from his intent reading.

"What," Andery responded, taken aback.

"They've been gone for almost two weeks now. I know they went into the Antarctic Circle, but beyond that, I have no idea. But you're going to find them and bring them home."

"What if they don't want to come?"

"Oh, they will."

"Why?"

His brother glanced toward Jen and something electric seemed to thrum.

From the corner of his eye, Andery took in the slightly angry cast to Jen's face before she met his brother's stare head-on and nodded. Andery almost turned to look at her, but realized that would be a mistake he would pay for until the day he died. Even that small moment was likely more than she ever wanted another person to see of Nicholas bringing her into line. He set aside his delight at her humbling as Nicholas turned back to him.

"Because I have an offer they will not refuse."

EDGE OF THE ANTARCTIC CIRCLE
5 JANUARY 2808

The landscape swept under them like an endless flow of pristine silk, frozen in the act of undulation. The sun sat bloated and low on the horizon, as the VTOL chased its shadow across the large expanse, broken only by an upthrust rocky promenade; a lonely, silent sentinel to nature's death and rebirthing process.

The cold ate into Andery with steel teeth, despite the extreme-weather gear, breath blooming in the rear cabin of the Cobra Transport. Though his personal experiences with the couple he now hunted were few and far between, from the moment he'd first seen them on the *Prinz Eugen,* he held them in the highest respect. That they, of all the hundreds of warriors present, dared to stand up to Nicholas only cemented his views. And this. Going out into the depths of winter...that required a whole other level of commitment.

No wonder Niki wants you, regardless of the ripples it might generate in his plans.

"The heater ever going to work on this blasted VTOL?" he finally said into his boom mic.

"*Aff.* When command gives us the extra fuel, you bet, sir. Right now, though, we barely got enough to do the job of tracking down these AWOLs, much less burning it on heat."

Andery grimaced past his boyhood saying gone amok (the man likely didn't even know where it came from) and nodded. "I understand."

"Sir," the copilot interrupted, "I've got thermal readings below."

"Not more ghost bears," he began. "How many can you see in a week, for heaven's sake?"

"No sir, signature's different. Bring us back around, Karl, I think we've got two humans."

"Out in the open?" Andery said too loudly, causing them all to wince. "Sorry," he muttered, but he hadn't expected that. *Not at all. In this cold, they should be holed up somewhere deep.*

The VTOL swept out and around like an orca trying for a hairpin turn, when it was forward movement where it excelled. On the second pass, the unmistakable human heat signature could be seen staining the cold screen yellow. "They're cold, Captain. Real cold."

With a nod, the pilot swept the Cobra Transport around one final time, then maneuvered into a landing a scant twenty meters from the pair. Even prepared for the blast, Andery trembled as the ramp dropped down and the full strength of Strana Mechty's arctic winter slammed him with terrible, bone-shattering force. He gasped several times, lungs refusing to suck in the numbing cold, and he turned away to catch his breath. With a headshake of disgust over his fear of heading out into such cold, he finished strapping on his snowshoes and plopped clumsily down onto the endless plain of white.

Regardless of all the training sessions, Andery felt on the verge of tripping over ludicrously clown-size feet as he made his way toward the two. Despite being swathed in synthetic materials that protected them from the cold, Hans and Sandra leaned on each other heavily; a sure sign of exhaustion staved off through sheer force of will. However, as the two shambled to a halt in front of Andery, they slid apart, forcing themselves erect though wearied to the point of breaking. Sandra uncovered her face first, and Andery sucked in a breath at the haggard woman standing before him. Despite (or perhaps because of) the shocking transformation, Andery's respect soared to new heights as she squared her shoulders and spoke defiantly.

"We return. But we return to challenge Nicholas's decision to split us between Clans. Among the frozen wastes we have found the true nature of the strength we bring to Nicholas's new vision, and that strength is unity. *Our* unity." As though this took all her strength, she staggered a moment, skin almost alabaster, lips pale red smears.

Andery slowly reached up, dreading this moment but realizing they deserved the respect of the same gesture in return, and undid his own face covering.

"Andery..." Sandra began, shocked at finding Nicholas's brother as part of the search party.

He squared his own shoulders, eschewing saluting as no longer proper, bowed deeply (thanks, Raymond) to show his respect and responded, delivering as though by rote Nicholas's message. "Sandra Tseng and Hans Ole Jorgensson. It is the decision of Nicholas Kerensky that your dedication to the oaths of fealty you swore to one another is something all new Clansmen should emulate. As such, you will not be separated."

Sandra gazed at him as though he had transformed into a wraith before looking toward Hans, who had just finished pulling his own face covering away, her shock mirrored on his roughened features—and then back.

With a cry of exaltation, she collapsed.

INTERLUDE TWO

MOSCOW
TERRA
TERRAN HEGEMONY
13 MARCH 2780

Nicholas stood in the small apartment, redolent with jasmine and cinnamon that wafted from his mother's cup of tea. He closed his eyes, basking in the evoked memories. Small islands of pleasure in a sea of years filled with desperation, pain, and fear.

"Nicholas," his mother said from across the room. He opened his eyes, taking her in as she sat on the couch, while he leaned against the wall. "Ah, it does seem odd to use your real name, does it not? But always remember, that can only be here. And only with you and I. Despite all that has changed, your father has too many enemies. You still must keep the secrets that have kept us safe."

He slowly nodded, finding he often still thought of himself as Koyla, even though a year had passed since his father, Commanding General Aleksandr Kerensky, had liberated Terra from the Amaris Occupation and done away with the need to hide. Mostly.

"When will..." he began, but couldn't finish the sentence, chest tightening.

Her eyes held such *knowing*, as she carefully shrugged. "Your father has not forgotten you, or Andery or I. But the Hegemony has been shattered. I've read the reports. A hundred million dead, five hundred million wounded, and a billion homeless." She blinked several times, eyes glinting, as her voice caught; more emotion than he could remember from his mother in all the years they fought to survive as 'Goons bled Moscow dry, for their amusement. "An eternity of demons flaying flesh is not enough for that monster Amaris, or those who enabled him!"

The anger and hatred that rose at the use of that name practically crackled in the air. Nicholas's own emotions reciprocally surged, bringing a warmth better than any spring day.

"And so your father must spend every waking moment trying to salvage what he can. To hold the Hegemony together, and pray that the House Lords won't scuttle his efforts."

"You think they will?" he immediately asked, rubbing his hand across his newly shorn scalp, the crew cut he'd grown used to in order to keep lice at bay, and now refused to give up. Through his mother's tutelage, he had an excellent understanding of the political machinations of the Great Houses and how they'd enabled the toppling of the Star League, far beyond the usual bent of a sixteen-year-old boy.

Then again, he knew instinctively he was not just any sixteen-year-old boy. Other memories invoked by the jasmine and cinnamon surfaced: meeting J at a park; chocolate ice cream; the first time his mother swore him to secrecy for his real name, Nicholas Kerensky; and that someday the commanding general of the entire Star League Defense Force would return, freeing them from hell and carrying him to greatness.

Yet his father had come, and they were still here in Moscow, in a small apartment. He'd heard the loud, angry voices as they'd tried to keep the fight from him and Andery. Heard his father telling his mother he could not possibly allow them to stay in a city so ravaged by war. And her emotional response; she refused to be forced from the city she loved after surviving on her own so many years. If he was ever done with Terra, perhaps she would leave, she'd said angrily. Until then, nothing would move her from her *Moskva*. Father had reluctantly agreed, though he'd left what felt like an army of soldiers; only a fraction remained of that initial group of loyalists.

And his mind understood. And even agreed. But emotionally? He hated it; it left him feeling...adrift.

"Of course they will. It's whether your father can keep back the wolves. And if anyone might singlehandedly keep five star empires at bay, it is Alex."

He nodded. His father. The commanding general. There was no greater man alive. Perhaps ever had been alive. He could do it.

In the meantime... "You made sure Andery was out playing, and there's only one soldier on duty, Mother," he finally said. *What is it you don't want Andery to hear? What do you want me to do?*

Her fierce smile of pride warmed him further.

"Always so quick to discern. So quick to see." She took her ritualistic sip of tea, closing her eyes for long moments, before opening them. The hard edge was back. The look he'd known most of his life; of survival, and hard things.

"War tribunals will be convened, Nicholas," she continued. "Your father hasn't shared specifics yet, but of course they will happen. I imagine by the summer the courts will have been sufficiently reestablished for such prosecutions. I'm sure there will be hundreds of names on the list, but ultimately only dozens will be held accountable. And the evidence is absolute. Most, if not all, will be executed."

She paused, taking another sip, her eyes questing and intense. As though trying to push Nicholas. Somewhere, in the back of his mind, was a hint that perhaps, in another life, a mother would not have such frank and brutal conversations with a sixteen-year-old boy. But it was such an amorphous thought, it floated away before he even became aware. Instead, his ice-blue eyes stared intently back at his mother, mind racing and racing, trying to see what she saw. Finally, it emerged. He didn't speak it aloud—such blurting was for Andery's annoying voice—but instead he looked at it from all angles, knowing his mother would have the patience to give him time to dive in and work through the problem thoroughly.

Finally, confident in his answer, he responded, "So few."

Her smile, if possible, grew fiercer. "So few. Beyond those at the highest echelons of Amaris's empire," she continued (never a capital *E* from his mother), "they'll use strategies from ancient atrocities. I'm sure they'll attempt to assess culpability of citizens and assign them to various bands of involvement.

But they'll fail to hold so many accountable. After all, there is so much work...just so much work to repair and to try to forget and to move on."

It'd been long since his waking nightmare, but her words hunched his shoulders. The sound of barking dogs echoed in his hears; the smell of his mother's blood as she bled in his arms assailed his nostrils; the feel of terror and anguish as gunshots extinguished life all around while he and his mother huddled in a copse of trees in a park he hadn't set foot in since that moment five years ago. He lost himself to the onslaught.

"My son," the voice reached out, shocking him back to a calm, safe apartment. Despite his best efforts, he shook, blinking rapidly as though to banish the phantasms from sight.

She had not moved, letting him overcome this with his own strength. But unshed tears filled her eyes. "But some of us cannot forget."

He scrubbed at the traitorous tracks on his face. "Some of us will never forget."

She nodded in response, placing the cup on the coffee table beside the couch, then reached into the pocket of her sweater and slid a small piece of paper across to the other side of the table. He moved away from the wall, reaching down to pick it up, and read the name written there. He knew this name.

"He helped us during the occupation," he said, confusion wrinkling his forehead. "Money and guns."

She shook her head. "Only to salve a sense of guilt, my son. Thousands died because he supported the Director Consulate of Moscow during the occupation. And that's just the incarcerations and shooting. How many tens of thousands died from starvation because he supported *that* woman?" If possible, her voice held almost as much loathing as when she'd invoked Amaris's name.

"He'll be brought up on charges. He'll be held accountable at those tribunals?" Despite a firm voice, Nicholas couldn't help the questioning tone at the end.

She slowly shook her head. "He won't, Nicholas. I love your father dearly, my son. And he is a great man who can and will still accomplish great things. But his love of the rule of law blinds him to what sometimes must be done."

"He killed the devil," Nicholas responded, blanking out that memory.

"He did. And it nearly killed the man we love, Nicholas. There will not be another." She pointed at the slip of paper in his hand. "*That* man is too insulated. Oligarchs always protect themselves with religious fervor. And he, I'm sure, will have an army of lawyers who can show the funds the Director Consulate used in her time in Moscow were stolen, without his support. Never mind the fact he could just as easily have carefully placed bureaucratic hurdles in the way to at least slow down her actions. To slow the deaths."

He slowly nodded. The rich had done very well during the occupation, while the rest starved and died, and killed each other to try to survive.

"And you can't leave because I can't cover you when the guard checks in."

"No, I can't."

"And everyone knows you by now."

"Correct."

"But not me."

"We've tried very hard to keep your face unknown. Almost everywhere you go, luckily, you're just an ordinary, annoying teenager to ignore." She smiled, her conviction he was anything *but* ordinary bright in her eyes.

"Your father—" she began, but he interrupted.

"Is a great man. And doesn't need to worry about this. Just like we don't worry him about...*other* things." He ignored the echoes of barking dogs and gunshots.

Her smiled blossomed further. His mother's proud, glorious smile. There was nothing so beautiful in all the world.

He stood up straight, feeling the mantle of their insurrection through most of his childhood settling back into place. The hated feeling of his life being *adrift* fading. Time for the hard things.

"What do you want me to do, Mother?"

"I've seen the fish-bone motifs daubed on doors of collaborators. I've seen the justice we, who survived their injustice, are meting out. When no other justice will ever be found. The people don't realize how involved he was with the Director Consulate. Not even those of our old cell. I believe it's time they found out." She reached once again into the pocket of her sweater, and pulled out an actual hardcopy photo, sliding it across the table as well.

He slowly reached out and picked it up. It was grainy black and white, but his gut clenched with renewed anger at what he saw. Looked back at his mother, and nodded once, firmly, as he'd done so many times before.

He moved to the back door, then the window—well hidden behind bushes that would enable him to escape the watchful eyes of their security guard—and slipped out without saying a word.

3 APRIL 2779

While technically spring, Moscow loved to keep its cold embrace a little longer than other cities at this latitude. It helped make its people stronger than others. At least that's what Mother had always taught him. For millennia, others had attempted to conquer these lands and this jewel of a city. And nearly always they were turned back. By the cold, and by the people the cold made hard. Able to do the hard things.

"You ready?" he said without looking in her direction.

"Of course I'm ready. I was ready before you were born," J spoke defiantly, even if in a whisper, at his side.

Never mind that he was older, that didn't seem to matter. He smiled as he glanced at her determined look, then grimness stole back over him. "We have to do this fast. Most of his guards are stuck in transfer by the accident Ivon set up right behind his car. He'll only have one, maybe two guards with him here at this house they've run to."

"You really think they won't shoot us?"

He ignored the hint of fear roiling his stomach. "During the occupation, you bet. But now, with the SLDF here? No, he won't chance murdering two teenagers. Especially when one's a girl," he finished with a wide grin, bracing for the coming punch. He winced, always seeming to forget how hard she could hit, despite her small stature. *Totally worth it.* "We can do this."

They gripped hands momentarily, in their usual ritual before danger, then shimmied up and over the wall. It wasn't the man's main estate after all, with its high walls, barbed wire, and many soldiers. This was one of his safe houses, that no one was supposed to know about. But after a month of hard work by the cell, they'd nailed down his whole schedule, found this house, and mapped out a plan.

Tonight, justice would be done.

They ran crouched low across the lawn, where the grass was slowly coming back to life. Reaching the edge of the small house—Nicholas snorted, considering five of his apartments wouldn't fill it—they slid up against the cold siding, catching their breath and waiting to see if they could hear anything. The timing had to be just right. The alarm system deactivated by the man's arrival, but before the guards checked the whole house; it had cost a pretty ruble, but the cell's hacker contact had been able to rig the alarm so they wouldn't know it wasn't reactivated once they got inside the house.

They heard the sound of the car pulling into the front driveway, then voices talking below the level of understandability, then abruptly they cut off as they entered and shut the door. Nicholas and J immediately opened the back door with a copied keycard and slid inside, to the kitchen. They quietly loaded random cans of food into her bag, and she crept back to wait at the door, keeping it ajar, while he filled his own bag with food. Despite his earlier bravado, his heartbeat ticked up until it seemed to thunder in his ears. The adults had gone over the plan with them again and again. But this was something they'd never done, striking at such power.

Just stupid teenagers grabbing food. Just innocent kids living on the street who haven't figured out they can eat at the SLDF's food kitchens down by the river. The mantra ran over and over in his head until footsteps neared the kitchen, and the most dangerous moment arrived.

"What the—" the large security guard spoke, pawing at the sidearm he carried, getting it out.

"We just wanted food!" Nicholas squealed in as loud and whiny a voice as he could think of—he just tried mimicking Andery in one of his tantrums. He took a step or two toward the door as the barrel of the guard's needler lined up with his head. No matter how many times a gun was pointed at him, his shoulders still itched with the sense of death a hair's breadth from dragging his soul kicking and screaming out of his body. *Can't run yet. Can't run. Where is he?*

"What's going on here!" the man he was waiting for bellowed as the oligarch marched into the room to see what the fuss was all about.

"We just wanted food!" Nicholas yelled again, making sure to grimace widely, showing off his dirty face and the mock rotted teeth.

The man's face moved from real concern to disgust and then anger. "You'll not get away so easily. Come steal my food! Next you'll have the other rats swarming over me. No, only way to stop that is to show what happens when you take what isn't yours."

Now. Nicholas sprinted for the door, J yelping in a wonderfully cowardly voice—he'd tease her about that forever—and sprinting as well. He knew he could get away from the old men. Knew it like he was a pilot in a light 'Mech sprinting away from an assault machine without weapons. For just a moment, the thought that he would start training soon, to join his father in the SLDF, blossomed teasingly. But he smothered it viciously. It was time for another moment of hard things. He pretended to trip, sprawling into the grass, wet and slightly slick from watering, tearing up dirt that got into his mouth.

He still could've got up and slipped away fast enough—took his pursuers forever—but he waited long enough for them to catch up as J ran to the wall and started climbing. As his mother had taught—and he had experienced, several times—he went limp and thought about anything else so his muscles wouldn't tense in anticipation: the gun blow to the side of his face still tore flesh, flashing bright lights and sending sounds hammering in his head like all the bells of Moscow ringing for Victory Day celebrations.

He never blacked out, but it was a near thing before he fully came to, hanging from the fist of the brute of a guard, and hearing the other man shout. "If you don't come back, little girl, we're going to shoot your friend," he yelled.

J started crying, loudly, on cue. Despite the throbbing pain, Nicholas barely kept a laugh from escaping. He'd never once seen her cry. Even when a man had split open her head, was about to kill Nicholas, and she'd saved his life by slitting the 'Goon's throat. *She does a good imitation.*

A smile did slide onto his face as the man moved to the back gate, unlatched it and pushed through, the brute following, still dragging a limp Nicholas. Despite the darkness, several streetlights still gave slight illumination to the back alley, and lifting his head he could see J, collapsed on the ground a dozen meters farther into the alley, where a cross alley met.

"If you make us come over there, it'll be worse, rat," the man spoke loudly, and J responded with an even louder moan.

Nicholas's gut tensed again, as the tableau dragged out for long seconds. *Did you read him right, Ivon? Mother?*

"*Yajtza,*" the man swore, then started walking, beckoning the guard to follow.

Nicholas let out an explosive breath of relief, causing his captor to shake him, as though a reminder he was in their hands.

Just as the man reached the junction, J quickly scrambled up, darting around the corner, and the man burst into a run, dashing in pursuit, the guard carrying him picking up speed, as Nicholas closed his eyes...

...as bright lights flooded from both directions of the intersection, spearing the oligarch, who stumbled to a halt, and the guard, just reaching the intersection, dropped Nicholas as he swept up his needler and raised his left arm to trying to shield his eyes from the bright light. In the confusion, Nicholas scrambled away, meeting up with the group of men and women already moving in from the opposite side.

"What is the meaning of this?!" the man yelled, blinking and desperately starting to back up. The crowd from the direction Nicholas had moved toward had already forced the guard to move closer to the oligarch, until the two were sealed between the walls of the alley and nearly fifty people armed with weapons, from broken bottles and baseball bats with nails hammered in, to a few pistols that had survived all the years of 'Goons trying to keep them from insurrectionists.

Ivon, a tall, scarred man who'd somehow survived police capture and the start of the firing squad park massacre from years ago, stepped forward. "You are here to be judged," he said quietly. There were no pitchforks or torches, or yelling and shouting. Just the quiet determination of hard people doing the hard things, when no one else would.

Confidence slipped from the man's face, and fear bubbled to the surface. "You can't do this! Do you know who I am?"

Ivon, whose face was shadowed by the harsh backlighting of flashlights, almost appeared to wear an executioner's hood, from Nicholas's viewpoint; his voice a match for that image. "We know exactly who you are."

Ivon glanced at the guard and pointed to where a narrow corridor opened through the crowd. Nicholas had seen so many reprisals the last few months. So many fish-bones daubed on doors, people beaten, even a few killed. But even Ivon and his mother knew it was time to try to begin curbing that violence, and it started here—albeit after one last important act of justice.

The guard took one look at his employer, shrugged as though in apology, holstered his pistol and slipped through the space and off into the night, as the people closed the gap.

"I can pay you," the oligarch said loudly, eyes jerking this way and that; so wide Nicholas almost couldn't see the pupils in the bright lights, even as his eyes finally adjusted.

"Amaris's own endless vaults of stolen gold would never be enough," Ivon said. The lack of anger in his voice seemed to frighten the man all the more.

"Help, someone help me!" he began shouting, looking beyond the wall of people around him at the houses that were all dark. Nicholas knew no one was home; part of the plan ensured every single neighbor on the block had a strong alibi that kept them away this night.

J slid her hand into his—Nicholas had long ago stopped trying to figure out how she could slide so easily between people, without making a sound—as Ivon stepped forward. The man tried to cringe away, starting to cry and blubber, but was seized from behind and held fast in place.

A large knife appeared in Ivon's hand, and he grabbed the man's hair with his left, dragging the blade across his throat in a slash, the crying cut off in a gurgle of spraying blood. The crowd parted behind Ivon, revealing a three-meter post lodged upright in the middle of the alley. It was quick work to lash the dying man to the post. Another stepped forward, a metal brand in his hand, heated red-hot by a handheld torch, firmly pressing a "T" into the flesh of the forehead that sizzled and popped as the flesh burned, the acrid smell evoking terrible memories for them all.

Ivon strode over, placing a strong hand on each of their shoulders, giving a squeeze, hard eyes catching theirs in the shadowed light. "We did what had to be done. And luring him out here means the police will ignore it, as we didn't violate the house." He chuckled darkly. "They'll call him stupid for going out into the night. Finish it, Koyla," (how he yearned for Ivon to use his *real* name) "and get that wound bandaged and hidden."

The crowd was drifting away, most of them already gone, as Nicholas let go of J's hand, reaching into an inside pocket and pulling out the last piece of the plan as he walked up to the dead man. Pulled out a safety pin, and carefully attached it to the man's blood-drenched shirt. He took a last look at the grainy photo that had pulled their entire cell back together again for one last bout of justice: the oligarch, naked, in the throes of ecstasy with the Director Consulate: the most hated woman in the Hegemony.

And walked away into the night.

BOOK THREE

"Moral maxims are surprisingly useful on occasions when we can invent little else to justify our actions."

—ALEXANDER PUSHKIN

CHAPTER 24

The day bled black.

Flames washed across one field of vision, while another showed viscous fluid oozing down the contours of the *Black Knight* as it stomped through the undergrowth. Andery could almost feel the vibrations of the impact tickling his spine and the cinching of the restraining harness as it kept him ensconced in the command couch. Fear of flames, and memories of a final horrible battle on Eden assaulted his senses, but he forced them away with an iron desire to see the outcome of the battle.

To *experience* it.

Despite endless regrets and protests, he would always be a warrior; he closed his eyes, longing for the sensations again. Longing for a battle (okay, perhaps just a mock battle), hands twitching to grasp joysticks. He swallowed dryly, tongue caressing sanded lips, before opening his eyes again to take in the multiple BattleROM images taken from the *Black Knight*, as well as still-mounted holocams throughout the training grounds.

The *Black Knight* abruptly picked up speed, as though it detected something not yet in view of a holocam, and Andery found himself swaying slightly, feet splayed as though touching pedals in sympathy with the weaving over uneven ground. A

Crab appeared from the undergrowth as though flushed from hiding by the burst of noise and speed from Dana's *Knight*. Twin lasers burned the air as they sought already damaged armor, one hitting to score a fresh mark, the other slashing wide.

Despite himself, Andery flinched. Though not at full strength (even Nicholas knew he must be careful with his *precious* newly minted eight hundred warriors), the weapons still packed a punch, and the wrong set of circumstances could end in death. They all acknowledged it. They were warriors, after all.

Eyes involuntarily flicked to take in nonexistent secondary monitors and the damage schematic. Feet twitching to adjust the movement of the 'Mech based on the wire diagram to present the least damaged side, pouring on the power with a left-handed throttle push to move at best speed on an oblique angled approach while bringing superior gunnery skill and the deadly PPC to play; azure fire scoured off armor in a blast of energy. A twitch of the middle finger and the secondary targeting interlock circuit sent twin beams of accompanying crimson energy; both found their mark across the dorsal of the elongated *Crab*, liquefying the small communications dish and further savaging an existing rent in the armor.

The *Crab*, realizing the damaged *Knight* still outclassed it, quickly tried to backpedal into the undergrowth, encroaching flames or not. But like a pit bull with jaws clamped tight, Dana wouldn't let her target go, and another azure whip flayed off armor, sending tendrils of destroying energy into the ever-widening crevice across the heart of the *Crab*. Before it made it completely back into the billowing smoke and collapsing trees, the *Crab* abruptly froze, then slowly toppled backward as the residual momentum overpowered the machine's balance.

Andery breathed raggedly through clenched teeth, as though heat eddies surged through a scorching cockpit, fueled by weapon discharges and a rampant fire, and scraped uncaring fingers through soft lung tissue; the chair seemed to vibrate from the concussion of fifty tons of myomer and metal meeting unyielding ground. Hands shaking slightly, he slowly ran calloused fingers across his temples, rubbing his eyes then running fingers jerkily through his hair.

"That was impressive," he finally croaked out. *Such battles. Such fighting. Such consequences. And once more I can have none of it.*

Over his shoulder, Dana responded, "Thank you."

He turned to find her still flushed from the battle, jumpsuit now hiding her nearly naked body, slicked with sweat from the scorching heat of not only the interior of the *Black Knight*, but also the raging inferno still barreling its way through the northern woods within the Aleksandr Beta Training Grounds. Fire crews were having a hard time curbing the blaze.

Their eyes met and electricity seemed to spark, a current lacking for years.

"Two more fights to go."

"*Aff.*"

"Not you too."

"Andery, especially me."

He may not like it, but he couldn't fault her reasoning and responded to her smile, with a wan one of his own. "I still can't believe you chose to fight a Trial of Position." He stood up, the adrenaline from the battle footage gun-cams making him slightly lightheaded, and he paused for a moment, eyes closed, hand outstretched to the holovid display to gain his balance. "After all you've done, you still feel the need to prove your worth?" He tried to ignore that he still struggled with imposter syndrome almost every day.

"Of course."

"To Nicholas?"

"To my people."

To my people? Of course. Her *people.*

"Other Khans have chosen this path."

"Not all."

"No, not all. But even if I were the only one, it would not matter. For I am all that matters in this decision. Nicholas may feel I am worthy of this post, but my people must feel I am worthy. *I* must feel it."

On the verge of opening his eyes, he kept them closed at the tone in her voice when speaking his brother's name. Didn't matter how much he flogged himself for an idiot, it still cut to the quick.

Soft hands abruptly pressed against his chest and he finally opened his eyes to find depths of excitement and passion reflecting his own high over just watching the feeds. The adrenaline. The close brush with death, regardless of powered-down weapons. The exaltation of victory; *that* never changed. She slowly raised onto her tiptoes and kissed him; her lips always the smoothest silk to his own perpetually chapped. The false heat of the holographic flames blossomed into real heat between his legs. *How long has it been?*

"*I* must know I am worthy of this honor. That I have it within me to wield this power in a way that will mold my vision to his," she responded, before kissing him again, hands moving to zippers and buttons.

Without any conscious thought, his own hands began their migration across clothing, while his mind fluttered like a leaf in the hot breeze of passion. *It's been how long? You almost can't talk to her anymore, and yet you're going to allow this to happen, aren't you?*

His hands found the zipper of Dana's jumpsuit, and he pulled it open and then down past her waist, where it pooled around her feet. Ragged breathing spiked as kisses became an impassioned quest for additional pleasure spots. The sweat-soaked T-shirt stuck against her flesh as he pulled it over her head, causing them to stumble for a moment, almost ruining the mood; almost gave him the power to break free from the pull of desire for an interaction he'd been without for so long; a taste of flesh too long absent from memory.

"And when you know you're worthy?" he managed past a thick tongue, his mouth already seeking her skin.

"I have had a vision," she moaned. "The Broken Sea calls to me."

As I call to you? But you never listen to me...

As their remaining clothing joined its companions on the ground and fevered touches pulled apart his essence until nothing remained, there was no response to the question; as a part of his mind endlessly cycled he fell, with a sudden premonition that once she fully took her Khanship, once she walked into the desert with her warriors to fully embrace her vision, another wall would rise between them.

He kept falling, tears leaking from blinded eyes even as he took his fill; a last supper before execution.

Always falling.

CHAPTER 25

SVOBODA ZEMYLYA
NOVY TERRA
STRANA MECHTY
KERENSKY CLUSTER
17 MARCH 2808

"A *surat* for your thoughts?"

"What?" Andery said, turning away from the circle of warriors to find Sarah at his elbow. "*Surat*? What?"

She shrugged, smile bringing the sun despite the cloud cover. "You ignored me the first time. Had to do something do get your attention."

He glanced down a moment, feet shuffling in the compacted dirt next to the construction site before responding. "Really? Sorry about that, Sarah. Just..." He shrugged, head tilting down toward the unfolding scene.

"I know. 'Course, not nearly as dangerous as a 'Mech battle, though. Right?"

"True enough. But it could be a lot more devastating to morale."

"And do you really care about that?"

"What?"

"Do you really care what their morale is? What ours is?" She managed to exclude him without a change of pitch or emphasis.

He opened his mouth to speak, then slowly closed it as she cocked an eyebrow.

"That's what I thought."

"It's not that I—"

She cut him off before he could get further. "Andery, I don't care. I can only imagine what all of this must feel like to you. After all, we've all got a Clan."

He winced, despite his resolve to get over it. For a moment, her uncompromising look felt irksome, until he realized, as usual, she never felt sorry for him or coddled him in any way. *In other words, she never treats you like a Kerensky. Isn't that what you always complain about? Even Dana, regardless of the other night...* He leaped away from that memory like a rabbit trying to escape a swooping raptor.

"And I don't." For some reason, it didn't hurt as much coming from Sarah.

"Exactly. You don't. You will." She shrugged.

"I will? I'm not so sure of that."

"Why?"

He took in her penetrating gaze, then turned toward the Circle of Equals at the bottom of the hill on which the primary construction site for this section centered. A crowd of thirty-eight warriors in white jumpsuits with blue armbands surrounded a central circle of two. Despite his knowledge of her hand-to-hand fighting skills, the other warrior appeared a giant to Dana's slight build; a good meter taller and wide enough he might just encircle a 'Mech's leg with his arms. The two bowed deeply, then began to circle each other. Andery cocked his head. *Thought for sure Jacob would run right in.*

"Why?"

He continued to ignore the question as the morning sun tried vainly to beat against his brow, but winter's mantle still hung on with sharp claws, unwilling to give way to spring just yet. He sharply sucked in a breath, the air pungent with newly turned soil, and leaned forward as though to join the circle as Dana launched the first series of attacks; a flurry of fists and kicks met by her opponent with casual ease.

"You can't join them."

"Don't you think I know that?" he spit out before he could curb the frustration. He sighed heavily, turning back toward Sarah while trying to keep one eye on the unfolding trial by combat below. "I'm sorry."

"There's that temper again. Haven't we talked about it?"

"Sure. Of course we have. It's all I get to do. Talk."

"Now we're moving beyond anger into bitterness-land, Andery."

He searched her face for some humor, but found only frank appraisal. And perhaps something else. While he'd playfully entertained thoughts now and then of what that something else might be, it cut particularly hard after the encounter with Dana. *An encounter that felt like a good-bye.*

How could he feel so dirty and yet abandoned at the same time? "Am I?"

"Yes, you are. Andery, come off it. This isn't like you. Anger's one thing. But this self-pity? Doesn't become you."

You have no idea. You think you know me, but only Dana knows me. Knew me... It cut with a pain he'd not experienced in long years. Since Eden. *Father.* He shrugged as though to pass it all off as unimportant. "Sure."

She grunted in frustration, but allowed it to pass. "You never answered my question."

"You're right. I didn't."

"Do I have to drag it out of you?"

"You don't have to do anything."

She growled again, louder, frustration plain. "Andery, what the hell is the matter with you? I like being with you 'cause we can talk easier than anyone else I know. Hell, easier than with my own warriors right now. Still." Andery could almost hear the shrug in her voice. "Knew this was going on, and thought you could use the support."

"You shouldn't be here," he said, straight and cold.

"Neither should you."

"No, I shouldn't. Clan Coyote business after all. But Nicholas will forgive me." *I'm such a disappointment, after all, there's not much further I could fall.* "But you. He might revisit his decision to honor you by naming you Khan of Clan Wolverine."

He turned fully away from Sarah, as though a physical rebuke to accompany his verbal pronouncement, and away from another series of feints and counterstrikes, with blows finally beginning to land as tired defenses lagged.

Instead, eyes roved over the entire region Nicholas had named Svoboda Zemylya. As though a microcosm of Strana Mechty. *Land of Dreams. How appropriate. To use our ancestor's language to tie this land to you, Niki. Too bad Russian didn't allow for a more possessive form. After all, this isn't so much the land of dreams, as it is the land of* your *dreams.*

Despite his bitter sentiments, the sheer majesty of the land couldn't be taken for granted. The park began almost twenty kilometers north of the edge of Katyusha City and encompassed a hundred square kilometers; as ever, Nicholas thought in grand terms. A verdant but mostly flat land, broken with numerous copses of p-trees dotting the landscape; the region screamed with vitality and nature's beauty. A perfect place for the perfect park.

But now a host of man-made structures joined nature's handiwork, dotting the plains that newly cast off the white of winter, starting to pull on the light green of spring. Though he could not see them all from his current vantage point, his name allowed him to visit, albeit usually at a distance, all twenty-one structures, each in various stages of construction. The twenty Clan Halls surrounding the central hub of the park and the final structure: the Hall of Khans. While some were almost completed—the Ice Hellions seemed to be taking their namesake to heart and were in a frenzy to complete their smallish, spartan hall—others, like the Jade Falcons, were making theirs so big they were only past laying the foundation and were still framing; *leave it to Elizabeth Hazen to have such an inflated sense of her superiority.* Still others, like the Coyotes, were too busy cementing their leadership to get much beyond laying a foundation either.

Yet they were all training, all forging themselves into the ultimate weapons, into his vision, and so Nicholas kept his hands off. More importantly, those Clans that chose to fight to affirm Nicholas's nominations for their Khanships showed an extra zeal in accepting the new Trial-based warrior society. After all, how could Nicholas possibly gainsay such fervent commitment? A commitment centered on him.

And, of course, in the center of the park, the Hall of Khans began to rise. Five times the size of even the large Jade Falcon hall, only the barest hint of walls could be seen yearning toward the sky. Unlike the Clan Halls, made of almost every material under the sun and comprised of architecture from plain to ornate, the Hall of Khans appeared to be built to withstand the ages. Mammoth granite blocks—which required multiple IndustrialMechs to move—lay like exposed bedrock, while others almost as large were laid out to begin the outer walls.

Touring the site, Andery couldn't help but contemplate history and the gargantuan cathedrals built during the Dark Ages of Terran's ancient past. While those structures couldn't compare to man's modern capabilities, they were made by hand, conveying a sense of superhuman dedication; beliefs incarnate in stone and woodwork to last the ages.

He should've known Nicholas would tap into such an ancient tradition, with every single element of this all to be hand-carved. *That was a masterstroke, Niki, saying that the full foundation can be worked on, but construction of the walls will not begin until we have conquered the Pentagon Worlds, and stones from those planets will be brought here. A fusion of all your "Clan space" into a unified structure. But will your beliefs last the ages, Niki? Is this your cathedral? This gargantuan construct? And if it's your cathedral, what will be at the center of Katyusha City? Or will this be your palace, Emperor Niki, while your cathedral waits to be built in the central square?*

A cheer arose, dislodging his sarcastic thoughts; he turned back to find the throng of warriors surrounding Dana with a wash of enthusiasm and support that expanded until it floated so high its eddies swept across his legs.

The ache of longing for things that always seemed to be out of reach rose to a fevered pitch.

Abruptly he realized someone was offering him a modicum of understanding and acceptance and he was spitting on the outstretched hand. He turned, ready to repudiate his harshness…

…only to find empty space beside him. The ache centered and focused and rose until he gasped for breath.

That's why I'll never find a place, Sarah. I'll never find acceptance. Why?

Because…me.

CHAPTER 26

BETA DROPPORT, KATYUSHA CITY
NOVY TERRA
STRANA MECHTY
KERENSKY CLUSTER
20 MARCH 2808

Navy-suited warriors filed onto the bloated-looking DropShip.

The sun, hotter than usual this early spring day and barely above the horizon, caused the vast DropPort tarmac to waver in the heat, and misty rain to burn off in monster swaths akin to fog. The scene felt surreal as the warriors swirled in and out of visibility before marching up the ramp into the *Vampire*-class DropShip. Despite its forty-two-meter length—not to mention twenty-eight-meter height—it remained strangely ethereal behind curtains of mist, as though a mirage in the morning heat.

In spite of everything, Andery managed a tight smile. *Leave it to Dana to make the first significant change to a Clan. Doing away with the white jumpsuits and colored armbands, and fully embracing Nicholas's chosen color for Clan Coyote. Is this what Nicholas truly wants? How far will he allow this to go?*

He sneezed abruptly, causing several warriors to glower in his direction with dark, hidden eyes. One warrior in particular scowled until his forehead disappeared under a knot of pinched skin and eyebrows joined in a craggy line, almost obscuring powerful, practically glowing eyes.

I shouldn't be here. He shivered.

"Pay no mind to my warriors, Andery," Dana spoke calmly at his side. "They have become overprotective of me."

Andery tried a casual nod to the last man, but received not so much as an eyeblink in return. "And that one?" he said, nodding in the direction of the man as he disappeared up the ramp.

"Ah, Gerek Tchernovkov. He, more so than any other, seems to have taken me under his wing. As though I am too young to know what I am about."

Out of the corner of his eye he could see a playful smile lying behind the amused tone, and once again the wall of the world Dana now moved in rose precipitously; gave him vertigo, causing him to wobble slightly.

"Andery, what is wrong?" she asked, concern showing on her face.

He looked back toward the grounded DropShip, shame spilling red across skin still light despite years of exposure to harsh sunlight, still incredulous at his own weakness. "Nothing. Too light a breakfast, I suppose." In the back of his mind, he noticed she didn't touch him; his mind dived for ignorance, reached for another subject. "Why not take a *Cobra*? The *Vampire* seems overkill for just a hop to McKenna."

A long pause followed his question. Andery knew Dana was onto him, but she chose to respond regardless. "We do not know how long we shall be down there. Need the supplies and possible lodging if the terrain proves too much for what I have in mind."

"And that is?" He looked at her and found a blank face, and the wall reared once more. "Sorry." He raised his hands as though entreating her to accept his apology.

She smiled sadly, too-knowing eyes wide. "Nothing to be sorry about. It simply a Coyote matter."

"Will it be so hard in Nicholas Jungle?" he said, again latching onto another topic, albeit related. "Why not simply use one of Nicholas's facilities down there? I'm sure he'd be willing to cough up some space and supplies."

"We are not traveling to the jungle."

"Uh. After your win yesterday, you said you needed to take your warriors on a...tribal sabbatical, I think you called it. On McKenna."

"Yes. I did say that. But not in the jungle."

"Where?"

"The Broken Sea."

Andery grunted as though sucker punched. "What the hell?"

She raised an eyebrow at his incredulousness. "I told you before that is where we are going. Would I joke about something like this?"

"No. No, you wouldn't. But what are you thinking? That desert's an absolute hellhole. No wonder you want the *Vampire*. Should take two or three of them, because sure as hell that wasteland is going to destroy one of them, stranding you all."

"But that is my home."

That brought him up short. "I forgot. Southwest."

"Right. While you may have been raised in Moscow on lost Terra, I will always be more familiar with deserts."

"But, Dana... This is like no southwest desert I can think of. Daytime-nighttime temperature differentiation is beyond belief, not to mention the acidic sand currents, and let's not forget the—"

"Andery!" she cut him off. "I am well aware of all that. But this is my Clan. My tribe. My choice. While we have trained hard and have begun building our Clan Hall, it is time we follow a path *I* know. A path to forge us into one."

Her eyes beseeched understanding, and while hesitant, he responded with what he hoped was support in his eyes and a fleeting smile.

"Then be careful." "*Beloved*" dangled unsaid, its lack a cavity of hollowness against the wall of her Clan and their growing separation.

Her eyes held his before she responded, "Of course."

Then Dana turned away without a backward glance.

KATYUSHA CITY
16 JUNE 2807

He startled out of his sleep, gasping.

"Andery." The voice spoke again, a dark body outlined against the light from the hallway. Memories of his brother and of Jes, waking him up in darkness to terrible events, rose hard and sharp-edged.

"Andery. Nicholas requests your presence."

He blinked several times, and the outline dissolved into a harder shape that bore no obvious resemblance to either his brother or the woman who had tortured him with longing and betrayals for so many years.

"What time is it?" he mumbled, grimacing at the scum of film on unbrushed teeth.

"0200 hours."

"Thank you. I'll be out in a moment."

The other soldier bowed and departed. Casting off the smothering effects of fatigue from too many days of hard work among the civilians in the city to try to forget, and too many sleepless nights of inability *to* forget, Andery dressed quickly. A splash of water and fingers through his mussed hair, and he was out and down the corridor toward his brother's quarters.

Stifling a yawn that popped eardrums and jaw cartilage, Andery knocked, then waited. A moment later, a blank-faced Jennifer answered the door, fully dressed in a crisp jumpsuit. She allowed him to slip in; the look in her eyes kept him silent.

He stopped dead when recognition of a beloved, familiar face broke across him like a wave over a parched soul. His eyes found Dana and he opened his mouth, feet already starting to move forward, when a hand gripped his upper arm in an iron shackle. He turned to see blazing eyes and a hard shake of Jennifer's head. But it was not her look that stopped him, but the fact she had touched him; something which had never occurred before.

As he took in the atmosphere of the room, his elation at finding Dana here cooled, allowing him to understand something was happening.

"Continue," Nicholas spoke.

"It was as I said, Nicholas. During a cleansing ritual, my entire Clan witnessed a portent we knew heralded the end of our sabbatical and required us to return immediately, so I might share it."

Nicholas nodded gravely, eyes latched onto Dana with the full force of his personality. While others might have wilted or lost themselves in such a powerful gaze, Dana seemed to expand, her own energy rising to meet his.

Andery clenched his teeth; dark thoughts began to swirl.

"We saw a pack of wolves and a pack of coyotes tracking a group of five *tallasi*," Dana said. "The bovine creatures were obviously terrified, running for their lives. But they had allowed themselves to wander too far from the acidic currents they can naturally endure, and the predators had them."

"You have not told me what this has to do with leaving your sabbatical, or your imperative to tell me about it," Nicholas responded with a little more force.

Dana nodded, as though conceding the point. "Something drove us all to follow. We then noticed the pack of wolves seemed to have vanished, while the pack of coyotes charged the *tallasi*, driving them toward a dried-up riverbed. When the group entered the rough terrain, the wolves emerged as though from ambush, and the two packs destroyed the *tallasi*."

"You still have not told me what this is about."

While Nicholas's voice did not rise in volume, Dana flinched as though prodded.

Yet Andery's attention latched onto something that had been bugging him for some time. He'd noticed Nicholas's slowly evolving speech pattern before, but tonight it stood out. As though Nicholas gained a slightly different accent...no, that wasn't right. A different way of phrasing that made his speech sound more formal. As he watched the two of them converse, he thought that Nicholas aped Dana's stilted speech pattern. No contractions, slightly odd phrasings...*what are you up to, Nicholas? This can be no accident.* Dark thoughts once more tapped creeping fingers across his skull, and he surreptitiously attempted to peek at Jennifer's face.

*Is there something going on here? Something...*He couldn't believe *that* of his brother. Of all the things he believed his brother capable of, this did not fall into that category. Not because his brother *couldn't* do something like this, but because Andery didn't see any advantage in it. Only discord would result if he was ever discovered in an affair. No, despite Jennifer's reaction to the scene, that was not a path Andery would walk even in his own mind (echoes of his own feelings toward Sarah made sure of that).

"They worked together, Nicholas," Dana continued, voice overflowing with awe. "Not just worked together, but they worked almost as though one animal. As though there were no wolves and no coyotes, simply predators accomplishing their mission. And when we ventured closer? The animals were sharing their kill." She finished almost in a whisper.

Nicholas finally nodded, eyes half-lidded as though deep in thought.

"It is a sign, Nicholas. A sign of what should be between two Clans."

He nodded again and after a long pause responded, "It is."

Andery rubbed his weary face, a sudden desire to be anywhere but here arising as he watched his soul mate commune with his brother on a level he would likely never achieve. *And do you really believe, Niki? I've lived with Dana for years, and often can't bring myself to believe in her visions. What about you? Do you simply play along? At least I've always been honest with Dana;* tried *to be honest. Will you be the same?*

He doubted it.

CHAPTER 27

CIRCLE OF EQUALS, NEAR KATYUSHA CITY
NOVY TERRA
STRANA MECHTY
KERENSKY CLUSTER
13 AUGUST 2809

Andery stood, looking across Nicholas's growing power.

Halfway between Katyusha City proper and the Svoboda Zemylya lay what had been a burgeoning city outpost of the original colonists. Several city blocks, including a new highway overpass that connected this back to old Strana Prime, like an arterial lifeline, already prepared to lay down several additional such outposts as they spread across the Novy Terra continent.

And now, it lay vacant. Despite the strong protests of civilians—including Carlotta's growing influence—Nicholas's force of will for uniting all into the megacity proper of Katyusha carried the day. And so this small city lay deserted. A ghost town. Awaiting the chance to find a future use, or fall into disuse and decay.

Which it apparently is now.

His eyes swept down from contemplating the vacant buildings and windswept streets—the rains and the stinking polyps would be coming soon—to see the two groups facing off against each other on crossroads almost exactly central to the entire vacant area. The animosity palpable, a dozen men and women in teal green single-suits and a nearly equal number in brown: warriors of Clan Steel Viper and Clan Wolverine.

"And why are we here again?" Andery said softly to the woman at his side, while looking at another woman across the street, whose eyes clawed at his with a radiance that nearly made them glow, despite the noon sun overhead.

"Khan Ellie Kinnison called me a liar," Sarah McEvedy replied, chin thrusting toward the woman attempting to savage Andery with her eyes.

"So," he said, breaking eye contact and watching as two sets of warriors from each side carefully walked a ten-meter circle around the center of the crossroads—using a locator transponder for accuracy—and used brilliant white spray paint to mark off the area. "Who cares what she says?"

"My warriors care. She disparages my honor, and so disparages the honor of my Clan," she said loudly, causing her warriors to stand up straighter, while scowls on the Steel Vipers' faces deepened.

"So," Andery responded, dropping his voice low; even he wasn't obtuse enough to ignore the latent violence that flared in looks and postures. "Don't tell me you think Nicholas is looking over your shoulder here?" He paused for a moment before continuing. "Then again, he probably is. But when has that stopped you from challenging him?"

"Not nearly as often as you," she responded in the same low voice; he could feel the smile in there, despite keeping her warriors from hearing this part of their discussion. "You're just a bad influence on me, when it comes to your brother. But regardless, this has very little to do with Nicholas, and everything to do with my warriors, and all of the Clans."

Andery cocked his head, waiting, but the silence stretched as the warriors continued to paint the large circle across the ferrocrete. *She's making you think, stupid. Think.*

He kicked it around from several angles. Though he was amidst all of them year after year, he was not one of them. *And never will be.* And that made all the difference. Caused him to take too long to find the answer. He nearly bit his tongue in frustration as he finally understood the truth.

"The competition isn't just within each Clan anymore. I've seen the way Nicholas fosters competition between the Clans."

"Exactly," she responded softly, the smile even more evident, as though she mocked him for such a slow response. "His vision of how to create the finest warriors. For four years he vetted all of us through live fire exercises. And yet that is not enough. His new society will be built upon a bedrock of competitions and trials for every aspect of our lives."

He couldn't tell if there was exasperation in her voice over that growing truth, but decided this wasn't the time to explore it with her.

"And she's directly attacked the leadership of Clan Wolverine. If I let it go, she'd do it again. And more important, others will come. It'd be a feeding frenzy that would weaken us beyond the point of no return. And despite all of our posturing, we are just eight hundred warriors. We have to be very careful, or missteps could be disastrous."

Andery could only nod in complete agreement. *The thoughts no one says out loud.*

"Nicholas loves his trials. And I love the idea of rubbing his face in it as I create a brand new trial. You really are rubbing off on me. I'm sure—whether I like it or not—this will become commonplace. I'm happy to leap into the deep end right now and make it my own."

Andery nearly ground his teeth, anger surging; he couldn't tell if it was because she had been forced into this situation, or for the enthusiasm that laced her words, despite any reticence she might claim.

"You realize this has very little to do with you," he said, glancing back at Ellie, who appeared to ignore Sarah completely, eyes still raking him. "She has gotten strangely possessive of my brother. And she hates my disagreements with him. But she's not willing to challenge me. Not a *Kerensky*. And it wouldn't look good to challenge my Dana. But merely a friend? Someone who's spoken words similar to mine? If Ellie can defeat you, it'll be a strike against me. You're simply collateral damage."

"Andery," Sarah responded dryly. "First, it's a good thing I'm not a jealous girl. Because you just stepped in front of me and took all the action. Second, I'm not upset only because, well, you're spot-on. But hey, I'm happy to be your punching bag. I have been for your words long enough, why not throw some fists in the mix?"

"I'm sorry—" Andery began, realizing the towering arrogance of his response, but she cut him off with a raised hand.

"I said I understand, Andery. And it's fine. Besides, I sure wish she could lip-read. Because if Khan Kinnison heard you call her Ellie, I'm not sure even your name would protect you from a fight."

They both chuckled as the warriors finished the circle and shared a final nod as Sarah stepped up to its edge.

"This day, a new trial is born," Sarah exclaimed, her previous laughing voice instantly replaced by that of a leader forging a Clan of devout followers. She stabbed a finger across the distance. "You, Khan Kinnison, have impugned my honor, repeatedly calling me a liar in front of the Clan Council. I declare a Trial of Grievance this day against your own lies. We shall enter this circle, and shall fight until only one stands victorious. And in that victory, the lies will be laid bare, the truth upheld through the victory of combat. And the troubles ended."

When did you learn to be such an orator? Andery thought, impressed at the way she captivated both groups with her words and stance.

She swung her hands up in the air, clapping them in a sharp bang that echoed strangely through the vacant buildings; all present held their breaths. "Khan Kinnison. You are challenged. Do you accept?!"

"*Aff!*" she replied with venom.

"*Seyla,*" the whole group of warriors stridently responded.

Bile scorched Andery's tongue, souring his stomach every time he heard his students' joking use of his childhood prank firmly embraced by the Clans. *Centuries from now they'll still be using that, with none of them aware it was just childhood gibberish. Much less our mother's prayer, Niki. How could you do it!* It hurt to contemplate how Nicholas's society continued to slice and parse and drag him into pieces to be subsumed into the whole.

The two Khans moved into the circle, the warriors forming two half-circles around them, and soon the grunts and meaty slaps of heavy hitting physical violence filled the crossroads.

Andery's disgust made him look away, taking in the whole scene, looking around at the empty city. His vision expanded and he knew—he *knew*—this area would eventually be laid to waste as endless trials moved from fist-a-cuffs to 'Mech combat as the years marched and Nicholas's Clans inexorably ground forward, devouring everything in their path.

Andery contemplated the loss of the bright hope this place once held compared to its doomed future, waiting until the victory was declared the way he knew it would be. He glanced back to see Sarah wiping away blood from her face as she stood over the unconscious form of the defeated Khan of Clan Steel Viper, right arm held triumphant in the air as her warriors cheered with abandon.

Andery's mood lighted as he once again beheld this beautiful, dynamic woman. *You think you're strong, Ellie, but I was there when Sarah killed her own troops under the force of her conviction.* His stomach slowly soured all over again as the admiration sparked other feelings, and he turned away, shame flooding his face.

CHAPTER 28

"Another block in your foundation," Andery commented.

"Hm?" Nicholas responded, distracted.

And why shouldn't you be distracted, Niki? He sighed, and scratched morosely at his old wound, knowing the move habitual, and not caring enough to stop.

"Yes, another block in the foundation. You have an issue with that, Andery?"

Andery's eyes found Jennifer's. "Of course not. Just a statement."

"Mmm..." Lips pursed while her eyes pounded relentlessly. As though the more time passed, the less she hid her disdain and dislike.

To avoid *that* look, he gazed toward the recently finished Clan Wolf Hall, and the gathering of Wolf warriors at its front. Unlike the huge Jade Falcon edifice still under construction, or the almost quaint Ice Hellion Hall long finished, Clan Wolf seemed to have struck a balance somewhere between; small enough to give the impression of power in the Svoboda Zemylya park where it rightly belonged, with the Hall of Khans at the center, but impressive enough to show Clan Wolf's confidence in their place in Nicholas's new society.

While the side and rear exteriors followed spartan lines, the front façade made up for the rest of the structure's plainness. Ten columns on both sides stretched up from the peaceful flagstone walkways bordering most of the building, up several series of rough-hewn rock steps, toward the entrance to the building proper. Surprisingly, the columns supported no roof, but were clearly a finished element of the building. With an artistic flair he hadn't expected from warriors, frescoes and bas-reliefs covered the front façade, its two low walls running out along the sides of the wide steps and the entire floor open to the sky, mirroring a mountainous terrain, down to evergreen boughs and rocky mountain vistas. Andery expected any moment to catch the shiver of moving pines and the scents of a hard, cold peak just beginning to recognize the inexorable march of spring, with green-spotted valleys and a smattering of colors against the harsh white as flowers poked through. Finally, the artistry and magnitude of the homage to their totem's origins led to a humble door that resembled nothing so much as an entrance to a cave.

Andery nodded at the almost perfect blend of grandeur, power, and humbleness. *A perfect home for the perfect wolf. The perfect warriors? No wonder Nicholas seems to be paying particular attention to this Clan.*

"You ignoring me?"

"Of course not," he said after clearing his throat. "Simply amazed at what Clan Wolf has wrought."

"You mean Nicholas?"

While she kept her chin up, Andery almost smiled at the lowered tone. *You're well on your way, Jen, but you've still got to play it safe now and then, don't you? You and Niki.*

"I'll concede Nicholas began it all, but the warriors of Clan Wolf should be given their due. Your brother, as Khan. He and his warriors should be given the honors this day."

"Of course. Of course. Jerome has always been dedicated to...me."

The strange inflection, as though she were going to say something else, gave him pause. He remembered a long-ago conversation with her brother and the obvious tension there; *as if I have any rocks to throw at sibling rivalry.* He opened his mouth for a clarification and a snarl filled the air; a primal, electric, and powerful scream of defiance and rage. The very air seemed to hesitate, while the hair on Andery's neck stood straight, shivering with a desperate need to flee. Glancing toward the far edge of the gathering of Wolf warriors, past the flagstone paths, he found the origin of the beastly sound.

As though in a surreal dream, Andery abruptly wondered if he'd suddenly shrunk in size; breath and pulse quickened, sweat beading across his brow.

A Strana Mechty wolf.

It stood what looked like almost ninety centimeters at the shoulder, and would top a hundred fifty kilograms if eyes didn't deceive. Almost twice the size of its predecessor (and no matter how much Nicholas denied it, Andery *knew* the wolf *must* be part of his genetics program), the wolf stood next to Jerome Winson as though a warg sprung whole from ancient mythology.

Despite his distaste for Jennifer (he always wondered how two siblings could look so different), Andery held only admiration for the towering, broad-shouldered and dark-haired Jerome Winson. Seeing him standing next to such a mammoth beast— his confidence almost visibly radiant—brought his respect for the man up another half-dozen notches.

"Ah. Winson. You never fail," Nicholas breathed softly.

"No, he never has," Jennifer responded.

Andery glanced between the two of them before giving in to the inevitable question. "Don't tell me that's a pet."

Ice-blue eyes found his. "Not a pet *per se*. A pet assumes domestication. Assumes anyone might walk up to it and scratch behind its ears and wait for the wag of a tail. But I assume you do not wish to try that on *this* pet?"

"Um, no."

"Exactly. No. This is more a...companion of Jerome's. Something to bring a new level of commitment from Clan Wolf. From all the Clans. To master one's fears and the terrible dangers of befriending a Strana Mechty wolf to bring it here and keep it from rending all who step too close...that is consummate skill."

Andery nodded at the logic, absorbing the excited tone in Nicholas's voice at this important milestone. *Ah, you would've been a masterful snake charmer, Niki. Simply masterful.*

Nicholas stepped away, moving among the ochre-colored single-suits of the Clan Wolf warriors, his own white a patch of frost in a sunset-touched desert. With formality, he paused with each warrior, exchanging words, then nodding gravely and moving on, leaving a wake of bright eyes and upturned lips. Déjà vu wrung Andery with an abrupt sense of their father doing the same thing countless times. *While you have struck out on your own, you still learned from the best, Niki. From the best.*

Finally stopping in front of Jerome Winson, he exchanged a longer conversation before actually bowing slightly; throughout the entire dialogue with the Clan Wolf Khan, a low growl reverberated around the clearing as the wolf crouched low, hackles half-raised, teeth partially bared in a snarl.

I wonder how Jerome feels. He was a big brother to both of us so long ago. And now he's a faithful follower of Nicholas? Does that really sit well with him? Andery could never bring himself to ask.

Beads of sweat rolled down across his eyebrows and into his wide, staring eyes as Nicholas turned and bowed the lowest yet to the wolf, then sank to one knee and calmly stretched out his hand to the beast. The wolf responded by crouching lower, hackles shooting completely erect and teeth bared fully as the growl rose in volume and dipped precipitously in tone, until it rubbed against the hindbrain and the primal human animal repressed for ten thousand years surfaced: time spun to a stop as forty-two sets of lungs seared with the need for air as long moments stretched and the desire to flee crescendoed, Nicholas's outstretched hand an immobile rock to the fury it taunted.

Explosive exhalations rocked the gathering as from one instant to the next the wolf crawled forward to lick Nicholas's palm, bump its moist nose several times, followed by a chin-to-ground maneuver that could only be interpreted as a bow; then the wolf fell back into a sitting posture at Jerome's side.

Despite his knowledge that the scene was completely manufactured, the whole episode still worked its magic on Andery, eliciting a tingling of adrenaline and endorphins as he saw his brother through the eyes of those present, before he could master the emotion.

Snake charmer indeed.

Andery wiped his forehead and rubbed the sweat from his palms on his pants, while Nicholas slowly stood, moved to a point where all eyes could find his, and spoke. "While I founded the Clans as a whole almost three years ago, it is fitting that each Clan has chosen its own path along the way I have laid out for us. For while we are one in spirit, we are a multitude in mind, whose whole shall be so much greater than the sum of its parts. And while each Clan has shown its own preference for when and how they shall declare themselves 'founded', I find it appropriate beyond mere words that Clan Wolf has not chosen to simply see the completion of its Clan Hall as its official founding. No, I take intense comfort in the knowledge that you all truly grasp the vision I hold and impart to you, for you have chosen your founding to be on this day, September twenty-ninth. The day the Great Father cast down the evil of the Amaris Empire and freed the Terran Hegemony from the Usurper's grasp. So, too, shall we free the Pentagon Worlds, and one day the Inner Sphere from the evil of the Great Houses."

He raised both hands, one pointing toward the wolf, the other palm up, as though offering the crowd a blessing; the similarities between Nicholas's gesture and pose and how Windham had spoken to his congregation during church ceremonies couldn't be more obvious, sending a shiver down Andery's spine at the continued rise of his brother's own mythology.

He finished his benediction, voice strident, eyes blazing. "Here, with the Strana Mechty wolf, we see what may be the epitome of a true warrior—cunning matched with instinct and stealth, joined with a final, terrifying attack. For this mighty creature, I have named you. You *are* Clan Wolf."

There could only be one response: a near-frenzied chorus of howls erupted for long minutes.

CHAPTER 29

COLDRILL VALLEY
NOVY TERRA
STRANA MECHTY
KERENSKY CLUSTER
23 MARCH 2812

The Coldrill Valley was a beautiful spread of copses of p-trees and fertile lands that held numerous farms built by colonists who had left the confines of the original Strana Prime to be hardy farmers and herders. Andery breathed in the sights and smells of a place he'd never visited before, keeping the other sounds at bay for another minute, before they pulled him back to this moment.

Eyes fell from pastoral scenes to several hundred angry people standing in front of as many warriors, a mix of most of the Clans in their bright-colored jumpsuits, along with Nicholas, Andery, and representatives from the civilian leadership of Strana Mechty.

Behind them, a massive land train idled on the well-worn trail that traced an arterial path from Strana Mechty to this valley and others, transporting foodstuffs to the city and returning much-needed supplies back to these valleys. And beside it stood a single BattleMech, Dana's *Black Knight*, the bright light blue color of Clan Coyote making it stand out harshly against the background.

A powerful statement. His eyes roved over the civilians, many of whom carried various farming implements, but the intent was clear. *Will we need that statement? Dana, what will you do if my brother calls upon you here? Niki,* would *you call upon her in this moment?*

"Andery," Councilwoman Carlotta spoke up, as both groups eyed each other with animosity. "You really need to listen to Justin. Please." Her usually cold face and tone held a hint of urgency that pulled his attention fully toward her, then to the other man he'd met earlier in the day on the long ride out. Justin carried too much weight, dour features strangely juxtapositioned against a cherubic face. Carlotta had introduced him as a senior labor leader, and a liaison with many of the farmers from this and other valleys.

"Justin," Andery said, tone carefully neutral, trying to focus on the man as the noise grew.

"Andery," the man responded, tone equally respectful. "The rumor mill has been churning for weeks. And now Nicholas himself arrives, with a large group of warriors, and even a BattleMech?"

Despite his mostly deferential voice, frustration was turning his eyes dark. *To anger, Justin? How much do you sympathize with them?*

"Did Nicholas really believe this would end any other way?" he continued. "This is their land. Deeded to them by right of colonization under the aegis of the Commanding General of the Star League Defense Force. Under *your* father."

Andery could almost ignore the painful spike he felt anytime his father's name was invoked. But he also noted Justin did not use any of the new terms Nicholas had created to rebrand their father. "I'm well aware of the situation," he finally responded.

"Then why is Nicholas here?"

He knew exactly why his brother was here. *And so do you—you just want me to say it out loud.* And despite the uncomfortable itch that lay between his shoulder blades in a place he could never relieve, in this instance, he understood Nicholas's motives. There were still plenty of pressures within Katyusha City—though Andery still hoped with leadership like Carlotta's, the civilians would eventually find a pressure relief valve—but on the whole, Nicholas had gained significant control over the largest population center on Strana Mechty; it would only solidify in the years to come. And it was time to extend that hold. Nicholas's words rose as though an invocation: "*They hold us hostage, Andery. They may not think in such terms. But the farmers who grow most of our food are beyond our purview. This cannot be allowed. All must be brought under the Clan way, or the Clans will not survive.*"

Staring at both Justin and Carlotta, he was unsure what to say. Then Nicholas's loud voice rose above them.

"Good people of Coldrill Valley," he began, his usual potent voice and charisma at work as he moved to the front of his warriors, only a short distance from the farmers, who stared daggers of hate. "We have forged a new society in Katyusha City that is transforming our way of life. That will ensure we do not fall into the bitter jealousy and hateful rivalries that led to the destruction of the Star League and the Star League-in-Exile. We will forever banish such failures to our past."

No, Nicholas, you won't end them. You'll just elevate them and keep them small-scale, always fighting among ourselves in ritualized trials of combat. You know this. And most of the Khans know it. But do the rest of the warriors? Do the civilians yet understand that you will overshadow them with your supremacy while combat becomes a daily way of life?

The sound of lowing cattle could suddenly be heard echoing up from the valley to the hill they stood upon; a surreal moment of calm in the chaos that surely was coming. *Will they really fight with a BattleMech at Nicholas's back?*

"It is time for all to be brought into this society. It is time for all of Strana Mechty to be joined to my Clans. As such, I have divided the continents of this world into enclaves that will become homes to my twenty Clans. This will not happen overnight. It will take time. Time for all of you to adjust. Time for you to determine how you and your progeny will acclimate to our new society."

"How can he not see it," Justin muttered at Andrey's side, momentarily pulling his attention. "Time is irrelevant to a farmer. They already think in terms of seasons and generations. The land is all that matters. The land as an inheritance for their children and their children's children. If you take that away—"

"From this moment on," Nicholas's voice boomed even louder, combining with Justin's voice, "Clan Blood Spirit is deeded the rights to the Coldrill Valley in perpetuity as their new enclave."

"—nothing else matters," Justin finished.

The moment stretched out and Andery felt the cool wind brush his skin, as the last vestiges of winter still clung here, and he swore he heard those cattle in the distance one last time before the animal howl of the farmers soared and they charged forward, brandishing their weapons, their fear and hatred writ large.

"*No!*" three voices shouted together as Carlotta, Justin, and Andery joined as one, watching horrified as the warriors surged past Nicholas—who didn't move a muscle—and met the oncoming civilians. There were no gunshots and the *Black Knight* never moved (*thank heavens!*), but despite the farmers being healthy and well-muscled, the warriors were masters of every type of combat, years of live fire exercises and continual trials having honed them into perfect weapons. And these farmers had not only dared ignore a decree from their new prophet, but threatened him with violence .

Dana's voice echoed in his ear: "*How this is handled will determine all the rest. Nicholas cannot be anything but ruthless here, so that all others will come into the Clans with very little violence.*"

As though to make up for that future, this moment was brutal and decisive; nearly all were injured and more than a dozen civilians died as Andery refused to look away, unshed tears filling his eyes.

CHAPTER 30

NEW NEUBLE DOWNS PUB, KATYUSHA CITY
NOVY TERRA
STRANA MECHTY
KERENSKY CLUSTER
15 APRIL 2813

Andery passed through the doors and stopped as though poleaxed.

Under an audio and olfactory assault, years dropped away between one eyeblink and the next and a hundred memories effervesced, drawn by the inexorable pull of fresh-made breads, bubbling stews, grilled meats, and endless aromas of a dozen different microbrews; juxtaposed with boisterous talking, the ubiquitous low-level clanking of utensils on plates and, of course, the clack of billiard balls.

"Andery," the waiter said as the short, balding man ghosted by, navigating the throng as though born to it.

He nodded back, so much more comfortable than he'd ever been in the old pub; moved into the miasma. While so many of the smells and sights of the new pub made Andery wonder if even the cooking staff had been transplanted from the original built more than twenty years ago on Eden, the layout was different enough to jar him from such reverie. *No, probably not the same at all. Most of them likely didn't make it. Maybe one of the primary chefs, with the recipes still in his head. And the owner, with a memory for what worked so well last time. Only way the food could match my memory so well.*

The melancholy flared momentarily, as it always did when thinking of those lost to the horrors of the Pentagon Wars, before he gently nudged it back into its place: deeply embedded in his soul.

"Andery, game?" Karla called, smoky eyes and delicious body beckoning.

He continued moving, waving once in response. "Not tonight, Karla. Don't have any money for you to take."

"You've always got something I can take, Andery." She laughed boisterously before waving an assent and turning back to the billiard table she crewed alone.

"Shark, that one," a new voice intruded on his left, almost causing Andery to jump out of his skin.

Andery turned to find Raymond Sainze at his elbow, having come from the direction of the restrooms. "Sheesh, Ray, about gave me a heart attack."

His Combine heritage peeked through momentarily as the man bowed slightly in apology before he broke into a most un-Combine-like wide grin. "But she's still a shark."

Andery glanced once more at Karla, then joined Raymond as they both walked to the back and their usual booth. "Yeah. But regardless of that, and how much of a flirt she is, she doesn't treat me like a Kerensky." The last came out in a subdued tone, as he smoothed a hand down his jumpsuit.

Raymond, in an unusual emotional display, clapped his shoulder as they neared the table. "I know, Andery. I know."

"Andery, Ray. Thought you guys would never show up," Windham said, almost yelling from his seated position not a meter from where they stood.

"Can you ever not be loud?" Stephen responded from the other side of the table.

"Of course he can't. He has to yell to be heard past that warthog he has permanently attached to his face," Carson rejoined, setting everybody laughing.

Andery slid into the seat, the cobwebs of his earlier memories still lingering as he took in the uniforms—more colored single-suits—that still looked odd to his sensibilities, despite the years. After all, what were a few years to a few dozen? The teal of Stephen's, Ray's orange, Windham's light purple, Carson's yellow and black; the potpourri of colors matched the hodgepodge of the pub, and made Andery's stark white stand out all the more.

Even in one of the last places on Mechty you allow your warriors to freely rub shoulders, you still force me to stand out like a sore thumb, eh Niki. It should have been a question, but it always came out like a statement, as though Andery knew exactly what his brother was trying to do.

As though by some unheard signal, they grew silent, as first Raymond, then the rest raised their cups and bowed their heads in memory for one of the first of the Pub Gang to die. Finally, as the silence stretched and eyes darted surreptitiously, Andery finally cleared his throat (abruptly needing the drink to wet his parched mouth) and spoke.

"Jason Everly. You may have failed the final testing, but you will always be remembered until the last of us passes away." Emotions swelled across the table in various forms. Andery pushed his own down, knowing that flood would only pull up the bitterness over the overblown riot and his senseless death at the hands of the Para-police.

"He probably joked with his last breath. *Phe-nom-en-al,*" Carson said. The lot of them startled for a moment—Andery almost aghast at the comment—before smiles and warm chuckles carried away hollowness and the darkness of death. Good memories. Good memories of a life lived to the fullest. And most of all, it was exactly how Jason would've cut through such a dour moment.

"What you guys having?" a voice interrupted.

Andery glanced up to find a middle-aged waitress, slightly rounded figure, with her hair pulled so tightly back into a bun it made her face seemed stretched like cooled glass. The orders came quick and easy as "the usual" rang almost verbatim around the table. As ever, Andery avoided the older woman's sea-green eyes (*what is it about every woman I meet and sea-green eyes!*) and dove into a discussion between Windham and Ray.

"That doesn't seem credible," Windham said.

"Why?" Raymond fired back.

"Because the riot was an isolated case. As terrible as it was, it's been almost two months now, and there's been no further disturbances like it."

"Windham. We were all on Eden. We know our history back to the Inner Sphere and even beyond, into ancient Terran cultures and nations. It *will* get worse."

Trying to ignore those eyes that still haunted him after all these decades, Andery jumped in regardless of his own feelings on the subject. "Before it gets better."

"What?" Raymond said, looking at him.

"It'll get worse, before it gets better."

Raymond stared, as though unable to make a decision one way or another. But he wouldn't go down the negative path, open pub or not. *After all, we're all fanatical, right? Even if we're not as fanatical as most.*

Andery nodded. *I understand. As sad as it makes me, I understand.*

"But the rioting was over land rights. That hit a little too close to home for them...after having nearly their entire city bulldozed to the ground to make way for our new Clan metropolis. They've put up with almost everything else. Why would this be different?"

"This is different."

"Why?" Andery chimed in. Out of the corner of his eye, Andery saw the waitress finally leave, and Carson and Stephen fell into their own conversation.

"Because Nicholas is beginning to accelerate things."

"It's been accelerating all along."

"Not like this. The expansion of the fosterlings programs. And you've heard the rumors. Of what's coming." Raymond lowered his voice, as he took a quick gulp of water.

"Not that rumor again," Windham said, waving it off. "Not even Nicholas could seriously contemplate destroying the family unit. Why would he?"

Raymond shrugged, as though to say, *"how could I know what the great Nicholas is doing?"* which only intensified Windham's scornful look. Andery covered his nervousness with a grab at his drink, as the waitress returned and plopped down a hardwood cutting board with a steaming loaf of black-pepper wheat bread. The heat shimmering off the fresh-from-the-oven loaf wafted to nostrils, making saliva gush.

The others tore into the loaf with abandon, while Andery's fingers caressed the hardwood of the mildly greasy tabletop, the whorls of the grain providing a natural path for his fingers to follow while his mind wove back across the knots of time to a hidden bunker and a smoke jaguar and his brother's look of triumph, and words couched as prophecy.

"Say what you will, Windham. But the rumors have to come from somewhere," Raymond responded after finishing a slice and carefully wiping his mouth.

"Of course they do. From people who've got nothing better to do," Windham shot back, almost spitting out crumbs before finishing his own slice. "You'd think they aren't busy enough or something. That'll change, I bet."

"Now, gentlemen, about enough of that, don't you think?" Carson broke in.

"But Carson," Windham said, eyes twinkling with mischief, "you keep forgetting, regardless of how much time passes, you don't get to order us around anymore. You're just a Clan warrior like the rest of us."

Carson's eyebrows began to lower before the huge smile escaping from behind Windham's beard brought creases to Carson's face as well, causing them all to erupt into a fit of laughing. "You'd think after how long now, I'd have lost that."

"Yup, just a bunch of Clansmen." Stephen's words came out a little strange, as though still unused to the term.

Except me. Andery bowed his head momentarily. *Always except me. You allow them all to join a Clan and deprive me of the same right. Do I care if you and Jen aren't in a Clan either? That you're saving yourself? Please. That works for you Niki, and for your wife, but not for the little brother.*

"It will take a while longer for us to get used to this, no matter the years that pass," Raymond said.

Andery glanced up to find a knowing look sent his way; friendship and a hand always outstretched in support. Without a word, he gazed around the table, seeing his fast friends, there through good times and bad. Especially the bad. It buoyed his spirit.

"Yeah," he finally responded, after swallowing a lump of emotions.

The rest of the heads around the table all nodded.

CHAPTER 31

OUTSKIRTS OF KATYUSHA CITY
NOVY TERRA
STRANA MECHTY
KERENSKY CLUSTER
2 NOVEMBER 2814

Andery sat in the uncomfortable chair. *More torture device than furniture.*

"Warrior Kerensky," Mayor General Carlotta said.

"Warrior Andery," he responded. *No one applies Niki's subtle influences over the last year of losing surnames to* the Kerenskys, *but I'll be the same as everyone else.* He ignored the fact that *that* was impossible.

The woman blinked slowly. Though soft of voice, Carlotta reminded Andery of a wintry peak, all hard planes, chiseled features, and enough ice to give Nicholas a run for his money. "Of course. Warrior Andery. Thank you for coming to our meeting."

"Of course, Mayor General," he responded in kind—glad he didn't stumble over the new title, though he'd interacted with some of these leaders, especially Carlotta, for years at this point—nodding to the semicircle of people (more like a high court inquiry than a gathering of civic leaders). "But to be honest, I'm not sure why you didn't request Nicholas's presence. If you're looking to air grievances, they should be directed to him." All knew Nicholas had delegated Andery as liaison to the colonists years ago, but he was hoping to put them back on their heels. *Let's get this right out into the open, shall we?*

Without breaking eye contact, Andery received the distinct impression the woman wanted to look toward the other four in the room, but instead she paused for a moment before responding.

"I felt...*we* felt, this would be better directed to you. As all such discussions have been."

Andery swore his chair—sitting in the center of a stark room bereft of any adornment beyond a cheap oil painting of a sunflower on the left wall, a window behind the ramshackle line of desks in front of him (the wan sun hardly making a dent against the dirty scabs on the window), and hardwood floors water-stained and musty from disuse—began to sprout nails on the seat.

"What she meant to say," another voice broke in, turning Andery to his left to see a balding gentleman with loose skin—as though he'd lost a large amount of weight quickly—and a nervous tic under his dull brown left eye, "is that you have done so much service directly with the ci...community." The man shrugged, but the slump of his shoulders barely registered the movement through his smudged and wrinkled suit.

Civilians, you mean. Not warriors. Don't want to go there, do you? "And you are?" Andery responded, still somehow uncomfortable with his role of dealing with these civilian leaders regardless of the long years of that exact work.

"Merchant Factor Dawson." The man tried for gravity, but only came across as weak. *Niki would likely strike you dead with fear, right? That's why you asked for me. This is what's running the civilian sectors in Katyusha?* Dismay swelled his unease. *I knew it was bad, but this?*

Sarah's words haunted him. He'd casually noted her continual harping on how ineffective the "civilian guidance" duties seemed to be, even after all this time, and that pressures were building...which coincided with too many conversations with Windham and the others. But he'd always been able to subsume such suspicions under the pressure of his other duties. Pushing himself day and night. Especially as he had interacted with Carlotta for some time now, and considered her very capable. But now, on the chair as hard as basalt, his spine already aching, the truth began to emerge, despite his best attempts to ignore it. *And perhaps despite Carlotta's best attempts to keep things on an even keel.*

"I'm sorry, Warrior Andery. I should've made introductions right away." Carlotta spoke without a hint of apology in her tone.

She pointed to her left, Andery's right. "This is Master Technician Jefferson." The wraithlike man nodded, teeth a white crescent in a thick, bristling beard.

"You've met Senior Laborer Justin before." Despite his title, the man was very heavy.

"Senior Technician Jules," she said, moving her hand to her right; the petite woman nodded, blue eyes striking against her dark skin and flowing black hair.

"And of course you know Master Teacher Paul." High forehead, thick limbs, but the only easy smile and friendly eyes in the group.

Andery nodded to each in turn, noting the conspicuous absence of any scientific leaders. *But you've taken all of them under your wing, Niki. Taken them under your care and lavished on them all the splendor and comfort of Katyusha proper, while forcing the rest of the civic leaders to just make do.*

His thoughts danced across the hot tin roof of reasons why his brother treated the scientists with such singular attention, and memories surged—of a jungle and a terrifying cat and secret lab for playing god; a science report of DNA screening and aptitude tests to determine ideal pairings he was never meant to see—forcing him to swallow heavily and dredge up the will to focus on the here and now.

A slow review of the leaders, and Andery couldn't stop his mind from supplying the rejoinder. *But you do this to yourselves, as well. Your choice to meet in this rundown facility, outside the official boundaries of Katyusha. As though to make a statement. And what statement would that be?* He almost smiled at the obviousness of it all. *Have you fully joined them after all these years, Carlotta? Or did they drag you down to this level, and you don't even realize you're on the cusp?*

"Now that that's over with, can we get on with it?" Justin said.

"Please, Justin," Paul responded. "There is no need to be uncivil. We all know how much Warrior Andery has aided the community. And he came upon our first request. We should provide him an open forum to hear our concerns, not force him on the defensive at our first words."

While Andery's teaching was almost exclusively with the military, he'd coordinated some curriculums with Paul for nonmilitary training; yet his eloquent words didn't fit the room.

Justin's pudgy lips twisted in disdain, but he didn't respond, much to Andery's relief.

"The reason we asked you here is to voice our concerns over some of Nicholas's latest...announcements."

Andery did smile then, despite the gravity of the situation. *You so wanted to say orders, didn't you. Or better yet, proclamations. From the king?* The look in their eyes told Andery he was not too far off.

"Okay." He gazed steadily. *If you're going to force me into this painful seat, then I'll make you work for it.*

"Warrior Andery," Jules said, her tone light and lilting, with an accent he couldn't place. "Our intention is not to grill you. But we have concerns. Concerns brought to us by others. And we feel it is our responsibility to present them to you. We certainly don't want the...unpleasantness of two years ago to occur again."

Andery just managed to keep a grimace from his face. *Your euphemism for the land-rights riots is awful. And is that a threat?* "And why not wait until the next Clan Council? Such concerns should be aired there," he responded with a level voice.

She looked askance at Carlotta, then straightened, as though coming to some inner decision, and said, "Because we feel intimidated and outnumbered there."

"Jules!" Jefferson cried, horror painting his tones large in the bare, small room.

"What?" she shot back. "He should know the truth. Right up front. If we want him to deal straight with us, we need to deal straight with him."

Jules went up a notch or two in his estimation. His eyes roved over the rest, wondering if he needed to revise his initial impressions across the board. He found Justin chewing on his lip, an almost petulant curve making him appear like an oversized child. *No, not all impressions.*

"And I appreciate that," he cut in before Justin found a way to interrupt once more. "I appreciate that you might feel intimidated by the new warrior halls and how the Clans," he chose his words carefully, "are eager to demonstrate that the responsibility you have placed in the warriors is well-founded."

Justin snorted, causing Jules to look at him fiercely and Paul to shake his head as though wishing he could chastise an errant student, but knowing "in front of the class" was not appropriate.

Carlotta didn't bat an eye, her cool blues seizing on Andery, though she responded first. "We're grateful you see our point of view."

He nodded respectfully. "And so?"

"It's not a single thing, Warrior Kerensky."

"Warrior Andery," he responded.

She again blinked slowly, as though thrown off guard for a moment. But she returned to the subject, laser-focused. "Warrior Andery, it's not a single thing. It's a host of things. Piling up one upon the other, in such a short time, until we can't breathe. Until we feel...we all feel...that we're losing ourselves."

He nodded, but kept silent. *Work for it.*

"Warrior Andery," Paul began, leaning forward on the desk, as though to beseech understanding. "Your brother's proclamations continue to grow. As the Mayor General says, it is not any single proclamation, but the combined weight that wearies. Just the last six months have seen a reorganization of how the civilian sectors work with the Clans. New titles. New spheres of responsibility. The introduction of work chits. Even the dating program he instituted last year has the air of...especially when he has now paired that with incentives for those who produce 'viable offspring.' And the banning of surnames along the way. It all has an air of *arrangement* to it. Conversely, the mores of the community are falling. You'd be shocked at what is found on our streets at night."

I doubt it. Just get to the point. It's all about yesterday's announcement. So get to the point. His sudden loss of patience for the group surprised him, regardless of how much he might empathize with what they must be going through.

"We, all of us," Paul said, hand languidly indicating the other leaders, "understand Nicholas's vision, and have accepted it."

Out of the corner of his eye, Andery caught a dark cloud cross Justin's face. *I somehow doubt that.* But he kept his lips sealed on that observation.

"But we would ask your brother to...perhaps...slow down."

"Slow down?" Andery said. "Slow down? It's been almost seven years since Nicholas formed the Clans. How much slower do you want?"

Paul shifted uneasily. "I suppose Nicholas has not moved as fast as he wanted."

Andery snorted, and Paul nodded. "But Warrior Andery, you have to understand it from the civilian point of view. The military is different. You are trained to follow orders—"

"No matter how...strange those orders may be," Carlotta broke in.

"Exactly." Paul nodded.

"I see," Andery said. *Come on. Spit it out. The real issue.*

"But the civilians," Paul continued, "they are not..." he cleared his throat, as though uncomfortable for a moment, then continued. "They are not trained as the military is. And so for them, it feels as though the changes have been nonstop. One on top of the other. Displaced from their homes, their allegiances changed, the new and odd ordering of the S...military. New titles...and the fosterages, and the selective courtships, and now..." he stopped, flustered.

Andery could almost see the beads of sweat squeezing out of Paul's skin, his loss of eloquence and the near slip of calling the Clans the SLDF (a big no no) a clearer indication of his concerns than any mere words. *I don't think I've ever seen you at a loss for words.*

"And now what?" he finally said, priming the pump. Despite his eroding patience (too much time around Jen and her complete lack of sympathy for the civilians?), the man's obvious concern forced Andery's hand.

"And now the announcement that *all* children will be fostered."

Finally. "Fostering has been going on since the Exodus."

"True," Carlotta spoke. "But this is different."

"Why? Fostering has increased significantly over the past several years. I would argue not a single family doesn't have at least one child fostered. And the results have been impressive. They speak for themselves."

She nodded, conceding the point. "Yes. However, it was only encouraged before. And while the structure of this new emerging society almost demands fosterage if our children are to have a solid place in its future, it is a subtle thing. A thing most, as they work hard to help forge this new...vision...can't quite see. But now there's no more velvet to hide the steel. Yesterday's announcement...has—"

"Nicholas is destroying the family!" Justin cut in, voice angry and loud, yet filled with anxiety, as though he hoped to shout over his own fears. "He's purposefully trying to destroy all semblance of civilian life and remake us into his vision. It's all a rocket sled to hell!"

"Justin!" Jefferson said, aghast.

"What? Jules is the one who said we should shoot straight with him. Isn't that right?" he said, petulant look thrown at her dark-featured scorn. "So I'm shooting straight. We all want to say it, and I'm the only one saying it."

He looked back at Andery, eyes skating this way and that, as though searching for the confidence to continue. *No wonder you didn't want to speak in front of the Clan Council. Their combined anger and disdain would've killed you, Justin...and would've wrecked the rest of you.*

"Nicholas is trying to destroy our families...and...and...we won't let him."

Dead silence echoed louder than words as Andery surfaced from his own thoughts of trust and his position among the civilians, unsure of what he'd just heard. He cocked his head and leaned forward casually, unconsciously mimicking his brother in that moment.

"What did you say?" Without looking directly away from Justin, he could see the stunned and sickened looks wash across the rest in the room. But what disturbed him most was that the truth of Justin's words was visible in too many of the five leaders' eyes.

Justin blanched at the quiet tone of authority, mouth hanging open like a bovine wondering where the next lump of grass might come from, jowls shivering sympathetically with a heart beating so loud Andery could almost hear it. "I said...I said that *we* just can't sit by and allow it to happen."

"I see." And he did, and it sickened him. Memories enfolded his senses until he couldn't breathe, as the giant crowd in the hold of the *Hermes* pressed against him and they plotted mutiny and Nicholas and Jes Cole manipulated him into acting as the accelerant so the rebellion could be controlled. The chair's nails grew to spikes, striking his body with terrible pain.

Not again. Not again. Not again. I'm the spark. Is that why you've allowed the pressure to build, Niki? Because you knew it couldn't happen smoothly. Your vision. That some would rebel. That if you allowed it, the leaders would rebel and then you could cut off the snake's head to deflate the entire thing? Seeing the manipulation so clearly, unlike last time, didn't make the pain any less intense.

Bile made him start to gag and he leaned forward, abruptly breathless, the stink of nervous sweat—not from Justin or the others, but his own—swirling in nostrils flaring with the need for a fresh breeze. With savage need, he surged up to pace in front of the gathered leaders, causing them to all visibly jerk away from him.

"Don't do this."

"What?" Carlotta said, voice struggling to maintain her calm detachment.

"Don't do this. Don't force it. I know it's been hard. You may feel it's been easy on the warriors, but it hasn't been. It's been hard for them as well. Hard for us all. But wasn't it hard when we first landed on the Pentagon Worlds? Wasn't it hard then? And we stuck with it. And look what we created. For a few brief years we found our paradise. This can be the same!"

He glanced up, searching their eyes, pleading; stopped pacing, standing bereft and almost forlorn in front of them. "Please, don't follow this course."

He noted whose eyes turned inward, marking them as moderates, possibly swayed by his plea. But despite his fear, Justin's eyes held the gleam of one who would not back down from the potential to seize power. *All about power for you, eh Justin?* It sickened him.

"Then try to get your brother to slow down. His announcement that all children must be fostered by the time they're five? Five!" Justin's voice gained power when Andery didn't respond, and the others failed to interrupt.

"I will talk with Nicholas," he said, knowing his words would fall on deaf ears, but hoping (*right, sure*) that this wouldn't happen. Not again. Not again in his lifetime. Not when he would be at the center of it, and he would lay awake for an eternity of sleepless nights, with the weight of dead eyes boring through him. "Just, please don't do anything rash."

"Of course not," Justin replied.

Andery *just* managed to keep his wince invisible. If that had come from any of the others, particularly Carlotta, he might have believed it. But from Justin...*so it begins again.*

He strode quickly from the hall, hoping to make it outside before vomiting.

CHAPTER 32

The colors seemed to blend together, until a whirling kaleido-scope reigned.

The parade marched solemnly down the main thoroughfare of the Warrior Quarter in Katyusha City, toward the central plaza. The cold and wisps of snow curling lazily through the air seemed apropos. *As though the very world mourns with us.*

Andery stifled a yawn behind a gloved hand, the fur edge tickling his nose and causing him to sneeze. Despite cupping both gloves over his mouth, the sound still barked out.

Jennifer glanced his way, wicked eyes taut with disdain, turned back to the spectacle.

He managed to keep his face from reddening, but just. Instead, he peered intently off the podium he occupied—Nicholas just to his right, a half-step in front, with Jennifer to his right, a half-step back—at the marching groups of warriors and the civilians on either side; the throngs mashed up against the buildings, a wave frozen in the moment of cresting.

As though a patchwork field of myriad flowers sprung to life, warriors marched in clean lines down the giant lane running from the apex of the Warrior Quarter all the way to the city center, their colors as bold and purposeful as their booted feet striking ferrocrete. Passing in front of Nicholas's reviewing stand, the warriors of Clan Cloud Cobra swept past, led by Windham (for once without a smile, face serious, eyes intent), feet in lockstep, light blue suits a solid wall of projected force. *Water. Like a wave. But in motion, compared to the civilians' arrested movement. Inexorable.* They marched on, followed by a small procession of civilians in the same colors; those who had volunteered from the civilian ranks to work directly with Clan Cloud Cobra (he'd not believed it would happen so easily, but Nicholas only chuckled at such doubt when he'd made the announcement two years ago, and now every Clan had a dedicated following of civilians, laborers, technicians, and more), followed by the next group. The bright, almost ostentatious green of Goliath Scorpion, led by Cyrus, passed in the same vein; legs, arms and strides in lockstep. *So perfect, so in unison, almost...*

...frightening. Yes, that's the word.

Andery's eyes hooded as he tried to stay focused on the spectacle Nicholas had orchestrated for the people, but he was so tired. So many long hours over the last weeks trying to stop what he knew had to be coming. Startling awake almost every night in an empty apartment, horror ripping at his soul until he dry heaved with the exertion of not blacking out...and yet... nothing. Weeks drifting by, and not a hint of anything other than muttered discontent.

Despite the weariness that hung like a dead and bloated albatross around his neck, he refocused as Elizabeth and her Jade Falcons swept by; he looked for and found his old student Samuel directly behind Elizabeth, chin high, eyes powerful as their Clan's namesake. *You've done well for yourself, Samuel.* Despite any lingering resentments over the problems involving Samuel so many years ago, he nodded. *Good for you.*

Mind wandering with fatigue, in and out of focusing on the here and now, a new thought percolated. Why no 'Mechs? Or vehicles? He knew the entire pageant, while ostensibly to mourn and commemorate the assassination of First Lord Richard Cameron in 2766—when, from Nicholas's point of view, the Star League began to go wrong—was a demonstration of the growing power and might of Nicholas's Clans. A way to wow the civilians into further acceptance of the invisible chains he bound them with. And what better way than with a parade of 'Mechs? And vehicles. *Nothing like the heavy impact of one hundred tons of myomer and metal close by to cow civilians, to spark awe.*

The dark yellow suits of Clan Star Adder, led by Khan Absalom, passed the stand, followed by the yellow and black of Clan Mongoose. He felt a moment of wistfulness as he found Carson (*wait, no, that would just be James now; have I finally accepted Niki's proclamation of no surnames?*) walking amid the warriors. While he knew Nicholas strove earnestly to create the ultimate meritocracy, the years that Absalom had contrived to keep his friend from truly commanding his own division...he couldn't help wondering if Absalom had somehow managed this as well, pushing James into obscurity once more.

On that thought, his eyes moved beyond the passing Mongoose warriors to find Dana and her Coyotes. Her eyes gleamed with fervor even at this distance, searching and finding Nicholas as all forty warriors saluted right, toward Nicholas; her eyes never wavered once toward Andery.

On the verge of screaming at the affronts to his sanity—losing complete control over his lack of sleep—repeated soft coughs echoed on the wind, and out of the corner of his eye Andery caught several warriors in the Mongoose line stumbling. Stunned, he began to turn his head—the stumbling *so* unusual—as Nicholas abruptly heaved back as though yanked from behind, blood spattering across Andery's face, the horrifying warmth of the droplets almost a relief from the cold. His own blood threatening to tear from his veins, his eyes corkscrewed around, unable to center or focus, sleep deprivation and shock preemptively annulling any sudden action.

Bedlam. Chaos. Hysteria.

Yet it all seemed distant. As though viewed from outside his body. As though Andery floated on a cushion of ambivalence, and watched in wry amusement as those below raced to and fro.

Andery...Andery...Andery...Andery!

The scream finally shattered his detachment, and the sounds and confusion swirling around exploded fully into his senses, the shouts and cries so loud he could barely hear Jennifer's screams. The coppery stench of the high velocity

blood splatter on his face made him gag, bringing further
disorientation; steam rose from each droplet, almost making
it look as though he were shedding his soul.

Nicholas.

Perhaps he was.

Nicholas. *Nicholas!*

Blood covered his brother's chest and face in a monstrous
splash of crimson, as though from a bucket of paint cast from
the audience. The red stained the white of Nicholas's jumpsuit
in sickening contrast, as though to emphasize the mortality of
every man...even Nicholas.

"Andery!"

The voice pulled him further up from his detached state,
blazing eyes reminding him of something, but the urgency of her
voice brooked no sidetracks of concentration. Before he knew
it, he found himself in a moment becalmed from screaming,
stampeding civilians (had the gunfire ceased?) by a wall of bodies
facing outward, ready to kill. Kneeling over the wounded and
unconscious body of his brother, Jennifer's face thrust before
him, all the power of her will blazing in sea-green eyes that
captured him like a moth to the flame.

"Andery!" she said, words implacable as a marching
BattleMech army, "you know who did this."

He began to shake his head, mouth sliding open in denial.

"Yes, you do!"

"No. I don't."

"Gods!" Her voice flogged him, as only she seemed capable
of; powerful and godlike in her own right. "Andery, still selfish
after all these years. Yes, you do know. And you're going to
take care of it."

"What...why should I—"

"They tried to *kill your brother, Andery*! What else do you
want? Who knows how many others they might have killed?
How many others will die because of your inaction! If Nicholas
dies, the Clans die!"

The force of her accusations impelled him away, stumbling
upright and back through the phalanx of warriors surrounding
Jennifer and Nicholas; some turned in unison to hoist his brother
up and rush him from the stage; he saw a host of other warriors

spreading out through the crowds, calming them...forcibly when needed...bringing the mess under control and trying to find the gunman.

"They'll find the gunman!" he yelled at Jennifer as she moved off the back of the platform and toward a waiting hovercar.

Her face, splattered in blood, hair coming undone out of its bun, glowed with projected power. "But it'll just be a gunman. You have to ferret them out. The leaders. This has to end. Do you want us to fall into the fighting of the Pentagon Worlds? Do you want that blood on your hands? Do you want the death of the Clans on your hands?!"

She turned, leaving him looking down at his brother's blood on his fingers, making them sticky. *How sticky blood is. How sticky...*

In a haze, he found himself down off the podium, moving among the warriors and civilians tending to the wounded. *She asks me to go on a headhunting mission. Not to arrest. But to annihilate. To hoist their bodies up at the city gates, drawn and quartered as though by decree of a medieval Terran king. How can I do that? How could I live with myself?!*

The sound of a siren cut through the air like a scythe, announcing the arrival of emergency vehicles. He stumbled. Fell painfully to his knees as the crowd spun past him, carrying wounded civilians toward the oncoming ambulances.

Dana's vision surfaced abruptly into memory, of crumbling towers and bursting lights and pain. He glanced around, his skin prickling with the knowledge that this could very well be the fruition of her vision. *Was there anything we might have done to prevent this?* He tried to gather his wits, rose to his feet.

Despite the painful admission, Jennifer was right. *Nicholas... if you die...all for nothing. We're not ready to survive without you...* And despite all too often never feeling like he really knew what he wanted, or what he thought of his brother, in this moment he knew that to be true. He *knew* it.

A woman and two men (civilians?) slowly rose, heads shaking over a body covered in blood on the ground, and moved on to work on another body a few steps away, whose chest rose raggedly. So at least one casualty. *Is that what you wanted, Justin? On your head.*

Andery moved closer, needing the support of this death to help firm his decision, when a sudden premonition walked harsh fingers across his neck. As he drew near, the yellow and black suit glowed for a moment, as though the sun managed to peek through the perpetually overcast sky of a Mechty December. Cold breath a claw digging into nostrils and back of throat and lungs as he gasped for breath, he stumbled painfully to his knees again, as emotions finally gave way to the shock of the shooting and the possibility of losing his brother and the looming rebellion (again!) and tears blurred his vision, wiping away the image of Carson's bloodied face, eyes and mouth open as though on the verge of smiling and offering a comforting hand to Andery (so many times through the years; the elder brother Nicholas could never be)...

...he seemed to explode into an inferno of rage and anger and sadness as it all cycled around again, and his voice rose until he thought his vocal cords would rip and tear and he would drown in his own blood...

"NO!"

CHAPTER 33

"Who did this, Carlotta?" Andery said, voice stripped of emotion, matching the bone-chilling cold—power for the entire city had been sabotaged twenty-four hours earlier—that puffed stark white plumes from everyone's mouth as they stood in the front room of Mayor General Carlotta's apartment.

Always reserved, cool, and competent, now she practically begged, tears crystalizing on her cheeks as she shivered in her nightclothes. "I don't know. I don't know. I promise! None of us could've been involved in this, Andery. Please. You have to know this. How long have we known each other? None of the civilian leadership could be involved!"

Her fear and babbling washed over Andery and away, never touching him as he stood statue-straight, rifle in hand—holding a weapon had never felt so natural—with twenty warriors at his back; five in the room, the other fifteen securing the building.

It had been frighteningly easy for him to step forward and assume command of a squad of troops to ferret out the insurrectionists. He'd originally attempted to draw most heavily from either the Coyotes or Wolverines—at least those warriors knew him better than most, given all the time he spent with Dana and Sarah—but both Khans had been adamant: one warrior from each Clan, or there would be riots among the eight hundred. Yet when the Clans' leaders had stepped forward, he'd denied them, saying no Khans would be allowed; their leadership was crucial in this pivotal moment. *We live or die right now.*

Instead, all the other warriors drew lots, and with the full support of every Khan—even Ellie, much to his shock at the time—he'd sworn them into his emergency command. He didn't know their names. Would never want to know their names. Shadows to accompany the shadow he'd become.

"I don't believe you," Andrey continued. "You're more aware than anyone of what occurs in this city."

"But not this!"

"A name. Give me a name. Where does this lead?"

"I don't have it!" The whites of her eyes practically glowed in the low-level flashlights that lit the room.

Andery closed his eyes. The anger and fury and pain surged until he almost didn't recognize himself. And underneath it all... fear. Robbed of a childhood by those who would tear down power. Something built over a lifetime, torn down again. And if Nicholas died, it would all have been torn down...once...more. *It will burn and burn, and we'll all die. There is no other place we might go.*

Despite his distaste for so much of what his brother had wrought, the vision before Nicholas's eyes was slowly emerging for Andery. A vision he'd purposefully ignored for literally years, unwilling to attach his name to all that would come. Yet he could no longer deny that this vision was better than any other path, where only death and pain existed; they teetered on the brink, toes on the edge of those other paths, darkness rising all around. Resolution settled across his shoulders finally, willingly accepting what had been in front of him for so long—he was a master of self-denial—and memories rose of hard decisions made long, long ago.

Of hard things.

He opened his eyes, now filled with harsh resolution, stepped forward, and jammed the rifle's butt into her gut. Carlotta cried out in pain, collapsing to the floor, and long minutes passed as the soldiers around him waited in tense silence, her muffled cries and gasping breath finally coming under some control.

The look of pain and betrayal in her face when she finally looked up at him was simply one more scar he would bear unto the grave. "Carlotta, give me a name."

"Paul," she gasped, snot covering her mouth and chin, starting to harder in the cold; face blotchy from the pain and tears. "It could only have been Paul."

He canted his head. *I was expecting Justin. Not Paul. I've known Paul far longer. I suppose it's always the quiet ones you never expect.*

"You will be taken into custody," Andery said, turned, and swept out of the room into the night, his twenty shadows following.

29 DECEMBER 2815

Andery walked past a new group of civilian prisoners being unloaded from the back of a truck—several very much the worse for wear—and up the steps of Nicholas's command post, his shadows following. He immediately knelt and pulled up the bloody hair of the overweight dead man sprawled on the steps. Unseeing eyes stared from the cherubic face of Senior Laborer Justin, his throat cleanly slashed from ear to ear.

"This is Laborer Justin?" The paramilitary officer spoke from a step above.

Andery glanced up to find him backed by several other officers. A loose affiliation of military that did not make the cut for the eight hundred warriors, they'd served as unofficial security and police. The new armbands, weapons, and determination on their faces spoke of hard changes. Implacable changes. Yet they shied away from Andery's eyes; refused to look at his shadows.

Andery wouldn't think about that; only confirmed what was already known. "*Aff.* This is Laborer Justin. He was found like this?"

"Yes. I mean, *aff*," the officer stumbled. "Sometime after midnight. His body was dumped here. This means...it is..." the man trailed off as Andery looked at him, and melted like wax under a blowtorch, his eyes finding his toes.

Andery looked down at the dead man again, and stood, turning away. One of his shadows stepped close, becoming his second-in-command, talking quietly as they moved away from the command post, the terrified civilians being arrested, and the still dark, cold day. "We were told it was Master Teacher Paul. Why is Justin here? A peace offering?"

Andery slowly nodded, putting the pieces together. "I thought it was Justin from the start. But if it is an offering, from who? From Paul? Or from one of the others?"

"Does it matter? We still must find Paul. Especially with the mayor general's testimony. He cannot escape. There is no place to go. We simply must squeeze harder," she said, voice as cold and emotionless as his.

Andery nodded again. *There is no place for any of them to go. They will be squeezed harder.* He moved toward the makeshift jail (the standard cells had quickly overflowed with the arrests), and entered the building, walking down long halls before coming to a room that contained the specific citizens he'd ordered arrested. Stepped into the room without closing the door, knowing his shadows flowed behind.

Time for more answers. More hard things.

10 JANUARY 2815

The single light bulb in the basement sputtered under the cycling current as the city's power grid fluctuated; back online, but still in need of repair. Despite the heat above, however, the basement had been dealt a catastrophic blow of several pipes bursting due to the cold, spraying water in every direction, then freezing. The strange, dirty stalactite and stalagmite icicles would've fascinated old Andery. But new Andery only had eyes for the miserable wretch tied to the chair he'd been collapsed in when they surged into the room.

"Andery, p-please..." Master Teacher Paul spoke. The cultured tones and always immaculate look were gone after a week of living on the run, sprinting from one rathole to the next, the entire city hunting him. "I didn't do this. I didn't do this." He shook his head, the lump on the side of his face left after several punches from one of his shadows growing larger, purpling.

"That's not what Carlotta said."

"She's a crazy slag," he mumbled. "It wasn't me. You have a body."

The five shadows tensed along with Andery. "And how do you know that, if you didn't give it to us?"

Paul managed to focus at the sharp tone, eyes flickering among the shadows that breathed death, and started to shake as the bright flash of ammonia in the dank space betrayed his loss of bladder control. "Everyone knows. Everyone knows! Yes, I was in those meetings. I voiced my displeasure. But never this."

"Then who? If not Justin, who?"

"I don't know. Have you found Jefferson or Jules?"

"Not yet."

"Doesn't that say something?"

"That assassins hide well."

"No! It says they were in it together. I've been hiding by myself, knowing you'd be coming for us." He tried to look at Andery directly, but snapped his gaze away, preferring the shadows to what he saw in Andery's face.

"And do you know where they are?"

"Last I heard was out by the new substation. But that was days ago. I don't know?"

Andery held up a hand to forestall a shadow stepping toward Paul with intent, confident they'd get nothing more. *We've broken him. Which means his info may or may not be actionable.*

But he had to follow up. He'd already started down this road. He had to keep moving. He flowed up the steps, out past his other shadows, and waved to the paramilitary police that they could take the man into custody; they knew which cell to place him in, under extra lock and key.

OUTSKIRTS OF KATYUSHA CITY
14 JANUARY 2815

"Sir, you shouldn't be leading the breach," another of the now nearly ubiquitous paramilitary officers said, eyes skittering around as though he had trouble keeping them on Andery's face.

"Yes, I should."

"And if you are killed?" The man sounded scandalized, his tone practically shouting: the near-death of one Kerensky was bad enough, but this?!

Andery shrugged. "Are you going to stop me?"

The man stepped back from the soft-spoken reply, eyes darting first to Andery and then to his shadows, and then to his feet. "No, sir."

"Secure the perimeter. No one gets in. And no one gets out."

The man nodded and Andery carefully moved back to look out the window at the building across the street. It was quiet now, but he knew there was an ambush awaiting them. As there was last time. *Paul would need another talking-to.*

Once more, a shadow slid forward to become his second-in-command. "Five warriors each, from cardinal points, hitting simultaneously," the woman spoke softly; Andery never looked them directly in the face, and they accepted it without comment.

"Thirty-second mark," he said, sliding to the edge of the door that opened directly on the street, feeling the countdown proceed until he heard the *click* in his earpiece and exploded into action through the door.

Andery sprinted across the street, diving into a slide on the ice and scraping his skin even through the heavy-weather gear as he banged up against the stairs that led into the dilapidated building. Small-arms fire popped in the cold morning air, along with the bright flashes and brief, deep-throated hums of laser rifle shots that tried to find his sprinting shadows, but at least on this side of the building, all five made it safely across. Andery clicked his throat mic three times, and a fusillade of return small-arms fire exploded from multiple levels of the building he'd just exited, windows shattering in both structures, as several squads of paramilitary soldiers offered him support.

He counted exactly twenty seconds and leaped to his feet, running for the shattered ground-floor window, which had received the brunt of the firefight, confident the supporting teams would cut off when he told them. *After the last example I had to set.*

He dove through the window, tucking into a roll cushioned by the carpet and the extra padding of his winter gear, but his shoulder still screamed from an old wound. *And I'm getting old. Too old for this game. And yet they follow and I lead...*

Almost before he was back on his feet, sidling up next to the doorway that led out of the room, his five shadows joining him. They burst into the hall, catching an errant insurrectionist trying to flee; they was cut down with twin, controlled bursts. Andery joined them as they leapfrogged in overlapping lanes of fire, both front and back, as they quickly cleared the northern quadrant of the bottom floor.

Memories surfaced of a much younger Andery, terrified and fumbling in a similar situation aboard a ship. *Would Hazen even recognize me? Would she perhaps finally forgive? No. I don't think she's one to ever forgive. The best I could hope for is acceptance that I'd finally stepped up.*

"First floor secured," a voice spoke softly in his ear, as it would for all the shadows.

They reached a stairwell and Andery signaled with one hand, sending the shadows up, guns sweeping in every direction as he followed in the middle, the last soldier watching below in case somehow they missed one.

They reached the second floor as sporadic gunfire burst from other parts of the building; his other groups of shadows meeting stronger resistance than expected. *Could this finally be the last of them?*

Three clicks in his earpiece gave him five seconds, and they piled up low against a support wall in the center of the large, relatively open second floor as another fusillade of supporting fire hammered the building from multiple directions outside. Andery counted the seconds as dust settled down from the building, covering them like a light dusting of snow matching the empty streets of this portion of old Strana Prime.

The sound finally cut off. *Nearly a minute. They must have spied something we didn't.*

"Second floor clear," another voice chimed softly after another few minutes of sweeping for targets.

Andery signaled his shadows and they crept to the next stairwell, booted feet soft against the carpet and even the tile of the stairwell as they moved up to the next floor. Andery caught motion from the corner of his eye as they reached the top, and dropped to his knees as shots passed through where he'd just been standing; the rifle in his hands hummed, and the endless years of marksmanship practice drilled two holes through the insurgent's forehead, dropping her lifeless to the ground as three others leaned around the corner, spraying ammunition in a dreadful attempt at firearms use. They died just as quickly.

Distantly, Andery realized his heart rate was only slightly elevated. He squashed that thought deep down, where he kept old Andery.

He led the way toward the stairwell leading up to the final floor, finding no more insurgents after that brief spat. Just as they entered the stairwell, a yell on the commline finally sparked a response as he jumped slightly and his heartbeat spiked. "RPGs. They've got RPGs!" someone yelled.

Andery and his shadows dropped to the floor as other voices shouted, "Incoming, incoming!"

The concussive blasts pummeled them as multiple explosions tore into the floor above their heads. Secondary explosions crumped, cascading chunks of the ceiling down onto Andery and his shadows with bruising carelessness, eardrums screaming under the assault; a blast of heat washed over him until he felt baked by a scorching sun, despite the heavy covering and cold air.

The visual and auditory assault seemed to drag on for minutes before the sounds and vibrations stopped shaking the building and Andery finally sat up, glancing dazedly at his shadows to verify movement; skittered away from eye contact. He swallowed in a dry throat several times to clear the heat and dust, but couldn't find the moisture, and instead reached up to his throat mic and made three slow clicks for "check in."

A chorus of voices responded, and much to his surprise all twenty shadows were still alive. *Devil's own luck there. Nicholas's own luck? Is there a difference?* He strangled the bitterness and pushed it down beside old Andery as well.

He glanced up to find a massive, gaping hole in the ceiling above them, looking straight up through another hole in the ceiling above that, up to the overcast sky above. Flames licked everywhere as the building still rumbled. He slowly stood, dusting himself off as his eyes sought any sign of life, but the flames were starting to spread, and the whole building was about to be engulfed. *We have to get out of here.*

No one could've survived that. Did that get the two of them? Did that get the last of them? How would we ever know? He finally scraped some moisture into his mouth as they began quickly heading back down the stairs.

"Shit."

**KATYUSHA CITY
3 MARCH 2815**

"How did she escape?" Andery said to the paramilitary officer as they stood inside the empty cell.

The other man winced, as though Andery had slapped him. "We haven't ascertained that yet. She had to have had help."

Andery turned to look at the man, eyes demanding he concede the ridiculous obviousness of that statement.

The man winced again. "I'm sorry, sir. Of course she had help. But we're not exactly sure who and how."

"How long as she been gone?"

"Two days."

"There was no check-in for *two days*?" Andery said; the inflection of his voice did not change, yet the man stepped back, eyes darting toward his shadows, then away.

"There've been so many prisoners to process, as well as rotating those few who will be kept in permanent incarceration to other locales. Now that you and your team are..." he trailed off, unable to even pretend he wasn't looking at his shoes, "now that the violence is...done?"

Andery ignored the man's question, contemplating the empty cell, then turning away, calling over his shoulder. "You will inform me the moment you have any additional information."

"Yes, sir," followed him down the hallway and back out into the night.

Andery paused outside, realizing the power had been on for two straight weeks now, and he'd not heard of a single act of violence from the insurrectionists within the past seven days. The wind swirled through the streets, and he drifted listlessly, finding darkness to hide in, as he'd done over the last weeks since...that terrible day.

Minutes drifted into nearly half an hour as Andery stood silently, grateful he couldn't see the blood on his hands. *What I have done...what I have done, brother?*

"Is it done?" a shadow said, his second-in-command materializing next to him.

He slowly forced himself to meet her eyes. Forced himself to fully acknowledge her. He slowly unclenched muscles he had forgotten were tensed; forced his eyes to take in his twenty shadows, who all resolved into warriors. Warriors who had followed him without question. *Warriors who have seen my rage and pain and shame. Have seen my monster inside. But I should've known better, eh Niki? I should've known there is a monster in all of us. Even in the best of all of us.* Memories surfaced from so long ago, of trying to hide behind someone's leg, but he thrust them away.

He finally met each warrior's eyes, nodding formally, as though releasing them from the oaths that had forged a team to cut off the head of the insurrectionist beast and secure Nicholas's new society.

You wielded us all as a master surgeon, didn't you, Niki? He tried to find anger at his brother, but found only sorrowful acceptance. *And yet I didn't do this for you, Niki. I did this for Carson. I chose. You forced my head and yet I...still...chose. For Carson.*

Each warrior stepped forward, grasping Andery's arm in a strong forearm grip, eyes conveying fealty to him directly—not as a brother to Nicholas, but Andery himself. As old Andery slowly resurfaced, veins of new Andery pulsed through and created a different whole; he accepted the mantle that he would've run from not long ago. His mind rang with assurances of his worth from Carson and others over the years. His friends. His family. *Can I have worth when my life never seems to match the version of me in my head?*

His shadows left, leaving Andery to his own thoughts, as the cold worked its way into his skin and bones. Would he ever be warm again?

And what about you, Carlotta? How did you get out of the cell? And who helped you? Were you behind everything? Was it always you manipulating others? Or perhaps you are what you seem, caught up in the machinations of others and just desperately trying to survive? As the questions swirled through his head, he wondered if he would ever discover the truth. If he would ever see her again. And if he did, what he might be forced to do. He'd keep his ear to the ground—he knew they all would—but for now...he was confident this beast was slain.

He'd just need to be ready for the next one.

CHAPTER 34

"Manipulated. Again."

"You are an excellent tool for the job," Nicholas responded.

Andery breathed in the astringents of the plain hospital room in an effort to bring calm. His eyes ached like burned holes in his head from the lack of sleep over the past months; his hands shook, and he tried not to look at them too closely, confident of what he'd see. He desperately needed sleep, but when he tried, the claws reached for him and he was dragged off the beaten path of dreams, as though water swallowed down the windpipe instead of the esophagus, and all he saw, like reverse imprints seared into his retinas, were slit throats and bloody faces begging for mercy and fire and corpses and he awoke screaming, alone and covered in loathing. Andery clenched down on a sound threatening to tear free, terrified it could either be a scream or a laugh and it might never stop.

But it is done... He shied away from the ending to that sentence, which begged for his attention. *...for now.*

He glanced around the room, trying to find a semblance of calm. The space, quiet except for the whir of a few wall-mounted contraptions (he could care less about their function), reminded Andery of a cozy sitting room or suboffice; he expected a robed gentleman to enter any moment, chardonnay in one hand, pipe in the other, book under his arm, ready to prop up his feet in front of the fire for a few moments of peace. *And that's what you got. Beyond everything, some peace. A little time away from the pressure. While I waded through blood! Blood!*

He hid his hands. He wanted to yell, but reined in his emotions; kept his voice under tight control. For a moment, even wished cold Andery were back. Until he realized the warriors in the hall would be those with the most fanatical allegiance to Nicholas for this whole charade, so no need to hold anything back. Anything at all.

"You shouldn't be a king, Nicholas. You should be a prince. I'm sure Machiavelli would be proud of such an apt pupil."

His brother's eyes narrowed, the temperature dropping precipitously between them, but he didn't rise to the provocation.

"Why?" Andery spoke, feeling like a trained poodle, knowing the hoops he jumped through ahead of time, but forced by habit (the chair and whip and doggy treat long gone) to go through the motions.

"Do I need to spell it out? If so, then I have drastically underestimated you, my brother."

"Oh, you'd enjoy that, wouldn't you?"

"Please. Andery. You are the one trying to clothe yourself in self-doubt and recriminations. Not I. Besides, we are all manipulated. From the day we are born until the day we die, someone is manipulating us. Even those who believe they do so for good, it is still manipulation. School. Good manners. Habits. These are not genetic traits we bring to the table. Conditioning and manipulation are what they are, whether or not we wish to dress them in the civil terms of 'teaching' and 'civility.' Words can be their own ignorance."

"Stop that."

"Stop what?" Nicholas shifted in the comfortable chair, the bed such a room would normally hold conspicuously missing. As were the bandages Nicholas should still be wearing after such a massive chest trauma as the bullet that supposedly tore into his body.

"Stop aping Dana."

Nicholas smiled. "It took you this long to notice?"

"I've known for a while. Been a little preoccupied."

"Of course."

Andery sucked in a lungful of air, trying to keep his patience; only Nicholas could agree with you and simultaneously completely dismiss your words.

"And what if they'd been a better shot? You had the best body armor we can manufacture hidden under your suit... but what if they'd gone for a shot between the eyes?" He still fumed, even after he'd figured it out. Not just to be manipulated once more, but that his brother might take such a huge risk... if he had died, they likely would have all died in the implosion of the vacuum his vacancy would've left. *Why I made the only choice possible...*

That *was why no 'Mechs and vehicles. That might've scared off even the most ardent opposition. Had to make sure they would take the bait you offered...yourself.*

"There are times when you must simply leap into the void. When all your options lead to a pivotal moment and you must believe in what you are doing so strongly you will lay everything on the line. Including your life."

"And what about James?" he snapped. He'd ignored the sorrow for months, and the constant fresh wound of pain. *The older brother you couldn't be, Niki, and you took him!*

"He was as dedicated as any to the cause. I know full well how much he...meant to you."

What were you going to say there, Niki? Influence? Did you actually think he had too much influence on me? A memory wormed up and spread roots of doubt. Of words spoken by James long ago. *Was that why there was no Khanship for James... Nicholas knew? And I had James asking about Jennifer. Did that... No! No, I cannot believe he did that on purpose. I cannot! Because if I do, then why wouldn't you kill me too, Niki, when my annoyance factor overcomes my usefulness to you?* His stomach twisted at the thought that such *purpose* could have flowed from Niki or Jennifer, and he once more pushed away all those alternatives.

"He will be remembered, Andery. I promise you that."

Andery bowed his head, wrenching it tiredly from side to side, hearing the cartilage *pop* satisfactorily...desperate for a bed and a very large bottle of sleeping pills so that he might drop into a coma for a month...free of the memories of his actions and the deaths on his hands. He feared no amount of remembrance or *surkai* would ever overcome such self-loathing.

"Why...?" he asked, the word husky with pent-up emotions.

"Speech patterns are just as important as clothing, work habits, and social interactions. I am experimenting with the speech pattern my new society will adopt, and Dana is so dedicated to the cause it seemed...appropriate. Sure, changing speech patterns will take much longer than any of the other programs that have been adopted, but I cannot leave anything to chance."

"That's not what I meant!"

"It was not? Did you not ask about how I am altering my speech?"

Andery began to pace, pulling his eyes off his brother before he launched his verbal grenade, hoping to see "real" blood from Nicholas. "Why?" The word came out like ground glass, sharp and demanding attention.

Nicholas's voice dropped toward its usual roughness. "Again, do I need to spell it out?"

"No. You don't. Just as with every rebellion you've instigated, you did it to stave off a greater rebellion. Precipitate it, control it, channel it, use it to your advantage. It's the same story, Nicholas. The *same* story. Channel the anger through a few select leaders, allow them their *rebellion. Then* you move in, cut off the head, and the rest are more devoted than ever. It's worked brilliantly before, so why not this time?" he finished sarcastically.

"Especially as the insurrectionists handed us the perfect justification to assign every single man, woman, and child to one of my Clans," Nicholas sounded casual, almost philosophical.

Andery nodded slowly, having seen the announcements, and knowing it was one more mechanism to lock in Nicholas' vision. But the burning question couldn't be ignored. "But...why...me?"

"You?"

Andery grunted, refusing to look at the satisfied smile he knew graced his brother's lips, lighting his eyes. *Almost fifty years old and yet you'll forever be his little brother, right, Andery? Manipulated and driven no matter how hard you fight it.*

But you're not alone, are you, brother? And I've gotten at least that much from my years of experiencing your ways, Niki. You always have an ace in your pocket. But I figured out your ace this time. He snorted. *Not that it's done me any good. But this time, at least, I can say I figured it out, whether or not I still leaped through your hoops. It was* my *choice.*

He'd deal with that later.

He stopped, leaned his forehead against the wood-paneled wall, the grain tickling his skin, scent of pine and lacquer—despite the years of hospital chemicals—still faintly present.

"Nicholas..." As much a plea as any uttered in the last twenty years.

Silence seemed to stretch and the gulf separating them at the moment never seemed greater, despite (or perhaps even because) of the firm yet tenuous link of blood lashing them together. *The coin once again, Nicholas, you on one side and I on the other?* After all that had been done to him, he still felt that call. That pull.

Will you ever force me to break our link, Nicholas? Even with everything you've done, will there be a time that I'll be forced to find the end?

He couldn't answer; the silence like a tomb.

"How better to become what I need to be?" Nicholas said. In the sacred silence, the words came as a cold wind; the breath of the grave. "And how much better to have the instrument of my justice be of my blood, as though a sword wielded by my own hand...and yet not my hand directly. *That* is how this was accomplished."

Andery started to look toward his brother, then realized it would be too painful. Perhaps another day, when the pain of another betrayal and more blood on his hands as a result of his brother's machinations lessened. He began to laugh, as the realization dawned that it *would* lessen, as it always did. And he would once more follow his brother. *My choice. My choice...*

"Andery."

"To become what you need to be. You've never admitted it before. I've known all along. Have been terrified of it. But now, to hear it from you...somehow, I'm no longer terrified. Just disappointed that our lives have come to this."

"Come to what?"

"Lies. Gods and lies, Nicholas." *And blood*!

"We do what we must."

"No, Nicholas. *You* do what you must. You at least have *that*. I simply follow in your wake."

Despite his resolve that it was his choice, the bitter words hung on his tongue like the taste of death and ashes as he turned and left the room as a new thought arose in his mind: *I* can *do the hard things. Nicholas. I* can.

Andery shuddered again at the blood on his hands, and at the new thoughts that percolated in him.

CHAPTER 35

KATYUSHA CITY
NOVY TERRA
STRANA MECHTY
KERENSKY CLUSTER
21 MARCH 2815

He stood in front of the door to the apartment he hadn't visited in half a year, desperate to find shelter from the storm and with nowhere else to go. For an hour, and he burned with so much pain. He tried and tried to open the door and could not, as tears coursed down his cheeks.

How could he face her? The love of his life, when there was such betrayal in him. Thoughts of other women that confused him—Jes and Sarah; jealousy of Dana's devotion to Nicholas and wondering how he could fit; inability to believe in the core of her soul and her visions; the blood on his hands that made them feel sticky most days, though he rubbed them endlessly, subconsciously, in an effort to clean them that never bore fruit.

The door abruptly opened, his stomach surged into his throat and he became dizzy; he cast his eyes to the floor, feeling unworthy. *I should've died killing those people. I should've died. Nicholas could use me as a martyr, propping up my body in a glass case as he's done to Father, using me for all time!*

Further shame spread until, for the first time in many years, he was practically pink, the heat on his skin washing the last of the cold from his hours of walking this night. *Always rationalizing, aren't we, Andery? Always rationalizing your choices with what's been done to you. Never what you've allowed to be done.*

He couldn't hear anything over his harsh breathing and the staccato thump of his racing heartbeat, emotions threatening to tear his sanity from its mooring and cast him adrift in an ocean he'd never return from as he squeezed his eyes shut to hold himself together.

A hand touched his face and a memory burst bright and vibrant, realization blossoming. *Twenty years ago. Twenty...years... to...the...day. Twenty years ago we gave each other...each other.*

The tenderness in that touch and that magnificent memory—the best of his life—sparked tears anew that tracked down his cheeks again. He slowly raised his head to find Dana's knowing, loving eyes as open and giving as the day they met. As he once more stripped himself naked to reveal his whole self, Andery unlocked his eyes for her, and the pain and the doubts and self-loathing surfaced in a torrent. He tried to open his mouth, but the tears transformed into a wracking sob that robbed him of sight and hearing, and he offered all of the agony and anguish of his soul to the one person he should've been turning to all along. The one person who had never judged him. Who had never asked more of him than what he could give. And he knew. He *knew* in that moment of shared intimacy that so few ever find, that she knew it all: knew his thoughts of Jes and Sarah and his doubts about her and of all the blood.

And she forgave. And she loved.

He collapsed on the floor, weeping uncontrollably at the realization that such love existed and that she offered it to him, how unworthy he felt to be in her presence; accepting the gift and unloading his pain to be shared, as it always should have been.

I chose. I chose. And those people suffered and died because of me. I chose.

Loving arms drew him close as he wept into the night. He knew it wouldn't be alright tonight. It wouldn't be alright tomorrow. Or the day after. But it might just start to be okay the day after that. Or the day after that. And he'd do everything he could to make it so.

But for now, he kept all the blackness at bay by desperately holding on to his heart.

CHAPTER 36

KATYUSHA CITY CENTRAL PLAZA
NOVY TERRA
STRANA MECHTY
KERENSKY CLUSTER
9 JUNE 2815

Nicholas Kerensky leaned into the shovel, scooped a pile of dirt to the side.

Applause swept the central plaza of Katyusha City, provided by some fifty thousand strong. Beyond the crowds in the central part of the plaza, the newly finished, colorful administration buildings and city halls for each sector actually glinted in the sun, as though a type of mirror image for the Clan halls of the warriors.

You think of everything, don't you, Niki?

Beyond the city halls, the mass-transit system terminals formed the outer pentagon of the central complex, both those in operation for several years, and the new line junctions just completed for the Laborer and Merchant Quarters.

All gleamed with power and authority and...vision. *New and shining, as though washing away the dirt and blood that got us here. Except the very center, which you just broke ground on...will you finally announce what's going to be here?*

Andery watched as Nicholas handed the shovel to Senior Laborer Borin (he looked so much more the part of *laborer* than Justin; he didn't shy away from the pain of that death, but stood firm, trying to accept it), then strode down the corridor of thronging people toward the raised podium where Andery and Jennifer waited. At the base of their father's statue, the podium gave most everyone present a clear and unobstructed view of Nicholas, even without the giant holoprojection that allowed everyone to see his brother ten meters tall while simultaneously broadcasting to the entire Kerensky Cluster.

And unlike your last great address from this plaza, no need for a security team this time, eh, Niki? If you would be king...what better way than to be gunned down by an assassin, only to rise.... When your mythos is already larger than life, that can push you straight into godhood. Right, Niki?

Andery couldn't decide which pulled at his heart with more sorrow: that he still followed Nicholas' lead despite everything, despite the blood on his hands and knowing that he had been manipulated (*all* the manipulations)—or that the bitterness such words once might have evoked no longer surged, simply echoed with remembered pain.

You can only gag so often at putrescence before you're accustomed to it. He grasped Dana's hand, who squeezed his in return. *Especially when I chose. I* chose!

Nicholas reached the podium, grasped the edges firmly, white suit flaring in a halo as the noon sun beat summer into the soil of Strana Mechty, and began.

"*Today is a great day for us all. Years ago, I announced the transformation of those loyal warriors who followed to protect us from the horrors of the Pentagon Wars into a new organization. The Clans. Since that day, those warriors have trained and unified themselves into a fighting force unlike any in the history of mankind.*

"*All to serve the purpose of protecting you.*

"*And our vision.*

"*Of establishing a new order. To take back the dream others have trampled into bloodied soil and shattered yesterdays. Today, we have reached a pivotal moment in that transformation. A moment our descendants will look back upon with awe and wonder. Most importantly, with appreciation and gratitude.*"

Andery's eyes roamed the crowd, the groups of forty warriors of each Clan (not forty...oh James!) serving as blocks of power spread equidistant throughout the crowd. At another time he might have considered it a security measure; put the warriors where they can have the most impact in any situation; even the 'Mechs ringing the perimeter could not muster such an immediate response. But not today. If Nicholas kneeled and begged someone to slay him, all present, even the civilians, would likely fall on their own blades first.

Such was the power of his creation.

*A creation I helped produce! But do we want that? Do I want that? After all is said and done, Niki is still flesh and blood. He'll bleed. He's not a god, just a man touched by...*nothing came to mind, and thoughts roiled over the trial of conscience surging within...a trial he knew he was losing.

"*This day,*" Nicholas continued, voice deep with conviction, "*we commemorate what has gone before and what will come. As with any great endeavor, there are those who refuse to see. There were those who could not endure even the Great Father's vision, leading to the* Prinz Eugen *and the Pentagon Wars and the path we now follow. Some could not see the path we have chosen and shed blood in their confusion. The blood of those who have sacrificed everything to protect us. To protect our burgeoning society.*

"*Eight hundred warriors formed the Clans. And yet now, as we reach a new signpost in the road, one of those consecrated has fallen.*"

Andery's gut clenched hard, bile rising, tears threatening, as he knew what would come next; Dana's hand somehow kept him grounded. Knew it as a great honor for his fallen friend... saw it clearly as Nicholas's exploitation of events to further his own long-term plans.

"*As with any great endeavor, there are those who are willing to make the greatest sacrifice of all. To give their life. Their blood. To see us safe. To achieve the goal we all work toward. But unlike past societies, which remember their fallen only in dusty memorials and forgotten history books, this day we will create a living, breathing memorial to James Carson. A living memorial to all eight hundred warriors who have sacrificed everything to create a golden tomorrow for us all.*

"*Today I announce the creation of eight hundred Bloodnames. Surnames our descendants will compete for to bear proudly. So that a hundred years from now, a thousand years from now, Carson will be remembered for his sacrifice, his name a badge of honor. All you warriors...your names will be won and treasured, far more precious than any banners or ribbons or awards, which dim and fade with the passing of time."*

A stir undulated through the crowd as they took in this new proclamation, an announcement that might have sparked resentment among civilians only a few months ago, for once more pushing them further into a role subservient to warriors...

But not this day. No, not this day.

"Warriors, citizens, if there is no unity, nothing can be achieved!" Nicholas boomed. *"You have shown that unity. You have shown that we can move beyond the mistakes of those who cannot accept the vision we all embrace. We are unified in heart and soul and in mind. And on this day, two days before the anniversary of the death of the Great Father, it is time for a new leader to step forth. It is time for a new office to focus the unity and power of what we create, as we draw near to the point of Return. Draw near to when we can come out of our self-imposed exile and free those harrowed souls even now still fighting for their lives against despots and visionless warlords on the Pentagon Worlds.*

"This day, I am become ilKhan Nicholas Kerensky. Thus shall it stand until we all shall fall."

Regardless of Andery's internal conflict, the power and conviction of Nicholas's pronouncement moved him. Focusing not on his inner pain but on the crowd beyond, he saw the fervor echoed in a thousand eyes and more. And once again the image of the coin recurred: he and Nicholas, on opposite sides, forever so close, forever separated.

A rhythmic sound began in one group of warriors, expanding and swelling until it crested as a giant sonic wave, breaking across the podium in a thunderous chant, a shout at the heavens.

"Founder. Founder! FOUNDER!"

As it washed over him, he was almost relieved by the confrontations he'd endured in the last few months with his brother and Dana. But there was one more confrontation he had to have this day; squeezed her hand, as he'd told her everything.

One more pain to endure.

INTERLUDE THREE

NORTHERN TERRITORY
AMERICAS, TERRA
TERRAN HEGEMONY
25 NOVEMBER 2780

Nicholas stood outside the large compound wearing his new clothing; the luxury hotel nearly the equal of any oligarch's mansion he'd spied back in Russia. He'd not seen his father in months.

Now, after hours of flight, he stood in a strange place, with a full company of BattleMechs stationed outside, and hundreds of implacable-faced Star League Defense Force soldiers, fingers far too near the triggers of weapons at the ready, staring in every direction as though an attack was imminent.

Why are we here? Why would Father meet us here? He couldn't decide if he was more upset with Mother for not telling him why they were here, for not having food on the flight (The first of his life! It should've been more exciting!), or Andery for constantly jerking this way and that and practically hiding behind mother's legs. *Andery. Absolutely Andery.* He sneered at his brother, and stared back at the soldiers and the sprawling, large building behind them.

Who lives here? On the verge of asking Mother if she had something to eat, he heard a soft thumping in the distance, and immediately looked around, trying to find the incoming craft. As he craned his neck, excitement spiking that he'd soon get to see his father again, he caught sight of his mother; despite her calm expression, her finger twitched as though she were longing to hold her teacup. Unease prickled his skin. *Why are you nervous, Mother? You're never nervous!*

The *thwup-thwup-thwup* crescendoed until the helicopter swung into view over the tops of the swaying trees on the far side of the large lawn that ended at a wall. He didn't recognize the model, but it banked steeply, blade angles adjusting as it shifted out and landed not twenty meters outside the wall, easily seen through the gates where they stood waiting.

Almost the moment it touched the ground, the door slid back and his father, Aleksandr Kerensky, stepped out, followed by two soldiers, and walked toward them. They didn't run, but their pace was quick. Regardless, every line of his father's posture spoke danger as clearly as a shout from his days on the streets that 'Goons were coming.

From the corner of his eye, he watched his mother take a deep breath, as though preparing for battle, her face settling into the determined expression he knew so well. *Hard things are coming.* He immediately reached out and snagged the squirming Andrey before he could dart toward his father. "'Goons are coming," he whispered savagely, causing Andrey to blanch and immediately step behind him and stop moving. *Sorry, Andery. Something's happening, and you need to stay out of it.*

Aleksandr neared the gate and Nicholas watched his stride hitch momentarily, shock washing his features when he recognized his family, before his lips compressed in anger. He walked up them, waving back the two following him. The soldiers spread in front of the building snapped a crisp salute, which he returned, before they resumed their vigilance.

"What are you doing here?"

"We are here to witness."

"This is no place for you," he replied. "No place for the children."

His mother's beautiful, laughing eyes flashed lightning, her anger every bit the match of his father's. "You were not here. You did not live through it. You did not watch us being starved and beaten. We have earned the same right to witness."

His father's face paled and turned a little more away from his family at every strike of her words. Nicholas felt tears scratching at his eyes, emotions welling. *I've never heard Mother say those words. Never.* He'd said them to himself some nights, when the nightmares wouldn't stop. But he would never say them out loud. And for one single moment in his life, fury flashed in a new direction, and he hated his mother for the pain she had caused his father.

The tableau held, the sound of the whirling blades finally dropping to background noise as they continued to slow, and no other sounds came but harsh breathing, and blood flooding Nicholas's ears at the shock of such hatred directed at her.

"So be it. But I would've spared them this atrocity," he said softly, stepping smartly away from them, waving at a soldier (captain?), who immediately trotted over.

"There will be more atrocities, my love," she whispered. The tenderness in her voice immediately dampened Nicholas's anger, and his heart went out to his mother, who'd saved their lives over and over again. "But this is one we must witness if we are ever to survive," she continued. "What has come. What will come."

"Major," his father said, tone as implacable as the armies that crashed against the shores of Terra and wore down the enemy's defenses unto victory. "I want a firing squad assembled immediately. Bring out all of the prisoners." While his voice was not loud, his words exploded among the soldiers like a hand grenade, shock painting every face; joy quickly covering most.

"Of course, sir. But, um..." the soldier swallowed, as though he didn't want to keep talking, but did anyway, "may I ask? Why now? After all the requests for execution, why now?"

Silence reigned for several heartbeats before his father spoke, voice as harsh as Moscow in winter. "We unsealed the Court of the Star League."

The major's face slowly turned purple, and smiling faces in the courtyard fell into anger.

"General," the major said, voice rough with fury, looking around at his men before standing even straighter. "We won't have a powered down rifle, sir. Not a man here would stand for that."

What? A powered down rifle? Why would you have a powered down laser rifle? Confusion roiled in Nicholas. *Who are we shooting? Why did we fly all this way, making Father angry, just to see someone killed?*

His father slowly nodded as the major visibly relaxed, as though he'd braced for a different answer. He turned away, yelling. "Jaxom, firing squad as we practiced. Anya, barricades. Claretta, your squad, bring them. All of them. Now."

As though a kicked hive, the soldiers burst into action, with nearly a dozen practically sprinting up the steps, while others started to create a cordon of a half-circle between where they stood in the courtyard and the luxury hotel itself. Others ran to the side and picked up a heavy, tall barricade and marched it with much grunting to place it at the foot of the stairs, then repeated the maneuver three more times, making a tall backstop around ten meters wide. Finally, soldiers trotted to a large storage locker, where they pulled out rifles and quickly began inspecting them as they walked back to a line Nicholas hadn't noted painted on the grass, about seven meters from the barricade. He counted twenty of them as the last soldier moved into the line.

He'd only ever witnessed the 'Goons and their sloppy work—even so, they were still dangerous—but watching SLDF soldiers move with such quick precision left Nicholas's jaw hanging open. He slowly closed it, confusion still whirling, then turned slightly.

"Mother, I don't understand. Why are we here?"

She glanced at him, reaching out to rub his shorn hair, a sad smile on her face. "To witness, son. We are here to witness. For us. For all of Moscow. For all the sons and daughters of the Hegemony."

He opened his mouth to respond that her answer explained nothing, but noise drew his eyes as soldiers began bringing people out of the mansion, walking them down the wide front steps. Men, women, a teenage girl. Over a dozen people, and finally he saw. Finally, he understood.

Andery whimpered and held more tightly to his leg, hiding, as Nicholas growled from deep in his throat before he could stop himself. The older man with a thin mustache had lost much weight the last months of his incarceration. But his was a face known to every child of the Hegemony. To every child of the Inner Sphere: Stefan Ukris Amaris.

Nicholas took a step forward without thinking before he felt his mother's firm hand on his shoulder. He looked at her, and she shook her head, and he managed to nod back, coming back to himself. The Usurper. The man who had toppled the Star League, killed a hundred million people, and had made their lives hell. "I would kill him myself," he growled.

"I know, my son. But this is a cross your father must bear."

The prisoners seemed lost, unable to understand what was going on. Even as they were placed in front of the barricade, most had resignation writ large on their faces—from the teenage girl who glared defiance, to the oldest man, limping, with a shock of white hair, who simply stood and closed his eyes.

"No... No! This cannot happen. This cannot happen to me!" a voice wailed. The terror in his voice and abject squealing left Nicholas unable to understand what was occurring as he saw Stefan Amaris, the former emperor of a reign predicted to last a thousand years, on the ground, weeping like a frightened child. The soldiers, disgust in every line of their bodies, attempted to drag him back to his feet, but each time he simply flopped back into the dirt.

"Post," his father ordered, implacable cold limning the word, after watching a half-dozen soldiers try to lift Amaris up.

Through nearly ten minutes of soldiers bringing out a post, hammering it into the ground, and finally shackling the blubbering Amaris to it, Nicholas's anger turned to disgust and even verged on pity (*I refuse to feel that!*). *This* was the demon who had destroyed their lives? This pathetic man had tormented them for years? He simply couldn't make a connection between the towering monster of the Amaris Empire and this pitiful wreck.

Fear slowly etched the faces of the other men and women (his family?) awaiting execution, yet they all held their ground; angrily resolute to resigned, none of them could even look at their former emperor in the end.

Nicholas had dreamed of a day like this. Dreamed of a day he could bring the justice of the Star League down upon the 'Goons and all those who had turned the garden of Terra into hell. Yet, as the soldiers snapped their rifles to the ready, and the instant stretched and stretched and stretched, his mind seemed to fight itself, over what was right and what was *right*. *Is that what—*

"Fire," his father said, cutting off his thoughts as twenty laser rifles hummed nearly in perfect unison, and thirteen people jerked and instantly fell dead.

The sounds of falling bodies and rifles snapped to ready washed away, and the world seemed to hold its breath, letting Nicholas pick up his father's subtly murmured words, despite the distance. "There will be no sympathy for the devil."

"Major," his father spoke loudly after another pause, "preserve the bodies and ship them to the *Pride* until I can figure out what to do with them."

"Yes, sir!" the man responded, and immediately began signaling the soldiers into action.

His father turned and strode back toward his mother, stopping as he took in her defiant look, before turning his eyes on his sons. Nicholas shivered at the bleakness there. A barren, windswept land he'd never seen from a face that had always showed him nothing but love.

"You have witnessed," he finally said to them, sadness brimming in his voice.

Her hands twitched, as though she would reach out to him, but they stayed at her sides. "We have. And we will be witnesses to the Hegemony, to the entire Inner Sphere and beyond. That the devil is dead."

His father slowly nodded, pointed toward the VTOL, inviting them, and then moved on, not waiting to see if they were following.

Nicholas pried Andery from his leg, taking his hand—he did *not* miss someone else taking his hand—and followed. He'd been without his father most of his life. But he would follow now. He would follow forever. And nothing and no one would ever stop him.

He didn't look back.

EPILOGUE

KATYUSHA CITY CENTRAL PLAZA
NOVY TERRA
STRANA MECHTY
KERENSKY CLUSTER
9 JUNE 2815

As ever, the darkness of a late Strana Mechty night was not true dark. Not with the mauve-and-violet aurora borealis streaking the sky like wine stains from god's cup, the thrum of his fingers on the cosmos causing the rivulets to writhe and contort as though alive and sentient, laughing at the plight of mere mortals below. Even after all these years, the sight never failed to impress, but Andery's eyes were cast down at the small hole scooped by Nicholas's shovel. And inward.

Are you finally building your temple, Niki? You never did say a thing about it in your speech, just scooped the dirt and went on. But now that you've crowned and clothed yourself in the mythos of immortality, will you build a temple to celebrate your godhood? A pyramid, perhaps? Like a pharaoh. Yes...that would be appropriate, wouldn't it, Niki. God-king. And who will be your Imhotep? Every great pharaoh needs a great architect for their temple-pyramid.

But of course, he already knew *that* answer.

"Andery."

Surprisingly, he didn't jump at the voice behind him, though he didn't hear her approach. Even after this long, she was still too stealthy for that.

"I wasn't sure you'd come." But he knew that to be a lie. Knew she would come when he wrote the note. Knew she wouldn't miss the opportunity to rub it in.

"Of course I'd come. I always come when you need me."

He couldn't help his harsh bark of laughter at *her* style of wit. Yet razor-winged butterflies began a violent dance in his belly, twisting his mouth grotesquely. *After all these years...you still feel it. Still feel the pain. Stupid.*

"Ah Andery, after all these years..." her voice whispered, sultry and soft.

He did startle then, eyes flaring at her speaking his thoughts so uncannily. "Are you a mind reader now?" But he'd actually missed that tone. *Damn me!* But he had. He took a calming breath, thinking of Dana; *thank you for getting me through this.*

"Of course not. Omniscient is reserved for your brother. I'm just a soldier."

"You were *never* just a soldier."

"I beg to differ, Andery. I may have become a soldier earlier than most, but I've been a soldier, following my leader's commands, since it all begin. Nothing more. Nothing less."

"Nothing less." He tasted that on his tongue and could think of nothing more unpalatable, more untrue. *If only you* had *been less, this all wouldn't be so painful.* "How long?"

"How long?"

"You know."

A soft chuckle. "Since the occupation. I told you that once."

"I know." And did, and the knowledge made it worse. Just didn't make enough of a connection to find the truth. *Or perhaps I didn't want to find it.* Old Andery might have shoved that thought aside, but he tried to face it, even knowing it would take a long time to accept it. He moved his boot, disturbing the fresh pile of unearthed soil, the scents pleasing in the rapidly cooling air.

"So, from the beginning?"

"Pretty much?"

He actually *felt* the ambivalent shrug; a casual discarding of his feelings that struck like a laser, piercing and cauterizing. He closed his eyes, casting about for the reasons he wanted this confrontation. Knew the pain it would cause. *Perhaps because it* would *cause pain.* Perhaps he needed to lance the wound.

Finally cauterize it after all this time. Do away with it. And finally replace it with the love of another.

"Do you love him?" He had to ask.

The silence of a city fell, with the hum of ubiquitous machinery, honks of distant horns, muffled cries of children, the throb of passing trams: susurrations around the depths between them.

"That is not a term that applies."

"What?" He opened his eyes to the city's skein of lights against darkness, refusing to look, canting his head as though trying to hear her more clearly.

"Love. Andery, that's too small a word. You were there during the occupation, even if so young. In the depths of that horror. We were all children...just children...and we found each other...held on to each other...perhaps we'll need to create a new word for what he and I share together."

He slowly nodded, thinking of what he and Dana had; knew he'd never have been able to survive this confrontation without having reforged that bond.

"Andery."

"What?"

"Look at me."

"And the surgery?"

Another pause, the shrug again felt despite the relative silence and darkness. "I've lived in the shadows my whole life. Lived lies and worn masks. What's one more shadow? One more mask."

"And your *brother*?"

She chuckled again, this time with the grim satisfaction of a job well done. "We told you that man never fails."

"That you did. Was what *we* had ever real?"

"Of course. But so many died during the Pentagon Wars. So many soldiers lost, so many reassigned to new commands. Such confusion. She simply...ceased to be."

"And your *brother*? Jerome?" He realized, in that moment, that Jerome had never directly lied, though he had lied by omission. But the twinge of that lie barely scraped the surface against the backdrop of the rest of his life.

"He has been a good little boy, hasn't he; a soldier who follows orders to the end."

He laughed quietly, harshly. "And did you need to be so... nasty?" He tried to stave off the final question, one of the hardest of his life, but knew there would never be a start to healing without an answer. "To me."

"You might have figured it out otherwise. I am also a good soldier, following my orders to the end. Andery, look at me."

He gave in, then. Slowly turned, heart thumping despite his resolve, bracing for the pain, but hoping it would allow him to finally settle it all...put it all behind. Because the sun would still rise tomorrow and he would still be Andery Kerensky and his brother would still be forcing him along a path that eventually led back to the Pentagon Worlds and war. And he would still have Dana.

Though her face was mostly in shadow, the aurora borealis caught her eyes, causing them to blaze. *How could I have missed it? Right there the whole time. Despite all my questions, I still missed what was right in front of me.*

His brother's wife. Jennifer. Jen.

"Good-bye, Jes."

"Good-bye, Andery."

And he walked away into the night.

ABOUT THE AUTHOR

Randall N. Bills began his writing career in the adventure-gaming industry, where he has worked full-time for two-and-a-half decades. He's led the publication of literally hundreds of sourcebooks, rulebooks, boxed games, and more. This includes instrumental work on the seminal *BattleTech* and *Shadowrun* game lines; he was lore advisor on Harebrained Schemes' *BATTLETECH* computer game, and co-story developer for Piranha Games' *MechWarrior 5 Mercenaries* computer game. His most recent game publications include the *Dungeons & Dragons* Dragonfire deckbuilder.

His hobbies include music, gaming, reading (fantasy to history, theology to science), and spending time with his family and LDS faith. He currently lives in the Pacific Northwest, where he continues to work full-time (and then some) in the adventure-gaming industry while pursuing his fiction writing—Randall has published eight novels, a collection of fiction in *The Mercenary Life*, two Star Trek novellas, and a host of short stories.

He lives with his wife, Tara, and children—Bryn Kevin, Ryana Nikol and Kenyon Aleksandr—as well as a neurotic German Shepard named Ecko.

BLACK KNIGHT
HEAVY—75 TONS

CLINT
MEDIUM—40 TONS

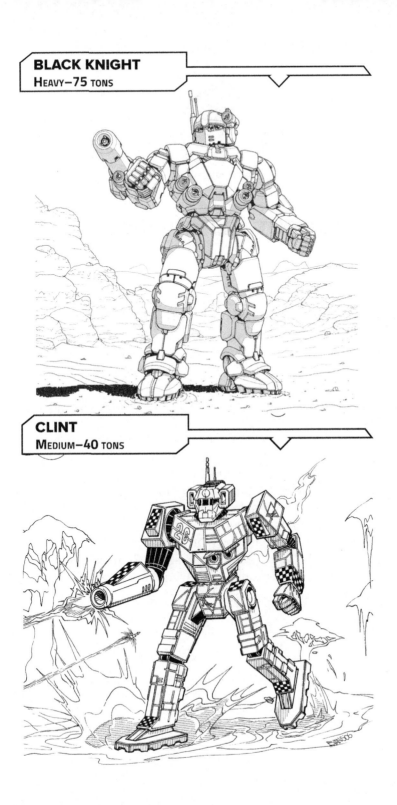

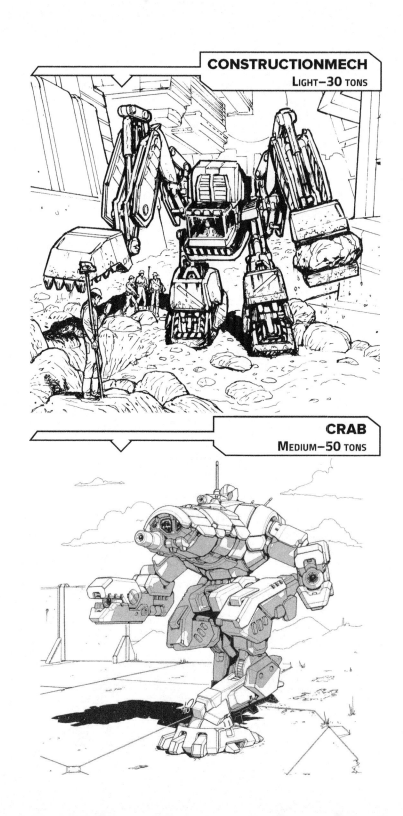

CONSTRUCTIONMECH
Light—30 tons

CRAB
Medium—50 tons

EXTERMINATOR
HEAVY—65 TONS

KINTARO
MEDIUM—55 TONS

LANCELOT
HEAVY–60 TONS

NIGHT HAWK
LIGHT–35 TONS

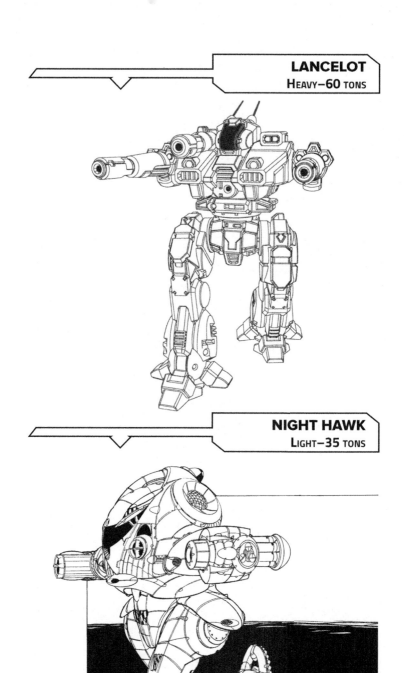

SENTINEL
MEDIUM—40 TONS

BATTLETECH GLOSSARY

AUTOCANNON

A rapid-fire, auto-loading weapon. Light autocannons range from 30 to 90 millimeter (mm), and heavy autocannons may be from 80 to 120mm or more. They fire high-speed streams of high-explosive, armor-piercing shells.

BATTLEMECH

BattleMechs are the most powerful war machines ever built. First developed by Terran scientists and engineers, these huge vehicles are faster, more mobile, better-armored and more heavily armed than any twentieth-century tank. Ten to twelve meters tall and equipped with particle projection cannons, lasers, rapid-fire autocannon and missiles, they pack enough firepower to flatten anything but another BattleMech. A small fusion reactor provides virtually unlimited power, and BattleMechs can be adapted to fight in environments ranging from sun-baked deserts to subzero arctic icefields.

DROPSHIPS

Because interstellar JumpShips must avoid entering the heart of a solar system, they must "dock" in space at a considerable distance from a system's inhabited worlds. DropShips were developed for interplanetary travel. As the name implies, a DropShip is attached to hardpoints on the JumpShip's drive core, later to be dropped from the parent vessel after in-system entry. Though incapable of FTL travel, DropShips are highly maneuverable, well-armed and sufficiently aerodynamic to take off from and land on a planetary surface. The journey from the jump point to the inhabited worlds of a system usually requires a normal-space journey of several days or weeks, depending on the type of star.

FLAMER

Flamethrowers are a small but time-honored anti-infantry weapon in vehicular arsenals. Whether fusion-based or fuel-based, flamers spew fire in a tight beam that "splashes" against a target, igniting almost anything it touches.

GAUSS RIFLE
This weapon uses magnetic coils to accelerate a solid nickel-ferrous slug about the size of a football at an enemy target, inflicting massive damage through sheer kinetic impact at long range and with little heat. However, the accelerator coils and the slug's supersonic speed mean that while the Gauss rifle is smokeless and lacks the flash of an autocannon, it has a much more potent report that can shatter glass.

INDUSTRIALMECH
Also known as WorkMechs or UtilityMechs, they are large, bipedal or quadrupedal machines used for industrial purposes (hence the name). They are similar in shape to BattleMechs, which they predate, and feature many of the same technologies, but are built for non-combat tasks such as construction, farming, and policing.

JUMPSHIPS
Interstellar travel is accomplished via JumpShips, first developed in the twenty-second century. These somewhat ungainly vessels consist of a long, thin drive core and a sail resembling an enormous parasol, which can extend up to a kilometer in width. The ship is named for its ability to "jump" instantaneously across vast distances of space. After making its jump, the ship cannot travel until it has recharged by gathering up more solar energy.

The JumpShip's enormous sail is constructed from a special metal that absorbs vast quantities of electromagnetic energy from the nearest star. When it has soaked up enough energy, the sail transfers it to the drive core, which converts it into a space-twisting field. An instant later, the ship arrives at the next jump point, a distance of up to thirty light-years. This field is known as hyperspace, and its discovery opened to mankind the gateway to the stars.

JumpShips never land on planets. Interplanetary travel is carried out by DropShips, vessels that are attached to the JumpShip until arrival at the jump point.

LASER
An acronym for "Light Amplification through Stimulated Emission of Radiation." When used as a weapon, the laser damages the target by concentrating extreme heat onto a small area. BattleMech lasers are designated as small, medium or large. Lasers are also available as shoulder-fired weapons operating from a portable backpack power unit. Certain range-finders and targeting equipment also employ low-level lasers.

LONG-RANGE MISSLE (LRM)

An indirect-fire missile with a high-explosive warhead.

MACHINE GUN

A small autocannon intended for anti-personnel assaults. Typically non-armor-penetrating, machine guns are often best used against infantry, as they can spray a large area with relatively inexpensive fire.

PARTICLE PROJECTION CANNON (PPC)

One of the most powerful and long-range energy weapons on the battlefield, a PPC fires a stream of charged particles that outwardly functions as a bright blue laser, but also throws off enough static discharge to resemble a bolt of manmade lightning. The kinetic and heat impact of a PPC is enough to cause the vaporization of armor and structure alike, and most PPCs have the power to kill a pilot in his machine through an armor-penetrating headshot.

SHORT-RANGE MISSILE (SRM)

A direct-trajectory missile with high-explosive or armor-piercing explosive warheads. They have a range of less than one kilometer and are only reliably accurate at ranges of less than 300 meters. They are more powerful, however, than LRMs.

SUCCESSOR LORDS

After the fall of the first Star League, the remaining members of the High Council each asserted his or her right to become First Lord. Their star empires became known as the Successor States and the rulers as Successor Lords. The Clan Invasion temporarily interrupted centuries of warfare known as the Succession Wars, which first began in 2786.

BATTLETECH ERAS

The *BattleTech* universe is a living, vibrant entity that grows each year as more sourcebooks and fiction are published. A dynamic universe, its setting and characters evolve over time within a highly detailed continuity framework, bringing everything to life in a way a static game universe cannot match.

To help quickly and easily convey the timeline of the universe—and to allow a player to easily "plug in" a given novel or sourcebook—we've divided *BattleTech* into eight major eras.

STAR LEAGUE
(Present–2780)

Ian Cameron, ruler of the Terran Hegemony, concludes decades of tireless effort with the creation of the Star League, a political and military alliance between all Great Houses and the Hegemony. Star League armed forces immediately launch the Reunification War, forcing the Periphery realms to join. For the next two centuries, humanity experiences a golden age across the thousand light-years of human-occupied space known as the Inner Sphere. It also sees the creation of the most powerful military in human history.

(This era also covers the centuries before the founding of the Star League in 2571, most notably the Age of War.)

SUCCESSION WARS
(2781–3049)

Every last member of First Lord Richard Cameron's family is killed during a coup launched by Stefan Amaris. Following the thirteen-year war to unseat him, the rulers of each of the five Great Houses disband the Star League. General Aleksandr Kerensky departs with eighty percent of the Star League Defense Force beyond known space and the Inner Sphere collapses into centuries of warfare known as the Succession Wars that will eventually result in a massive loss of technology across most worlds.

CLAN INVASION
(3050–3061)

A mysterious invading force strikes the coreward region of the Inner Sphere. The invaders, called the Clans, are descendants of Kerensky's SLDF troops, forged into a society dedicated to becoming the greatest fighting force in history. With vastly superior technology and warriors, the Clans conquer world after world. Eventually this outside threat will forge a new Star League, something hundreds of years of warfare failed to accomplish. In addition, the Clans will act as a catalyst for a technological renaissance.

CIVIL WAR
(3062–3067)

The Clan threat is eventually lessened with the complete destruction of a Clan. With that massive external threat apparently neutralized, internal conflicts explode around the Inner Sphere. House Liao conquers its former Commonality, the St. Ives Compact; a rebellion of military units belonging to House Kurita sparks a war with their powerful border enemy, Clan Ghost Bear; the fabulously powerful Federated Commonwealth of House Steiner and House Davion collapses into five long years of bitter civil war.

JIHAD
(3067–3080)

Following the Federated Commonwealth Civil War, the leaders of the Great Houses meet and disband the new Star League, declaring it a sham. The pseudo-religious Word of Blake—a splinter group of ComStar, the protectors and controllers of interstellar communication—launch the Jihad: an interstellar war that pits every faction against each other and even against themselves, as weapons of mass destruction are used for the first time in centuries while new and frightening technologies are also unleashed.

DARK AGE
(3081-3150)

Under the guidance of Devlin Stone, the Republic of the Sphere is born at the heart of the Inner Sphere following the Jihad. One of the more extensive periods of peace begins to break out as the 32nd century dawns. The factions, to one degree or another, embrace disarmament, and the massive armies of the Succession Wars begin to fade. However, in 3132 eighty percent of interstellar communications collapses, throwing the universe into chaos. Wars erupt almost immediately, and the factions begin rebuilding their armies.

ILCLAN
(3151-present)

The once-invulnerable Republic of the Sphere lies in ruins, torn apart by the Great Houses and the Clans as they wage war against each other on a scale not seen in nearly a century. Mercenaries flourish once more, selling their might to the highest bidder. As Fortress Republic collapses, the Clans race toward Terra to claim their long-denied birthright and create a supreme authority that will fulfill the dream of Aleksandr Kerensky and rule the Inner Sphere by any means necessary: The ilClan.

CLAN HOMEWORLDS
(2786-present)

In 2784, General Aleksandr Kerensky launched Operation Exodus, and led most of the Star League Defense Force out of the Inner Sphere in a search for a new world, far away from the strife of the Great Houses. After more than two years and thousands of light years, they arrived at the Pentagon Worlds. Over the next two-and-a-half centuries, internal dissent and civil war led to the creation of a brutal new society—the Clans. And in 3049, they returned to the Inner Sphere with one goal—the complete conquest of the Great Houses.

LOOKING FOR MORE HARD HITTING BATTLETECH FICTION?

WE'LL GET YOU RIGHT BACK INTO THE BATTLE!

Catalyst Game Labs brings you the very best in *BattleTech* fiction, available at most ebook retailers, including Amazon, Apple Books, Kobo, Barnes & Noble, and more!

NOVELS

1. *Decision at Thunder Rift* by William H. Keith Jr.
2. *Mercenary's Star* by William H. Keith Jr.
3. *The Price of Glory* by William H. Keith, Jr.
4. *Warrior: En Garde* by Michael A. Stackpole
5. *Warrior: Riposte* by Michael A. Stackpole
6. *Warrior: Coupé* by Michael A. Stackpole
7. Wolves on the Border by Robert N. Charrette
8. *Heir to the Dragon* by Robert N. Charrette
9. *Lethal Heritage* (The Blood of Kerensky, Volume 1) by Michael A. Stackpole
10. *Blood Legacy* (The Blood of Kerensky, Volume 2) by Michael A. Stackpole
11. *Lost Destiny* (The Blood of Kerensky, Volume 3) by Michael A. Stackpole
12. *Way of the Clans* (Legend of the Jade Phoenix, Volume 1) by Robert Thurston
13. *Bloodname* (Legend of the Jade Phoenix, Volume 2) by Robert Thurston
14. *Falcon Guard* (Legend of the Jade Phoenix, Volume 3) by Robert Thurston
15. *Wolf Pack* by Robert N. Charrette
16. *Main Event* by James D. Long
17. *Natural Selection* by Michael A. Stackpole
18. *Assumption of Risk* by Michael A. Stackpole
19. *Blood of Heroes* by Andrew Keith
20. *Close Quarters* by Victor Milán
21. *Far Country* by Peter L. Rice
22. *D.R.T.* by James D. Long
23. *Tactics of Duty* by William H. Keith
24. *Bred for War* by Michael A. Stackpole
25. *I Am Jade Falcon* by Robert Thurston
26. *Highlander Gambit* by Blaine Lee Pardoe
27. *Hearts of Chaos* by Victor Milán
28. *Operation Excalibur* by William H. Keith
29. *Malicious Intent* by Michael A. Stackpole
30. *Black Dragon* by Victor Milán
31. *Impetus of War* by Blaine Lee Pardoe
32. *Double-Blind* by Loren L. Coleman
33. *Binding Force* by Loren L. Coleman
34. *Exodus Road* (Twilight of the Clans, Volume 1) by Blaine Lee Pardoe
35. *Grave Covenant* ((Twilight of the Clans, Volume 2) by Michael A. Stackpole
36. *The Hunters* (Twilight of the Clans, Volume 3) by Thomas S. Gressman

77. *Isle of the Blessed* by Steven Mohan, Jr.
78. *Embers of War* by Jason Schmetzer
79. *Betrayal of Ideals* by Blaine Lee Pardoe
80. *Forever Faithful* by Blaine Lee Pardoe
81. *Kell Hounds Ascendant* by Michael A. Stackpole
82. *Redemption Rift* by Jason Schmetzer
83. *Grey Watch Protocol (The Highlander Covenant, Book One)* by Michael J. Ciaravella
84. *Honor's Gauntlet* by Bryan Young
85. *Icons of War* by Craig A. Reed, Jr.
86. *Children of Kerensky* by Blaine Lee Pardoe
87. *Hour of the Wolf* by Blaine Lee Pardoe
88. *Fall From Glory (Founding of the Clans, Book One)* by Randall N. Bills
89. *Paid in Blood (The Highlander Covenant, Book Two)* by Michael J. Ciaravella
90. *Blood Will Tell* by Jason Schmetzer
91. *Hunting Season* by Philip A. Lee
92. *Visions of Rebirth* (Founding of the Clans, Book Two) by Randall N. Bills

YOUNG ADULT NOVELS

1. *The Nellus Academy Incident* by Jennifer Brozek
2. *Iron Dawn (Rogue Academy, Book 1)* by Jennifer Brozek
3. *Ghost Hour (Rogue Academy, Book 2)* by Jennifer Brozek
4. *Crimson Night (Rogue Academy, Book 3)* by Jennifer Brozek

OMNIBUSES

1. *The Gray Death Legion Trilogy* by William H. Keith, Jr.
2. *The Blood of Kerensky Trilogy* by Michael A. Stackpole

NOVELLAS/SHORT STORIES

1. *Lion's Roar* by Steven Mohan, Jr.
2. *Sniper* by Jason Schmetzer
3. *Eclipse* by Jason Schmetzer
4. *Hector* by Jason Schmetzer
5. *The Frost Advances (Operation Ice Storm, Part 1)* by Jason Schmetzer
6. *The Winds of Spring (Operation Ice Storm, Part 2)* by Jason Schmetzer
7. *Instrument of Destruction (Ghost Bear's Lament, Part 1)* by Steven Mohan, Jr.
8. *The Fading Call of Glory (Ghost Bear's Lament, Part 2)* by Steven Mohan, Jr.
9. *Vengeance* by Jason Schmetzer
10. *A Splinter of Hope* by Philip A. Lee
11. *The Anvil* by Blaine Lee Pardoe
12. *A Splinter of Hope/The Anvil* (omnibus)
13. *Not the Way the Smart Money Bets (Kell Hounds Ascendant #1)* by Michael A. Stackpole

14. *A Tiny Spot of Rebellion (Kell Hounds Ascendant #2)*
    by Michael A. Stackpole
15. *A Clever Bit of Fiction (Kell Hounds Ascendant #3)* by Michael A. Stackpole
16. *Break-Away (Proliferation Cycle #1)* by Ilsa J. Bick
17. *Prometheus Unbound (Proliferation Cycle #2)* by Herbert A. Beas II
18. *Nothing Ventured (Proliferation Cycle #3)* by Christoffer Trossen
19. *Fall Down Seven Times, Get Up Eight (Proliferation Cycle #4)* by Randall N. Bills
20. *A Dish Served Cold (Proliferation Cycle #5)*
    by Chris Hartford and Jason M. Hardy
21. *The Spider Dances (Proliferation Cycle #6)* by Jason Schmetzer
22. *Shell Games* by Jason Schmetzer
23. *Divided We Fall* by Blaine Lee Pardoe
24. *The Hunt for Jardine (Forgotten Worlds, Part One)* by Herbert A. Beas II
25. *Rock of the Republic* by Blaine Lee Pardoe
26. *Finding Jardine (Forgotten Worlds, Part Two)* by Herbert A. Beas II
27. *The Price of Duty* by Jason Schmetzer

ANTHOLOGIES

1. *The Corps (BattleCorps Anthology, Volume 1)* edited by Loren. L. Coleman
2. *First Strike (BattleCorps Anthology, Volume 2)* edited by Loren L. Coleman
3. *Weapons Free (BattleCorps Anthology, Volume 3)* edited by Jason Schmetzer
4. *Onslaught: Tales from the Clan Invasion* edited by Jason Schmetzer
5. *Edge of the Storm* by Jason Schmetzer
6. *Fire for Effect (BattleCorps Anthology, Volume 4)* edited by Jason Schmetzer
7. *Chaos Born (Chaos Irregulars, Book 1)* by Kevin Killiany
8. *Chaos Formed (Chaos Irregulars, Book 2)* by Kevin Killiany
9. *Counterattack (BattleCorps Anthology, Volume 5)* edited by Jason Schmetzer
10. *Front Lines (BattleCorps Anthology Volume 6)*
    edited by Jason Schmetzer and Philip A. Lee
11. *Legacy* edited by John Helfers and Philip A. Lee
12. *Kill Zone (BattleCorps Anthology Volume 7)* edited by Philip A. Lee
13. *Gray Markets (A BattleCorps Anthology),*
    edited by Jason Schmetzer and Philip A. Lee
14. *Slack Tide (A BattleCorps Anthology),*
    edited by Jason Schmetzer and Philip A. Lee
15. *The Battle of Tukayyid* edited by John Helfers
16. *The Mercenary Life* by Randall N. Bills
17. *The Proliferation Cycle* edited by John Helfers and Philip A. Lee

MAGAZINES

1. *Shrapnel Issues #01–#06*

Printed in Great Britain
by Amazon

29440896R00159